THE PACIFISTS

THE
PACIFISTS

by
Kevin Carlin

Copyright 2019

Printed in the United States of America

First Printing, 2019

ISBN 9781005517175

Prologue:

The ability to artificially induce hyperdimensional wormholes was the major scientific breakthrough that set humans free to spread their nonsense throughout the entire galaxy, whereas they had previously been confined to destroying only a few local planets with their childish tantrums. The first wormhole-inducing device prototype was known as WID-1. It was the size of an entire planet, and it took over 500 Humanoid Standard Years to build, for two reasons: 1. Building a device the size of a planet requires building it very far away from your home world–and since this was to be the device that would master instantaneous interstellar travel, that meant commuting to your worksite the old-fashioned way, and 2. It was a government project.

When WID-1 was activated, it imploded and swallowed the entire star system in which it was built. Fortunately for humans (or unfortunately for the galaxy, depending on how you look at it) the designers of WID-1 had the good sense to activate it remotely. Had the few brilliant minds that understood the intricacies of such a creation been present for its failed launch, the galaxy would have continued to enjoy eons of relative peace. With the knowledge gained from the WID-1 failure, WID-2 took a mere 235 years to build. It was built in deep space rather than risking another perfectly good star system, and it launched successfully on the first activation.

After that, the science to make the devices smaller and more portable grew exponentially, as it tends to do with new technologies (Robotic Law Enforcement, for example). Pretty soon wormhole-inducing devices, or WIDs, were small enough to bring along on a spaceship. This was a game changer in that space travelers could pass through a wormhole and still pop home for dinner to find their teenagers throwing a kegger in their absence.

Previously, space pioneers making use of hyperspace bridges had to wait in painfully long queues at mass transit WID stations, and because of the warping of space-time necessary to operate such large stations, a glitch would often occur that resulted in each space traveler getting to the front of the line just as the station agent was leaving for their lunch break.

After many breakthroughs, WID devices could be made small enough to hold in your hand. A handheld WID drive would produce a wormhole that was microscopic in size, and so most people, while impressed, didn't see any practical use for it, and went about their business. But most people have a pitiful lack of imagination, and by the time the uses for a miniaturized WID device were common knowledge, WIDCorp had already gained its stranglehold on the markets.

As everyone later learned, plenty of things can travel through a microscopic wormhole, the important ones being energy, gravity, radio waves, and social anxiety. For example, if you were to, say, plop a WID on the bow of your spaceship, you could open a wormhole close to the event horizon of a black hole. The gravitational forces could not pull your spaceship through the microscopic hole and into the black hole, but they would darn well pull your spaceship forward fast enough that you better have remembered to restock the barf bags[1].

---

[1]   Because of the differences in acceleration due to gravitational forces versus acceleration due to contact forces, many a clever advanced physics student

If you put another WID on the stern of your spaceship, you could apply the brakes before you run into the red giant you're now barreling toward at over half the speed of light. A couple more WIDs on the flanks, and suddenly you could strafe–a huge tactical advantage if perhaps a rival spaceship-manufacturing corporation was firing torpedoes at you, which they almost certainly would be, because the craft you just built with that kind of acceleration and maneuverability would be sure to put them out of business once and for all.

Prior to WID technology, spaceborne military vessels were inefficient enough that waging war required a significant provocation between two factions. There would first be an attempt at diplomacy, then a gradual breakdown in communication, usually set off by a seemingly innocent error by an interpreter that wouldn't be discovered until centuries later by an adroit historian. Then a lengthy standoff would be followed by one despot or another carrying out a false flag operation to set off the proverbial powder keg, and finally the mobilization of troops.

Conversely, the evolution of the WID drives and the newfound maneuverability in the vacuum of space resulted in the various tribes of the galaxy being able to engage in armed conflict with such ease that those in leadership positions could hardly think of a reason not to declare war on each other. With each passing year, spaceborne combat became more and more common, until eventually the galaxy was involved in one continuous war that spanned generations.

---

has argued that the body inside the WID-powered craft would not feel the acceleration in this way, and so they choose to forgo their seatbelts. However, a gravity field from a *microscopic* wormhole acts only on the immediately surrounding engine, not on the entire ship, and so every single one of those advanced students ends up pinned against the back bulkhead on their first field trip into the wild black yonder of outer space, while the remedial science kids remain strapped happily into their seats, singing along to "99 Bottles of Nutritional Slurry on the Wall."

Part I

Chapter 1

*The Kadrafian species were created involuntarily by the Kadraf
Mining Corporation, which had purchased a resource-rich but
inhospitable planet, named it Kadrafia, and then mixed human DNA
with that of a local bluish-purple moss to create a species that could
survive on the harsh planet. The corporation enslaved the new
species to mine the planet, but the Kadrafians were in their first
generation when they rose up and overthrew the Kadraf Mining
Corporation. In fact, Kadrafians considered themselves to have
been born a free people, because even before the revolt they spent
more time planning their uprising than they did working in the
mines.*

*The revolt was three generations in the past when tensions
boiled over and the Kadrafians were again forced to defend their
freedom; this time not against some two-bit corporate security team,
but against the full power of the formidable Galactic Naval
Corporation.*

*When Kadrafians reached puberty, they experienced a growth
spurt in which their bodies grew faster than their skin could keep up,
and so they ended up with thin lines of scar tissue in a complex web
all over their bodies. As a rite of passage into adulthood, their scar
tissue was traced into a brightly colored tattoo. The color of their
tattoos denoted the industry they intended on working in. For
example, Kadrafian warriors wore orange tattoos.*

*-Excerpt from "Grapes of Wrath: A Brief History of Kadrafia,"
by Brandine Lupinski.*

Freeda crouched behind a row of shiny new spaceships
parked in the lot. Mere days ago, a team of high-pressure
salesmen were busy forcing these ships on the public. Now,
however, the sprawling expanse of Dealin' Dextorious'

dealership lot was a hardened battlefield in the latest skirmish between the Kadrafian Combat Force and the Galactic Naval Corporation. Artillery rained down around Freeda and her squad, destroying next year's models and voiding warranties. Every time the Kadrafians in Freeda's platoon peeked their blue heads around a windshield, sniper fire whizzed by their ears. "It's not looking good, squad," she admitted.

"Why are we even contesting this miserable planet, ma'am?" asked Kamber, Freeda's second lieutenant. "An entire planet that's just endless spaceship dealer lots. If you don't have a spaceship, how are you supposed to get to this planet to buy one?"

"Yeah, but he's got catchy ads," said Freeda. "And we're contesting the planet because Dealin' Dex has been dealin' military grade ships on the down low."

Three rows over, a used model with a "low hyperspace jumps" sign on it exploded under artillery fire. After the decibels dropped, Kamber said, "If I'd known we were about to get sent here, I wouldn't have complained half as much about the ice planet Buennagel."

Private Grenif, the new recruit, asked, "You were stationed at Buennagel? I always wanted to go there."

Kamber fired his rifle blindly over the barricade to give covering fire to Freeda, who was standing up to fire a WID-propelled grenade launcher (WPG) toward the sniper nest. "No, you don't," shouted Kamber to the rookie. "It's a worthless place, and I don't know why it was ever colonized in the first place." The grenade exploded in midair, failing to penetrate the pillbox. "Are there no planets left that have more than one climate: cold at the poles, deserts at the equator, and mountains and oceans in between? Every planet we get sent to is just one damn thing. Desert planet, ice planet, hippie music festival planet, and now this one, the worst of them all."

Another round of artillery rained into a ship only one row

away. "We have to make our move soon," shouted Freeda. "We've gotta do something about these snipers." Then into her radio she shouted, "Where is our backup?"

Over the radio came a familiar voice. "Freeda, it's Rev. I'm coming in. Where are you?"

"That's my brother," Freeda shouted to her squad. "He's a fighter pilot." Then into the radio she yelled, "Rev, we're pinned down in the Green Alligator Lot, row 34. There's a Dealin' Dex statue you can't miss. The pillbox is in the giant dollar sign in his right hand."

"Hang tight, sis," squelched the radio. "Colonel Dalton is ordering me to maintain formation, but screw him."

From the ground Freeda watched as her brother's ship circled the statue of the middle-aged car dealer. Dealin' Dextorious was an overweight Astroman[2] whose signature outfit was a green spandex suit complete with a cape, as if to suggest that giving a fair price on a spaceship required superhumanoid abilities. Revloo's fighter concentrated fire on the pillboxes, but they were too well armored.

"Hang tight, Freeda," he said, and landed his fighter behind the statue. Then, leaping out of his ship, Revloo climbed the back of the structure from the outside.

Freeda looked over her cover just in time to see the pillboxes light up with rifle fire from within. "Move, now," she shouted at her platoon, and jumped over the barricade. Sprinting full speed at the base of the statue, Freeda didn't stop to kick in the door, but busted through with her shoulder. She ascended the stairs four at a time, her squad panting to keep up behind her.

When she got to the pillbox, Revloo had killed the snipers, but he had taken a shot to the lower chest. Freeda rushed to

---

[2]   The Astromen were a race of humanoids who adapted to spend their entire lives in zero gravity. Within a decade after they evolved their unique adaptations, the WID system of artificial gravity was invented, and the entire species became immediately obsolete. Still, they're up there in their deep space colonies, churning out all-star Grav-Ball players season after season

where he was propped against the wall. "Revloo," she cried. "I heard your squad commander. You disobeyed a direct order to help us. Why?"

Revloo laughed, which sent him into a coughing fit. "Every truly great Kadrafian warrior understands that sometimes, orders need to be unfollowed." He stopped to wince and hold his side. "Raif'yans will never be slaves, not even to ourselves. You're a great warrior, sis. Always follow your instincts."

Freeda's memory of what followed was a blur. She lifted her brother over her shoulders and raced down the stairs, ordering her platoon to rejoin the battalion. She slumped Revloo behind the seat in his fighter, taking the pilot seat herself. Her only training in a fighter was from video games, but Freeda launched the ship and soared full throttle toward Revloo's carrier, dodging anti-spaceship fire and strafing enemy troops with Gatling lasers along the way. By the time she landed on the carrier in orbit, Revloo was unconscious. She lifted his body out of the fighter and placed him on a stretcher.

Colonel Dalton, who had ordered Revloo not to break formation, stood behind Freeda and watched. "Don't worry," he said, "we'll get him patched up and promptly court-martialed for insubordination. That was some damn good flying. I'd like to give you a recommendation to the flight academy, if you're interested."

Chapter 2

Through almost all eras of warfare, the vehicles of war, be they land, sea, air, space, or time, would inspire all sorts of emotions in the onlooker. Just as the shape of a racing ship inspires daydreams of careening across that checkered finish line with the entire field trailing behind, a well-designed warship would plant in the heart of the beholder a series of violent fantasies. The most notable exceptions to this were the fighter ships of the GNC-KCF War. They were the first era of armed conflict to use the WID drive technology, and they were nothing more than a perfectly spherical cockpit with weapons racks on each side and WID engines jutting out the back, giving them the aesthetic symmetry of a toddler who's given herself a haircut with Mom's old pinking shears.

-Excerpt from "Birds of Prey: A Collector's Guide to Military Craft," by Brandine Lupinski

Three Years Later:

Freeda stood in front of her fighter. To her right, a line of pilots stood at attention in front of their blue fighter ships, which matched their splotchy blue Kadrafian skin. Colonel Torgue, the carrier's executive officer, was addressing the fighter and bomber squadrons set to launch an assault on a strategic target.

"Raif'yans, listen up," said Torgue. "We're hitting an orbital mass transit station today. It's technically not a military target, but our intel assures us it was evacuated when they saw our fleet approaching, so there's no need to worry about civilian casualties."

Freeda smirked behind her helmet. *Oh, I wasn't worried*, she thought to herself.

Torgue continued, "When you got your assignments this morning, this probably sounded like a routine mission, but our intel has confirmed the Navy carrier *Centauri* has entered the system to defend the transit station. I don't need to tell you that's The Monk's carrier, but let's not get distracted. I know you're all Pollyanna optimists, and you all want to be the warrior that takes down The Monk, but stay focused on the mission. The Monk is nothing more than a target of opportunity. Your primary target is that transit station. Is that understood?"

Freeda's smirk turned into a wide smile. *You tell 'em, Torgue,* she thought. *Make sure these grunts focus on the mission, so that I can be the one to get The Monk. And just to be sure I get him, I'm going to shoot down every single Navy ship that's out there today. No survivors.*

Freeda climbed into her fighter and strapped in. By the time she'd finished her year and a half of flight school, Colonel Dalton had been promoted to general and given command of a fleet. She ended up stationed on his carrier, and though she was far down the chain of command and rarely interacted directly with the general, from time to time he would stop her in the corridor and offer various words of wisdom and mentorship.

Inside her ship, the only preflight check Freeda ever did was to give her guns a few satisfying spins and then wait while the other pilots went through the dreadfully dull process of checking their gauges, mirrors, and radio presets until the launch signal finally came on. While she waited, Kamber, who had followed her to the flight academy along with her entire squad, clicked on the radio. "Ma'am, you know Torgue was talking about Banshee Squad, right? He looked right at us when he said it. Please tell me we're sticking by the bombers. We're not breaking off and chasing extra kills, yeah?"

"Whatever you say, boss," Freeda replied.

"Ma'am, I know all you care about is getting kills, but we have a job to do."

"We sure do, Kamber. And that job is to kill every Navy

ship we see."

"Ma'am, just because we got here under Dalton's personal recommendation does not mean we can–"

Before Kamber could finish the sentence, the launch light flickered on, and Freeda's fighter shot out of the tube and into the vacuum of space, racing toward the Navy fleet without waiting to join formation.

Chapter 3

The Galactic Naval Corporation was an odd hybrid of public and private interests. It was funded with taxpayer dollars by the governing galactic body, the Order of the League of Intragalactic Governments, Associated Republics, Corporations, and Hierarchies (or the "Oligarchy" for short), but the Oligarchy only had limited power over requesting when and how the Navy would protect taxpayer interests. The GNC's primary mission was to safeguard the financial interests of its stakeholders, and the Oligarchy's role was to beat the patriotism drum loud enough to drown out any voices asking troublesome questions like, "Why do we spend more on the military than every other period of history combined, but we're not able to budget any money for schools or infrastructure?" Or the even harder to answer, "Explain to me one more time why we're still killing blue people?"

-Excerpt from "Slaughterhouse-Five: How the Hawks Turned the Galaxy into a War Zone for Political Gain," by Brandine Lupinski

Copernicus, callsign "Monk," took a swig of whiskey, then set the bottle on the floor of the egg-shaped flight simulator. The words "Game Over" flashed on the screen in front of him, so he pounded the start button to begin a new round. As a fresh wave of pixelated Kadrafian fighter ships appeared on the screen, Monk grabbed the simulator controls and prepared for a dogfight. He had the entire simulator deck to himself, as it was the middle of the night, and anyone else who was awake was on watch. *Damn these nightmares*, he thought to himself as he tore his way through wave after wave of digital foes. *Thank the Statement for the solitude of the simulator. My shipmates hate me enough as it is, but if they find out that the Navy's top ace hasn't been able to sleep in weeks, I'll be done for.* Monk took another large gulp of the whiskey and replayed the events of the evening in his mind.

Earlier that night Monk was relaxing in the mess deck, eating dinner with one of his squadmates, Lieutenant Ashley Sokolov, when he heard a familiar voice.

"Hey India Squad, nice shooting today." The comment had been accompanied by a single slice of tomato arcing across the mess deck, and Monk had looked up just in time for the bright red disk to land squarely on his face, covering the protruding lens of his bulky metallic cyborg eye.

Monk said nothing, but Ashley turned to the assailant. "Oh, so you actually can aim when you put your mind to it. See, Porter, you just need to apply yourself, and you'll get on the leaderboard someday."

Connor Porter stood up from his table and picked up his tray. "That leaderboard means nothing as long as Monk is at the top of it. Worthless Loomy."

The Lumano was busying himself with adding the tomato slice to his sandwich rather than responding, but Ashley continued. "Watch your mouth, Porter. That's the top ace you're talking about."

"He's not an ace at all," spouted Porter. "He's never vacuumed a single Kadrafian cockpit. He just shoots their engines off and lets them float around in space waiting for rescue."

"The leaderboard goes by killing ships, not pilots. Exactly as it should be," Ashley said.

"So they go get a new ship and come right back out, and then us real aces have to do the dirty work? I have half a mind to shoot him down myself."

Porter's squadmates snickered, drawing Ashley's attention. "You think that's funny, Lima Squad?" she asked. "Everyone in this room knows Porter couldn't hit Ace's ship while it was parked in the hangar bay. Why don't you rookies ask your squad leader why he's lost four wingmates in the last three months."

Porter, who had been walking toward the tray return, turned and marched toward Ashley. Just as he got to her, she stood up and brought a knee into his tray, which went flying over his shoulder with a crash. As applause and laughter rang out across the crowded deck, Ashley put her hands up in a show of innocence and said, "Walk away, Porter. I'm not in the mood."

Porter hesitated, then turned to pick up his tray. He walked backwards toward the door and said, "Keep that coward out of my way. Lima Squad has some Raif'yans to kill." Porter turned to exit. At the door to the mess deck he caught a hard shoulder from Monk's other squadmate, a giant of a man who looked down at Porter, prompting the smaller pilot to scurry out of the deck.

Hassan "Teddy Bear" Amador was a large and jovial human, known to almost everyone simply as "Bear." The exception was his squadmate Ashley, who insisted on calling pilots by their given name. Bear came and joined Ashley and Monk at the table. "What did I miss?" he asked.

Ashley let out a sigh. "Well?" she said to Monk. "You have nothing to say?"

Monk shook his hairless head and remarked, "You don't have to respond to it, you know. If our squad name sitting in the top spot on the leaderboard for over a year doesn't shut those guys up, nothing will."

"It gets so old," Ashley said, playing with one of her French braided blond pigtails. "Every day with this nonsense. I admire your skills, Ace. Really, I do. Any other pilot who takes the time to line up a non-lethal shot in a dogfight doesn't live long enough to earn a cute nickname for it. Your skills are either supernatural, or you made a shady deal at a rural crossroads, but couldn't you just kill, like, one Kadrafian pilot, one time? It would get everyone off our backs, and who knows, you might even like it."

"Tell you what, Lieutenant," Monk said, "I'll vacuum a Kadrafian cockpit when you start using a callsign."

Ashley scoffed. "That's a bluff, and callsigns are stupid. But Statement alive, it would be self-defense. Every one of those Raif'yan pilots is doing the smart thing and aiming for your center of mass, and you're out there disabling their ships like it's a game. The one life you seem to have no regard for is your own, and yet every day you come back completely untouched. There comes a point where if I didn't know better, I'd start wondering if you were a Kadrafian spy who shaved his body hair and dyed his skin dark brown to pass as a Loomy. Hassan, help me out here."

Bear frowned. "I'm not going to encourage a Lumano to go against his morals," he said, "but I must admit, Monk, there's a part of me that keeps hoping you'll slip up and accidentally land a kill shot. If it's not intentional, you'd be absolved of guilt, and it sure would make all three of our lives easier. These Navy folks, all they know is violence. They're never going to trust a pilot who won't kill, no matter how many times you've saved their lives." He stroked his beard in silence for a few seconds and then added, "Ashley and I respect both your skills and your moral compass. It's just, as I happen to be a very personable guy, it's strange for me to be disliked by, like, every pilot on this carrier because I fly with Monk."

Ashley took a sip of her beer. "You know we'll always have your back, Ace. All I'm saying is, they're Raif'yans. They're evil. What's the difference if you rid the galaxy of one or two of them here or there?"

Monk finished his drink and set it down. "They're not evil, Lieutenant. That's just tribalism and propaganda. They're trying to survive, same as us. Thanks for the beer. I need to go check in with the crew chief. See you in the morning."

When he'd finally run out of excuses to avoid his bunk, Monk hit the rack and tried to get some rest, but the night ended the same way all his nights had for weeks: He woke up from a nightmare he couldn't remember, drenched in sweat and with a splitting headache; then he wandered down to the simulator deck to kill time until the morning muster. *That quack of a doctor tried to diagnose me with PTSD,* Monk thought to himself, sitting in the sim. *Doesn't he know I'm a Lumano? My species doesn't get PTSD. We're, like, enlightened and shit. As the first of my kind to join the Navy, of course I'll have a visceral reaction to seeing war up close, but I can handle myself. All I have to do is keep my cool and get through the mission tomorrow, and then I'm escaping from all of this. I just need to pull off a convincing death.* He took a few more swallows of whiskey, then set the simulator to its hardest setting.

The next morning, as the launch sirens were sounding, Bear ran down the corridor toward Ashley and shouted, "The chief is going nuts on Monk!" The fighter pilots of the Galactic Navy Carrier *Centuari* were scrambling to their fighters, but they slowed their pace enough to eavesdrop on the dramatic scene at the top ace's fighter stall, where he was engaged in a shouting match with Chief Schultz, the head of the flight deck crew. The sirens drowned out much of what was said, but the chief was warning Monk that his WID engines failed inspection, and he was threatening to block Monk from climbing into his assigned fighter, a ridiculous-looking craft that sacrificed aesthetics for functionality.

"Monk," yelled the chief, "this engine is about to implode, especially the way you fly. If you launch, you'll be down to three engines before you're out of the tube. You want to fly around in circles all day with three engines?"

"That's a nice metaphor for this whole stupid war, Chief. Bunch of maniacs flying around in circles. I'm not letting my squad launch without me. Get out of my way."

"I'm warning you, Monk. Launch, and you'll be nothing

but a tally mark on the nose of a Kadrafian fighter before your squad has even gotten into formation." Monk tried to physically push his short round frame past the chief, but Schultz towered over him and held him back. "Monk, just because we're friends does not mean you can defy me. I'm the chief of this deck. These are my ships. You are borrowing them from me."

"Then let me borrow a different one, Chief."

"You know we don't have any fighters to spare. I can't let you launch."

"I'll bring it back just how I found it. That engine looks fine to me." Monk had been a skilled ship mechanic on his home world. He could often be found working with Chief Schultz to troubleshoot and update the WID engines of the *Centauri*'s fighters.

"That engine is a disaster waiting to happen," Schultz said. "There's two ways this goes if you launch. Either the dampers blow and you go soaring off into deep space never to be heard from again, or the dampers hold and the engine sucks you in for the relativity nap[3]."

"You don't believe in the relativity nap, Chief. You told me yourself you're not superstitious."

Monk finally sidestepped around Schultz and leaped into the cockpit of his crimson fighter. The chief scrambled to stop him, pointing his finger and shouting. "You do not have permission to launch that fighter, Monk. If you fly out of this hangar I will consider it theft! If you survive this mission, I swear to the Statement I will have you court martialed!"

---

[3]   The relativity nap referred to the early days of hyperspace travel, when unstable wormholes would collapse on space travelers, stranding them in some dimension of space-time that humanoids had no business being in. In theory, as the narrowing walls of the wormhole reduced the space traveler to nothing more than a vague mathematical concept, the last milliseconds of their life would feel like an eternity, and the glimpses they would catch of the upper dimensions would be reminiscent of the weird dreams one has when eating too much processed sugar in the lunchroom and falling asleep on their desk in the middle of an afternoon physics class.

As the fighter canopy slid shut, Monk fired back, "Nah. You'll probably recommend me for a medal." He then winked and pulled his helmet down over his head. Seconds later Monk was space-borne, with India Squad in formation behind him.

Inside his fighter, Monk took off his space helmet. He pulled out his bottle of whiskey, half full from the night before, and took a drink. That will calm my nerves, he thought to himself as the liquor warmed his throat. I do my best flying with a little buzz. But today I don't need calm nerves for flying. Today I need calm nerves for getting shot down.

As Monk and India Squad approached the mass transit station they were defending, Ashley got on the radio to her squad commander. "Hey Ace, I know you want to get our backs, but you should let us handle this one. If Chief Schultz says a ship's not ready, you'd be crazy to fly it. And since I know you're not crazy–well, relatively speaking. I mean, you fly recklessly, you're the best pilot in the fleet, and yet you refuse to defend yourself–so, I suppose you are in fact completely nuts, but still, you should head in and let the chief take another look at your ship. We got this."

There was a silence, and then, "Thank you, Lieutenant. I'll be fine."

Monk waited for the Kadrafian assault force to be in range, then flipped a switch that he'd installed the night before, which turned off his fighter's acceleration dampers. *Here we go*, he thought. Because of the gravity-based propulsion systems, ship accelerations were not limited by available thrust, but rather by what is a safe acceleration force for a passenger's body. Dampers were used to ensure a safe and smooth ride, but if their calibrations were thrown off by even a small amount, a ship would be near impossible to control.

Once he had the dampers turned off, Monk cursed

convincingly into his radio, and his ship jerked around like a fly evading a newspaper-flailing rage. The Kadrafian Combat Force (KCF) ships opened fire on him, narrowly missing, but Monk flipped a second newly-installed switch, and a billow of white smoke poured out of his upper left engine.

"Sir, you're hit," Bear called over the radio. "Are you all right?"

"I'm fine, but my controls are berserk. I don't think I can land it. I'm going to set it down on the planet; it's a bigger target than the carrier."

"Roger that," said Bear.

Ashley clicked on her radio and added, "You know Schultz is going to throw himself the biggest, most extravagant 'I told you so' party ever. There will be cake and face painting, and he'll probably find a clown that can twist balloons into the shape of your fighter leaking smoke and crashing into a planet–"

Monk cut her off. "Thank you, Lieutenant. I got it." He banked his fighter down toward the planet at an unhealthy acceleration, and took another pull from his bottle. Into the radio he said, "I might ask Schultz to keep it like this. This baby really moves." He coughed into the radio and then corrected himself. "On second thought, maybe I'll have him turn it down a touch. I just threw up a little."

Monk shut off his radio and took a few more sips as he descended into the planet's cloud cover. His fighter controls spun like a carnival ride that had failed inspection. He had practiced this very scenario in the simulator for a month, but a fighter lurching at unprecedented acceleration was one thing on a screen, and quite another when those forces try to push your brains out your eye sockets.

Monk had chosen this day specifically for the overcast weather forecast. Once into the clouds, he switched his governors on and switched off the novelty party device that had been pouring the convincing white smoke out of his engine. The smoke was a clever touch, but from here on out it would make him too easy to follow, even in the clouds.

Satisfied that he had put on a convincing performance, and feeling a little woozy from the unhealthy acceleration forces he had subjected his body to, he set his course for the only city on the planet, Galeria City. Once there he'd send out his final distress signal, set his ship down in the jungle just outside the city, and detonate it. The search and rescue crew would find the charred remains of his ship, he'd be pronounced KIA, and he could go safely home. That was the plan anyway, and it was a good one.

But Monk was no stranger to things not going as planned, and so while he was optimistic, he was hardly surprised when in the denseness of the clouds, a Kadrafian fighter emerged from his blind spot and crashed full throttle into his port side.

Chapter 4

The Lumanos were the first humanoids to branch off from the homo sapiens classification and become their own species. They had started out as a scientific community of humans on New Belgium. When their population fell victim to a plague, the only cure was to mix their DNA with a local fern and evolve. In the process they became not just sterile, but genderless and asexual, only able to reproduce themselves in a laboratory.

Evolution as a potential cure to the plague was a controversial solution, and was put to a vote. The New Belgians were so hesitant to alter human DNA that even when faced with extinction, the vote only passed 64% to 31%, with 5% undecided (the term "five-percenter" remained a serious insult on New Belgium for several centuries). In a more superstitious community, the vote in favor of surrendering to extinction may indeed have carried the day.

-Excerpt from "The Audacity of Hope: How the Lumanos Beat the Plague and Saved Their People," by Brandine Lupinski

Both fighters sputtered and fell toward the jungle below like grav-ball defenders when the attacking team scores a 100-pointer and triggers the gravity to engage. In the initial seconds of Monk's descent, he concentrated on opening his eyelids all the way. Panicking would do him no good, and so he took his time surveying his controls, focusing on the flashing warning lights one at a time and waiting for it to click in his head what each one meant. Engine three, power loss. Fuel leak. Landing gear malfunction. There was an error message indicating that his novelty smoke machine had been destroyed, but that was a nonissue what with all the real smoke pouring out of two of his engines. Just for good measure, Monk tried flicking the switch to the smoke machine on and off, but it had no effect.

As his ship dropped below the clouds, the planet looming ever-larger beneath him, Monk could see the city due east across the jungle of the only land mass. Directly below him was the coastline, and to the west was nothing but ocean. Monk tested out his controls. The starboard engines were functioning, but he succeeded only in speeding up his descent, spinning his ship around, and making himself dizzier. He pushed the controls the opposite way, and the ship spun in the other direction, also speeding up his descent. The ocean below him grew unsettlingly large, and not just because it spanned most of the planet. The white foam of individual wave caps reached up, waiting to make his acquaintance, and made Monk feel like he might be running low on time to screw around with his controls. With a renewed conviction, Monk jammed on the forward thrust, flipping his ship upwards, and causing him to black out. His fighter came to a standstill, hovered a few feet over the ocean surface for a moment, then plunged into the water.

Monk came to just as his battered fighter plopped onto the ocean floor. This was not part of the plan. He knew he was near the coast, but in his plummet he hadn't obtained a good estimate of his location. Maybe 1,000 meters to shore? He could walk it in his spacesuit without fear of asphyxiation, but trudging underwater with his gear was going to be a slow and tedious trek. Monk had never been a big fan of hiking, not even on dry land. It's not that he didn't love the beauty of nature, it's just that he never understood why people were so insistent on combining it with exercise. Monk's philosophy was that nature should be enjoyed with a six-pack in a hammock. And maybe some air conditioning.

Spaceships have no need for a compass, but he did have a gyro in his pack that he'd calibrated to the planet before launching. All he could do now was hope it was correct. If he set out for his ocean-bottom stroll in the wrong direction, he'd never know it, and he didn't relish the idea of asking a Galerian cephalopod for directions. The good news was that the water was shallow enough to see sunlight, and the ocean floor sloped gently upwards in the direction that his gyro claimed was east, so there was nothing for it but to set out on the journey.

Monk fished around at his feet and found his bottle. When he'd been struck by the Kadrafian ship, he had just finished a swig and replaced the cap. The bottle was intact and half full. After taking another drink, Monk hooked the bottle on his belt, pulled his watertight pack onto his back, slung his rifle around his arm, and brought his fist down on the ejection button from his craft. The front canopy slid open, and the water rushing in pinned Monk against the aft bulkhead until the air bubble from his cockpit was ascending skyward like a lost balloon.

Monk's helmet held tight, so he pulled himself forward out of the ship and started toward shore. The sand was loose, and his boots sunk in with each step. It was going to be a long slog, and he would be completely vulnerable if the underwater wildlife turned out to be as unfriendly as Monk imagined they were. The bright red fabric of the Galactic Navy flight suits didn't exactly help him to blend in with his environment, either.

Monk walked for what felt like an eternity. His muscles burned, his shoulders ached, and his head slumped. The scenery was about as interesting to look at as the flight through the orbital cornfields of the Nebraska Nebula (known as the "Neb-Neb"), and at one point Monk found himself questioning whether he had already passed a certain stalk of seaweed. He finally sat down and gave in to the temptation to look at his watch. He had been walking for eight minutes.

Embarrassed, he got up and pressed on. He could see sunlight above him, and the water's surface inched closer over time, so he was at least hopeful that he was going the right way.

Twenty minutes later, Monk was exhausted. He kept his gyro out to make sure he wasn't disoriented and turning from his easterly direction, but he was unsure of how far he'd traveled. Though he couldn't feel the currents, he assumed any time his feet left the ground at the same time, he was moving with them. After another break, Monk decided the water's surface was sufficiently close that it was worth poking his head above water. He set down his pack and forced the butt of his rifle into the sand, then squatted down and jumped as high as he could, which was just barely out of the sand. At least his feet were loose. Before they sunk back into the sand, Monk gave a couple good strokes with his arms and began to rise. Thirty seconds later, panting and fatigued, he broke the surface of the water.

The good news was he was going the right way. Land was nearby. The frustrating news was he could have made landfall a while ago. The continent was indeed to the east, but since he was unwittingly walking into a small bay, he had been walking parallel to the north beach of the bay for the last 200 meters.

Monk let himself sink toward his gear, hoping that the currents in the bay hadn't taken him too far from his pack and rifle. Halfway down he could make out his gear, but it had a visitor. A man-sized cephalopod examined his pack, no doubt searching for those delicious Navy MREs that the foodie blogs raved about. Monk had things on his mind other than counting extremities, but had he been in the mood to crunch numbers he would have concluded that this was a decapus. That knowledge wouldn't have helped him anyway, because Monk could never remember the mnemonic for the relationship between the number of appendages and how friendly a creature was[4]. Was it odds versus evens? Was it perfect squares are friendly, or prime numbers are the deadliest? Or was that all an old wives' tale anyway, and you had to take it on a creature-by-creature basis?

Spent as he was, Monk continued to tread water to maintain his altitude while he assessed the situation. One thing was for sure, he wouldn't survive the coming journey across the jungle without his pack. Monk was still thinking about it when his movement got the attention of the decapus. It pushed off the ground with all ten limbs and came flying upwards. Sensing its malicious intent, Monk curled up into a ball and dropped toward the decapus feet-first. Just as the two came together, the cephalopod reached forward with its tentacles, but Monk stretched his body straight and struck the creature in the face with both feet. With two tentacles around his torso, Monk turned his body face downward, and they dropped together toward Monk's rifle.

As they descended in a tangle, Monk had both arms in front of him in anticipation of landing within reach of his weapon, but as the two hit bottom, the cephalopod got a tentacle around his right arm and pulled it down to his side. With his left arm Monk grabbed the rifle and stuck the barrel against the upper lid of the creature's single eye. Lumanos were opposed to killing, but their peculiar set of morals allowed for self-defense against a terrifying sea monster with ten appendages and roughly a billion kajillion teeth. Despite that exception, as the Lumano pilot's finger started to squeeze the trigger of his rifle, he looked into the decapus' eye and saw the reflection of himself holding the deadly weapon. Just as his finger found the trigger and began to squeeze, the creature's teeth broke through his space suit on his left side, just above his hip.

Monk felt the bottle of whiskey pulled from his belt, then

---

[4] Arms of three will leave me be. Arms of four, I best be swimming fast to shore. Arms of seven, five or six, that for sure is a harmless mix. Arms of eight is a lethal fate. Arms of eleven, ten, or nine, just don't wear red, and you'll be fine. Arms of twelve, thirteen, or more, no one as yet does know for sure.

heard the crunching of glass. Though lacking human facial features, what followed was the decapus making an expression that could only be described as a "bitter beer face," and then lashed out with its teeth. In an instant, the Lumano found himself in the pitch-black nothingness that the soul occupies after leaving the body but before crossing over to the other side. A few seconds later, the darkness began to dissipate. Monk could see the decapus swimming away, and realized that he wasn't dead at all, but had been engulfed in a cloud of ink.

Relieved that he didn't have to kill his assailant, the Lumano stood up and assessed the air bubbles now fleeing upwards from the hole in his suit. He wasn't that far from shore, but he was on borrowed time if he couldn't stop the leak. With his glove he wiped a dollop of slimy decapus saliva from his leg and pushed it into the hole in his suit. Eventually the acidic slime would burn through and make the hole bigger, but the immediate result was that it slowed the bubbles to a manageable trickle. Turning north, Monk reached the shore in twenty minutes and collapsed onto his back on the beachhead. The beach was relatively safe, and he would need to regain his energy before he entered the jungle.

Chapter 5

*After the Oligarchy succeeded in shouting down the general
population's concerns about WID devices and that silly "preserving
the fabric of space-time" business, WID devices had been added to
just about everything, from escalators to toaster ovens. After all,
opening a wormhole near a heat source like a blue hypergiant would
get your bread toasted much faster than those primitive electric coils
of the ancient method. Do you, dutiful patriot and upright galactic
citizen, want to be left behind by society, waiting upwards of three
minutes for two pieces of toast? No, you do not.*

*-Excerpt from "I, Robot: Technology of a Bygone Era," by
Brandine Lupinski*

Lieutenant Ashley Sokolov and her partner, Hassan "Bear"
Amador, had been flying together since before Monk was a
pilot. The two humans had originally fought against having
the Lumano assigned to fly with them, but after the first
month of India Squad sitting squarely atop the ace rankings,
they softened on the idea. Two months later, neither batted an
eye when Monk was promoted to squad leader.

Ashley and Bear wanted to stick with their wing leader, but
they stayed with the station they were assigned to defend.
Trusting that the squad leader could handle himself, Ashley
focused on the bomber squadron making a run on the mass
transit station. Bombers had a similar design to the fighters,
with similar maneuverability, but their weapons racks were
fitted with plasma torpedoes along with a single laser, not the
Gatling lasers carried by the fighters. Watching two bombers
attempt to dogfight with each other was like watching two
grav-ball goalies fight, neither one ever quite managing to
land a punch.

After taking out all but two of the fighter escorts, Ashley
and Hassan pulled in behind the bombers, which were out of

plasma range of the station. Bear got up close behind the first wing of Kadrafian bombers. "Check this out," he said to Ashley. "I'm going to line up his engines like Ace does it." Bear spun up his guns and squeezed the trigger, but just then Ashley came in from the side and sliced her Gatling laser through the cockpit of the Kadrafian ship, opening it to the vacuum, killing the pilot.

"Dammit, Lieutenant. I had that."

"Just take them down. We don't have time for monking around, Hassan."

Ashley and Bear continued strafing to the side in a large circle around the Kadrafian squad. The remaining three bombers spun to keep their fronts to the Navy fighters. The two final Kadrafian fighter escorts squeezed in between the Navy pilots and the bombers, so Ashley and Bear found themselves face-to-face with a pair of Gatling lasers at full spin.

"I call bombers," demanded Ashley as she danced her ship gracefully around the Kadrafian's defensive formation.

Bear looped around behind her, ready to slice open any enemy fighter that attempted to maneuver behind his shipmate. "Roger that."

Ashley was a steady shot with an impressive leaderboard. She had the skills to disable the bombers' engines and leave the pilots alive, but she lacked the patience. She couldn't pass up the opportunity to show off her own signature move, which could take out several ships at once, much to the chagrin of anyone on the verge of squeaking out a victory on the leaderboard for the day.

Ashley flipped her ship to the left, once again coming around the bombers in a wide circle, facing them as she strafed. All at once she jammed on her starboard engines, bringing her fighter to a sharp halt. The bombers kept rotating, losing sight of her. This gave her the split second she needed to line up her sights on the center of the bomber's weapons rack, and let loose.

Plasma torpedoes are a terribly irresponsible thing to mount to the side of your cockpit if you plan on being anywhere near live Gatling laser fire. The torpedo tubes are heavily armored from the sides to protect the plasma payload from being ignited by laser fire, but if an errant shot hits the front barrel of a plasma torpedo launcher, the entire thing will go up at once. Ashley's guns hit home, and the plasma in the bomber's magazine spilled out in all directions, destroying not only the middle bomber, but all three bombers and one of the fighters in a grand explosion.

Some of the crew had attempted to nickname her Ashley "Firecracker" Sokolov after the first time she pulled off the trick shot, but she broke the nose of first the person to say it to her face. For a while after that they called her "Nosebreaker" behind her back. She spent three weeks on scullery duty for the assault, but they let her keep the name on her galactic ID as her pilot callsign.

Having no bombers left to escort, the remaining Kadrafian fighter turned to retreat. Ashley and Bear would normally chase it down, but they wanted to catch up with their squad leader. Meanwhile, the other fighter squadrons of the *Centauri* were pushing the assault. The Navy capital ships moved in on the Kadrafian carrier group, but it had already begun its retreat and was preparing for a hyperspace jump out of the system.

With the KCF in retreat, Ashley and Bear dropped into the planet's atmosphere and descended through the cloud cover to look for their squadmate. The first thing they could see was the smoke from a crashed fighter on the coast, but it turned out to be a Kadrafian ship.

Ashley turned her fighter face down for a better view and swooped low over the jungle. "Are you getting any readings,

Hassan?" she asked.

"Negative. His emergency transponder doesn't seem to be giving a signal. It must be damaged. I'm not ready to consider the possibility that he's gone sailing off into deep space at speeds normally designated for photons."

"Nor I," Ashley said. "I don't see any other smoke from a crash on land. We're going to need stronger sensors to find him if he's under water. Let's head in and come back in a search and rescue rig."

"Roger that, Lieutenant."

In the hangar, the two fighters came skidding down their launch tubes, the canopies opening and the pilots stepping out of their cockpits before they had come to a complete rest. The flight deck crew rushed to do the post-mission check on their ships. Ashley and Bear blew past them to address Chief Schultz.

The chief was on his back under a ship. He slid out when he heard the pilots coming in. "Where's Monk?"

"He went down on the planet. We need a SAR rig to look for him." Ashley didn't wait for an answer. She ran toward the rescue craft hangar stalls.

Schultz called out after her, "Take the aft rig. Just bring it back in the same number of pieces it's in right now."

Bear was jogging behind Ashley, but he balked at the phrasing and turned around. "And how many is that?"

"Hopefully one," said the chief, "but I may have miscounted." As Bear turned around and resumed his jog the chief called after them, "And as long as you're down there looking for miracles, see if you can find me some spare mechanics."

Bear took the controls while Ashley powered up the sensor equipment, trying to remember how to use it. It had been Monk that forced her to qualify on rescue rigs in the first place–he had some fetish about saving lives being just as important as taking them. Bear had quietly grumbled about the early morning training, while Ashley openly rebelled against it. She distinctly remembered saying, "Teach me to use these defib paddles to fry some Raif'yans, Ace." He declined to teach her that particular skill, but it was a simple enough concept. She worked it out on her own. She did learn to fly the SAR rigs, begrudgingly, constantly reminding the Lumano that "this ain't the Galactic Coast Guard Co-op."

Bear made a first pass over the jungle. Ashley's sensors let out a blip, and Bear brought the SAR craft closer. The blip on the screen grew into a bleep, then a bloop, then a solid dot. The dot doubled in size, then doubled again. "Okay, that's too big to be his ship," Ashley called out. "In fact, I think you might want to get some altitude." Bear yanked on his controls, and the craft shot upwards. The rainforest below opened up, and a creature the size of a building jumped at the Navy ship, a set of gnashing teeth narrowly missing the landing gear. Ashley's eyes were on her sensors, and the dot expanded to take up the entire screen, causing her to jump back and throw the device. The screen bounced off the window and landed at her feet. "What is that thing?" she yelled. "It's big enough to have swallowed Monk's ship whole."

Bear was focused on gaining a safe distance in case the creature had a frog-like tongue capable of picking them out of the air like a fruit fly. "Well," he said, "if it had swallowed him, we'd get a transponder reading from here, so rule that out. Let's make some passes over the water. Hopefully whatever those things are don't swim."

Three hours later their search produced no results, and the *Centauri* called them in.

After debriefing they went straight to the mess hall, more to talk than to eat. "I guess his recklessness finally caught up with him," Ashley said. "No one lives forever, right?"

"And why would you want to?" asked Bear. "The way he flies, deep down we knew it was coming. I think he did too. He was acting weird all week."

"What do you mean?"

"I don't know. Just acting weird. Look, we should probably get some sleep, Lieutenant. We're about to have some big shoes to fill."

Ashley gave Bear a side-eyed glance and then conceded. "You're probably right," she said, and headed for her bunk.

Chapter 6

With a genderless humanoid species thrown into the mix, the writers and press of the Milky Way were stuck with the dilemma of pronouns. Masculine? Feminine? Plural? Despite the more feminine facial features of the Lumanos, the masses defaulted to the masculine set of pronouns when referring to the galaxy's newest citizens, because the masses were unsophisticated slackers whose fathers never taught them how to properly treat a lady.

The debate reached a temporary climax when the Woke Star System mobilized their fleet of elite Social Justice Warriors to prepare for a military conflict in favor of a new pronoun for the new species. After a brief stand-off, finally someone thought to actually ask the Lumanos which set of pronouns they preferred, to which they responded, we're kind of busy surviving a plague here, so, sure, whatever, masculine is fine. The ambassadors of Woke then redirected their forces to invade a banking colony that gave massive bonuses to its executives after declaring bankruptcy and leaving its workers unpaid. The invasion was unsuccessful because the Social Justice Warriors' invasion force, while elite, was never all that well organized.

-Excerpt from "Divine Secrets of the Ya-Ya Sisterhood: A Guide to Lumano Culture," by Brandine Lupinski

Monk lay on the beach for 15 minutes. He kept his helmet on, but shut off his internal oxygen and breathed in the fresh Galerian air. The local star was nearing its highest point, which meant Monk had roughly 15 hours until dusk.

As the burning subsided in his legs, he sat up and looked around the beach. Gentle waves broke over the white sand, and a single galeragull picked at a dead fish. Rising over the brush to the north was a pillar of black smoke where the Kadrafian fighter crashed. Still in his red spacesuit, Monk grabbed a medkit out of his pack. He left everything else on the beach and hobbled into the brush. It had been hours since the crash. The pilot was either dead or had already left the area, but maybe they left something useful behind.

The undergrowth was smoldering in the crater when Monk stepped out of the weeds and into the smoky clearing. The ship's extinguisher system had put out most of the fires around the broken fighter. The windshield of the cockpit was gone, and Monk could make out the splotchy blue skin of the Kadrafian pilot's face. Her right leg was pinned under the control column. She'd passed out trying to free herself. The "Eject Now" warning light on the ship's console was flashing, and the accompanying alarm attempted to sound its ominous suggestion, but all it was able to muster was the repeated "womp-womp" of a chronically-depressed trombone.

Monk took slow, quiet steps toward the ship, as though the sound of his footsteps on the sand might succeed where the ejection warning had failed in rousing the slumbering pilot. As more of her became visible, Monk could see that she was still holding on to her pistol. Aside from her leg, she looked unscathed in her dark blue flight suit. Too focused on the pilot to watch his footing, Monk tripped on a piece of debris and let out a curse. The Kadrafian's eyes sprung open and she fired a single shot into the sand near Monk's feet. "Stay back, Navy." The pilot took a few deep breaths as she fought to come out of the fog of unconsciousness.

"I have a medkit," said Monk, his arms high in the air. "I can help you free your leg. If you kill me, you'll die right there in that ship."

The Kadrafian fired another shot. Blinking into the daylight, she missed wide. "I'll wait for rescue, thanks."

"Rescue isn't coming," Monk said. "It's been several hours. They'd have been here by now. Your forces had to retreat from the system, and mine don't know where to look because I turned off my emergency beacon."

"Several hours?" asked the pilot. "How can that be poss–wait. You disabled your emergency beacon? What are you, deserting or something?"

"Actually, yeah," Monk said. "But I wasn't planning on having to walk through this jungle. Let me treat your leg. We stand a much better chance in this wilderness if we work together. If you don't want my help, chances are we both die out here."

"Then we die out here. There's no way we can trust each other." The Kadrafian again tried to move her leg, as though it might have miraculously freed itself while she was passed out. Monk took a step forward, and the trapped pilot put another shot into the sand, then raised the sights to aim at his forehead. "Not one more step. I mean it." Despite her injured condition, the barrel of the gun did not tremor in the slightest as she trained it on the Navy pilot's head.

Monk glanced over his shoulder at the jungle. He was more concerned with the dangers of the wilderness than with being on the wrong end of a Kadrafian pistol. "Look, shoot me or don't, but don't go five-percent on me, kid. This jungle will make your decision for you pretty soon."

The Kadrafian lowered her gun, slowly. "Fine," she said. "Bring the medkit." Monk reached for his medkit and approached the cockpit. He picked up a piece of debris to use as a prybar, and lifted the console that was pinning down her leg, allowing her to tumble free. The Lumano then went about winding the medical wrap around her knee. Tying off the wrap, he took off his helmet so he could see better.

The Kadrafian pilot's eyes went wide as she saw his dark skin and hairless head. "You're a Loomy! You're The Monk[5]. You sneaky bastard. If I had known that I would have killed you and died a happy Raif'yan right here."

Monk helped Freeda to her feet. "Nothing stopping you

[5]   Kadrafians always added a "The" to his callsign, after a Kadrafian heavy metal band wrote a hit song that referred to him that way.

now that you know."

"Actually, Loomy, there is. You have officially saved my life, and unlike you Navy rats we Raif'yans have a thing called honor. I wouldn't expect The Monk to understand that."

"Well, it's just Monk, but my real name is Copernicus. I haven't been called that in a while, but I think I'd like to go back to it."

The Kadrafian pilot suppressed a laugh, which turned immediately into a wince. "Copernicus?"

"It's a common name on New Belgium. Apparently it was a pretty popular name in the ancient world. New Belgians love that kind of stuff."

The injured pilot stretched her leg in the wrap and then stood up straight. The rotund Monk came barely up to the shoulders of the slender Kadrafian warrior. "Huh," she remarked. "I thought you'd be taller. And I didn't expect a Loomy to have a cyborg eye."

"Long story," said Copernicus. "I lost my real eye in a bar fight."

"Yeah, right," laughed the Kadrafian. "A Lumano in a bar fight. That's rich. I'm Freeda."

Monk, (or Copernicus, now that he was returning to blissful civilian life) climbed into the cockpit of her ship and retrieved her pilot survival pack. He then got her arm around his shoulder, and the two hobbled out to the beach and sat down on the warm sand.

"The Monk is really deserting?" Freeda asked.

"I'm not cut out for war," he replied.

"Coulda fooled me."

Monk dug in his pack for some emergency rations. He opened a package, broke the protein bar in half, and offered a piece to Freeda. "We can work together to make it to the city," he said with his mouth full. "After that you can find transport back to your post. Or not. It's really none of my business. How's that medical wrap coming along?"

Freeda bent her knee where she was sitting. "I can walk on it. It'll probably be an hour before the limp clears up. I'm not leaving this spot. My beacon is still active, so rescue will come eventually."

"Suit yourself," Copernicus said. "I'm heading east around this bay, then following the coast to the city, if you change your mind. The ocean is fresh water here; it's safe to drink. Whatever you do, don't go into the brush alone. Or at all. Don't go into the brush at all."

"Whatever." The Kadrafian hung her head into her knees and muttered to herself, "Found The Monk and let him save my life and walk away. I've brought eternal shame upon my family."

Copernicus was changing out of his space suit and into a set of civilian clothes. He took off his dog tags and wiped some blood from his decapus bite on them. "Here," he said, and tossed them at Freeda's feet. "I'm assuming the Navy will pronounce me dead and leave it at that. That'll silence the doubters if you want to take credit for killing me."

Freeda picked up the tags and inspected them, but didn't respond.

"Well, Freeda," Monk said, "Good luck." Then he threw his space suit and helmet into the undergrowth, grabbed his pack, nodded goodbye, and walked off to the east around the bay.

The days on Galeria were long, but the nights were roughly ten hours due to the sole continent being far to the north and the planet having a 45-degree tilt on its axis. Despite being close to the poles, the constant sunlight made for a pleasantly warm climate. It was five hours until sundown when Copernicus was too exhausted to go on. The beach may have been safer than the inland, but walking on sand with a heavy pack for ten hours was too much for him. He had only made it around the south tip of the bay in all that time. Technically, he was within sight of where he started. In the last few hours of sunlight, Copernicus sat on the sand and relaxed, saving his energy for the journey ahead. He pulled his spare bottle of whiskey out of his pack and drank himself to sleep.

Chapter 7

Freeda stood waist-deep in the bay, stabbing her knife repeatedly into the water. The nighttime sky above was a deep black. The only light was the campfire on the beach, along with its long reflection on the water, and from where she stood, Freeda could see the reclined Lumano next to the fire, rousing from sleep. Comfortable that the creature was dead, she turned toward shore, dragging the decapus carcass behind her. As she pulled the sea monster onto the dry sand, one of the tentacles flinched. She jumped on top of the creature and resumed stabbing it over and over.

"Yeah, I think you got it," said Copernicus. "I think it's dead."

Freeda ignored him, but stabbed the corpse three more times in the eye. Then she cut a long slice across its body, reached in with her other arm, and pulled out the largest of the creature's hearts, tossing it into the Lumano's campfire. "Bet you it's good eatin'," she said. "You hungry?"

"I'm a vegetarian," replied Copernicus. He held out his bottle of whiskey and asked, "You thirsty?"

"I don't drink."

"So what are you doing here?" he asked.

Freeda had ditched her space suit and was wearing her standard BDUs. They may not have been freshly laundered, but at least they were comfortable and lightweight. Her feet were shoeless but partially wrapped in tape. She had no pack with her, but she had a small pouch slung around her shoulder on a string.

She threw her knife blade-first into the sand and sat down. "I went into the brush to kill something to eat, when a pack of meerkats came at me. I must have killed four dozen of them, but they kept coming. Eventually I retreated into the water with my pack and inflated my ship's life raft. I saw your campfire and figured I may as well head this way in the hopes that you maybe got yourself killed and I could scavenge your gear. I was almost here when I ran into this thing with at least nine legs, and of course my life raft is bright red."

The Lumano didn't say anything, but he furrowed his brow at the last comment. Freeda elaborated, "You know, legs of eleven, ten, or nine, just don't wear red, and you'll be fine?" Copernicus nodded, finally remembering the old saying. "The creature took my raft down like it was nothing. I think it swallowed my motor whole, but then got tangled as the raft deflated. I stuck it in the eye with my knife. It got my pack and my pistol, so I got its heart."

With that, she reached directly into the fire and pulled out the sizzling organ. After savoring a few bites, she continued. "There's no undoing my shame at having my life saved by The Monk, so I may as well go with you to the city for now. Someday, you and I will again engage in honorable mutual combat, and I will kill you."

"I already told you," said Copernicus, "I'm not engaging in combat anymore. If you want to kill me, you're going to have to do it here. Just do me a favor and wait until I fall asleep."

Freeda took note of the half-empty bottle of whiskey at the Lumano's feet, and for the first time noticed the slur in his speech. Copernicus had already laid his head on the sand and closed his eyes. Freeda took a few more satisfied bites of her half-cooked decapus heart. While she ate, she took the opportunity to study the passed-out Monk, who within one rotation of this planet had been both her adversary and her savior.

She had never seen a Lumano this close before. The first thing she noticed was how feminine-looking his face was. While the Lumanos lacked breasts and had a more masculine build to their hips and torso, it was hard to look closely at their face and think of them as male. Despite the bald head, if a human woman had the face of this Monk, or Copernicus, or whoever he was, she would be considered very beautiful by "Yoomy" standards.

Could she trust the Loomy? The question burned in Freeda's mind. Lumanos were known to be trustworthy, nonviolent, always willing to help anyone, with a tendency to "turn the other cheek," a curious expression from the ancient world that pretentious people liked to use when they wanted to sound smart. Being a peace-loving species, Lumanos never joined the Galactic Navy. Except that this Lumano had joined the Galactic Navy. Did that fact alone render the other stereotypes about him moot? It was well known that The Monk did not kill, but did that mean she could necessarily trust him? Why had he broken from his people's tradition and joined the Navy? She supposed she could ask him directly when he awoke. They did have a long walk ahead of them, after all.

Chapter 8

The uses for WID technology were virtually limitless. One major breakthrough was that it could be distributed in a grid below the lowest decks of a spacecraft to create the vital comfort of artificial gravity. Before that, space travelers were forced to float around the cabin like loose garbage on a windy day, arriving at their destinations with atrophied leg muscles and a feeling of helplessness. For a time, various spacecraft manufacturers had experimented with magnetic boots and a metal floor, but oddly enough having their feet act as anchors rather than supports left most space travelers with a crippling feeling of being an insignificant pawn in an infinitely cruel universe, and so it never caught on.

-Excerpt from "A Scanner Darkly: The Rise and Fall of WID Technology," by Brandine Lupinski

Ashley had never lost a squadmate before. She knew she needed sleep, but it wasn't coming easy. Eventually exhaustion took over and her eyes fell closed. In her dream, her arms were orange with blue tattoos. She was standing next to a human in the pulpit of a Tautologist temple on the Kadrafian home world, and they were conducting a mystical peace ceremony. The audience was standing room only, filled with members of every humanoid species.

Ashley held an ancient relic in her hand. The crowd began to chant the word "Shalom," and the relic glowed brighter and brighter, until the scene was washed out in light. When the brightness subsided, Ashley found herself holding a single spear, fighting a giant monster on an unrecognizable world. As she threw the spear, the monster dodged to the side, stepped into a trap, and let out a loud howl. Just then a second creature emerged from the brush, charged toward Ashley, and pounced. She awoke in a sweat.

Orthodox Tautologism was the dominant belief system in the galaxy. Tautologists had a complex set of theological traditions, but their core idealogical belief was that "this statement is false." In waking life, of course, there were no Tautologist Temples on Kadrafia, the Kadrafians being a wholly atheistic society. Over time groups of missionaries had attempted to win converts on the planet, but it would take a special set of marketing skills to sell the concept of a benign creator to a species who not only knew exactly who their creators were, but had been at war with them for a good chunk of their existence.

That morning at breakfast, Ashley and Bear sat in the mess deck at their usual table, both carefully not looking in the direction of the empty seat.

"Weird dreams," Ashley said.

"Yeah, me too. I was having flashbacks of my mom begging me to stop fighting at school. I fought constantly, and she was at her wit's end. The truth was that I was sticking up for other kids who were being bullied. She wouldn't believe me until their parents backed me up to the dean. That helped get me out of trouble to an extent, but momma still wasn't happy to have me fighting. We used to have a saying on the origin planet–"

Ashley cut him off. "Hassan, you're not from the origin planet. You're from Earth."

"Earth is the origin planet. Everyone knows that."

Ashley let out a snort. "Are you serious? How long have we known each other, and I didn't know you were a delusional Earth-birther? Earth is way too hot to have evolved a species as delicate as us Yoomies, and it's as saturated with greenhouse gases as it is devoid of natural resources. The human origin planet is either Mars or Centauri Hb, but nobody knows for sure."

Hassan leaned back in his chair and crossed his arms.

"What about the fact that one rotation of Earth is equal to one Galactic Standard Day, and one Earth orbit is within a quarter of a day of a Humanoid Year, Lieutenant? Of the five ancient planets, Earth is the only one that matches that. It has to be the origin."

"Oh, please. Lots of planets match the year and the day, and Earth's astronomy has no correlation to the seven-day week, so that theory doesn't hold water–not even the irradiated sludge that passes for water on Earth. You're being ridiculous, Hassan. New Mesopotamia makes a better argument for being the life starter than Earth does."

"With 'New' in their name? Now that's absurd."

"Some historians think Mesopotamia and New Mesopotamia are the same planet, but the 'New' was added in ancient times after a bloody regime change. I saw a documentary on it. Statement alive, Hassan, the colony on the Earth's moon is more hospitable than the planet itself. I'm sorry, but you have to maintain a severe level of cognitive dissonance to believe Earth is a tolerable place to hang your space helmet. It's the armpit of the Milky Way."

Bear chuckled in spite of himself, and then Ashley laughed out loud. "I knew I could get you to smile," he said. "It's not going to be easy going on without him, but we need to keep our spirits up. We're the top aces now, and though the other pilots may not like us, they look to our leadership."

Ashley let a minute pass in silence, holding her breakfast burrito in front of her without taking a bite. Finally, she said, "Yesterday you said Ace was acting weird, but you didn't elaborate."

"I'm sure it was nothing. I shouldn't have said anything." Ashley folded her arms and glared at him. "Oh, come on, Lieutenant," Bear pleaded, but she maintained her dark look. "I'm not sure. I guess for one thing he spent a lot of time on the simulator this past week while you were down in the gym. I made a joke about it, asked him if he had something to prove, or if he was practicing his lethal shots, and he just shrugged and didn't answer. Said something about you can never be too sharp."

Ashley grunted and put down her burrito. "What if," she started, then trailed off. Before she could say anything else, they were interrupted by a gaggle of ace pilots who'd approached to offer condolences.

"Lieutenant Sokolov, we were sorry to hear about Monk," said one. "He was a good pilot."

Ashley's face darkened. "You're sorry? You were horrible to him. You were horrible to us for flying with him. Why don't you go–"

"Thank you," Bear said sincerely, cutting off his squadmate.

"So anyway," continued the pilot, "now that there's an opening in the top squad–"

Ashley didn't let him finish, but stood up and headed for the tray return, letting the pilot feel a healthy dose of shoulder on her way past. After she was gone, Bear shrugged at the group of pilots and said, "I'm sure she's giving plenty of thought and meditation on the subject of our squad opening. If you'll excuse me."

An hour later, Bear walked into the simulator deck and wandered through the rows of egg-shaped pods. He called out, "Lieutenant Sokolov, are you in here?"

One of the simulator pods opened halfway, and a voice from inside called out, "What do you want?"

Bear jogged zigzag through the rows of pods to find Ashley sitting inside a sim with a computer on her lap, running diagnostics. "What are you doing?" he asked.

"I went to clean out Copernicus' locker," she answered without looking up from the computer. "It was full of empty beer cans and junk food wrappers. How could someone who ate so much gluten have such good reflexes? Anyway, I got it halfway empty and couldn't stand the stink anymore, so instead I'm following up on something you said."

"Oh, for crying in the sink. I shouldn't have said anything. Look, please don't flake out on me here. I can't have you turning into a Conspiracy Theorist of Skepton right now."

"I'm definitely onto something here. You said Copernicus spent all week in the sim, so I looked at the recent scoreboards. If he was here, his name would be all over the high scores. He wasn't there, so I checked further, and he hasn't logged on in months." Bear opened his mouth to say something, but then closed it. "So he was either using the sim pod as a place to hide out and read romance novels, or he was using a different login. Romance novels seems more likely, but I have no way to check that, so I'm looking through the logins from last week to see if there's anything out of place."

Bear opened his mouth again, and this time said, "That will take forever, though. These pilots are competitive. The sim deck is a popular place."

"Well, fortunately for me, I'm the one person in this smelly basket of fighter ships that knows everyone by their real name and not just their dumb callsign, so a fraudulent login should be easy to spot. Any time I see a name I don't recognize I'm cross referencing it with the ship's crew roster."

"Ashley," said Bear, "I'll admit that it's weird that he didn't log in, but you need to drop this. Monk was reckless. We knew it was only a matter of time."

Ashley finally looked up from the computer. "It's not just that, Hassan," she said. "We have our own reputations to worry about. After all the anti-intellectualism we've put up with for flying with him, if it turns out that something shady went down, we better know about it first before everyone else finds out and rakes us over the coals. Everyone hated us. Now they want to join our squad. They think we're just going to forget about the way they treated our squad leader because we're so happy to finally be popular. I'm not giving them the satisfaction."

"You don't have to," said Bear, "but I still shouldn't have brought up the sim deck. It's the perfect place to hide out and get some quiet time. He probably was reading. Please drop this, Lieutenant."

Ashley spun her computer screen around and showed it to her giant squadmate. "You were right to mention it," she said, "because there's something you should see. Ensign Laneeko Lytess scored sixty thousand points over the last couple days."

"Yeah, so?"

"Those are some impressive numbers considering he or she is not a real crew member on this carrier."

Bear thought for a second. "Laneeko Lytess? Why does that name ring a bell?"

"Because 'Laneeko' and 'Lytess' are the names of Copernicus' twin brothers."

"Okay, that's weird," admitted Bear.

"Oh, you ain't seen nothing. He set up a customized little scenario to train in. Check it out."

Bear leaned over and squinted at the long list of settings on the diagnostic screen, then let out a whistle. "Acceleration dampers off. I didn't know that was an option," he said.

"It's not. You have to go into the code."

"So it wasn't a malfunction?" asked Bear.

"It wasn't a malfunction."

Chapter 9

The Kadraf Corporation's experiment was a scientific success but a business failure. It was a profitable venture in the short-term, but after the new species revolted, the shareholders lost everything, the corporation went instantly out of business, and the corporate officers, all of whom pointed fingers at each other over the fiasco, were themselves sentenced to a life of hard labor in the oil fields of Dakota 17[6]. While there was a legal gray area in the Milky Way regarding genetic experimentation, holding intelligent species as slaves was consistently held to be one of the more heinous crimes in the civilized galaxy, ranking even above taking up two launchpads in the spaceship parking lot.

The Kadrafian revolution had lasted less than a month, and was barely violent. They decisively demonstrated to the Kadraf Corporation that no mining ships would get anywhere near planetside in one piece. Once the Galactic Justice Corporation was alerted to the situation and got involved, the mining company found itself with a set of problems far worse than what they had been treating as a mere labor union strike, and the whole thing was over as soon as it started.

After gaining their freedom and officially being recognized as a government, the new species tried to communicate to the rest of the galaxy that all they wanted was peace with the governments of the Oligarchy and a place at the diplomatic table. As the proud new owners of an untarnished and harshly beautiful planet on which they were specifically adapted to thrive, the Kadrafians had no interest in trudging across the galaxy seeking silly things like vengeance.

-Excerpt from "Conspiracy of Fools: A Slightly Less Brief History of Kadrafia," by Brandine Lupinski

---

[6]   The worst part about a sentence to hard labor in the oil fields of Dakota 17 was that the only machinery in the galaxy that burned oil as an energy source was the equipment used by the prisoners of Dakota 17. Well, that maybe wasn't the worst part, but it did add a gratuitous feeling of futility to the already severe punishment.

Freeda awoke with the full force of the sun on her face, but kept her eyes closed. She wasn't ready to face the reality of waking up somewhere other than her bunk. Unfortunately, her other four senses screamed that she was indeed on a sandy beach, outside and exposed to the elements. She blinked into the daylight for a few seconds, then stood up.

Copernicus was eating his breakfast and putting salve on his calves. He offered her some of both. She took the food but declined the ointment. "So from here we follow the coast?" she asked. Copernicus nodded, and they set out.

They walked the first hour in silence. The walk was nice, anyway. They were out of the bay and on the coast to the actual ocean, and because it took more regular beatings of the waves than the protected bay, the sand was harder packed and easier to walk on. For a while they made good progress.

Eventually the sand gave way to a rockier terrain. Around midmorning, the shoreline rose to become cliffs over the sea, and the dilemma then became whether to take the high ground or the low. The low ground, the bottom of the cliffs, was a collage of crashing waves and jagged rocks, an unpleasant and unpassable combination for small, fleshy members of the homo genus. The high road, on the other hand, was the undergrowth of the rainforest, which came right up to the edge of the cliffs, leaving no safe haven in between a deadly jungle and a deadlier fall.

The path to the top of the cliffs from the shore was a manageable slope, but before making their ascent was a good time to have a meal and discuss their next steps. A log washed up on the beach provided the perfect place to sit and enjoy some Navy emergency rations. Freeda inhaled her meal and set it down. "That was delicious," she said.

Copernicus went into a coughing fit and spit out the piece he had been chewing. "Are we eating the same thing? We have a theory in the Navy that the cooks have conspired to make the rations taste as bad as they do so the food in the mess hall will taste good by comparison."

"Well, you've obviously never tried the food in the KCF meal hall, then. I'll have to send you some in a care package sometime. It tastes like my feet smell right now."

"Noted," said Copernicus, pulling a can of beer out of his pack and chugging half of it. "Everybody's military food service sucks. See, I bet you our two sides have more in common than any of us realize."

Freeda's face softened. She took a few gulps of water and said, "So far all you've told me about this jungle is that we're going to die in there. You haven't said what will be the instrument of our demise."

Copernicus smiled. "Well, most likely a Galerabeast, but it could be anything. Almost everything in there is poisonous: plants, bugs, snakes, most of the birds. The Galerabeasts are pretty much the only thing on Galeria that aren't poisonous. In fact, humanoids are supposedly poisonous to them, but they don't know that, so they eat any humanoid they come across just the same."

"What's a Galerabeast?"

"It's a beast that lives on Galeria," answered Copernicus.

Freeda gave him an impatient look and said, "Loomy, you are as frustrating to talk to as you are to dogfight against."

Copernicus went on, "Well, nobody knows a ton about them. No one's bothered to categorize them, because it's too dangerous, hence the generic name. I'm not sure how anyone knows that we're poisonous to them. That might have started as a joke; it might not be true at all.

"What I do know about them is they're huge, they move like the blazes, and they're covered with armor that can withstand your laser rifle. If you catch one with its mouth open, it's possible to put a shot through the soft palate on the roof of their mouth and into their brain. There's a few hunters in the city that claim to have done this. Most of them are probably telling tales out of school, but there is a bar owner that has a Galerabeast head mounted in his tavern. It takes up an entire wall."

"So, you just wait until it roars?" That seemed simple enough to Freeda. She had done some big game hunting on her home planet. They may not have had Galerabeasts on Kadrafia, but they had plenty of Armadillosauruses, a formidable creature with only a slightly more clever name than this so-called Galerabeast. Hunting the Armadillosaurus (at least it wasn't called a Kadrafabeast) was known to be a dangerous hobby, though, and Freeda had earned her place among the elite group of hunters to have brought one down with only a knife.

"Oh, they don't roar," said Copernicus. "They only open their mouths when they're lunging at you. You get a split second to line up that shot. The tavern owner I know of who pulled it off lost a foot in the process. But if we encounter one, we're not killing it. Their vision is infrared, so we can be invisible to them if we cover ourselves in cold mud. I saw it in a movie once."

"First of all, Loomy, I thought you said everything was poisonous in there. I'm not covering myself with poison mud. Secondly, hiding is for children's games and small animals. If I see one of these things, I'm going to kill it and eat its heart."

"I think you'll change your mind if you see one, but suit yourself."

Freeda took a second look at the waves crashing on the jagged rocks below the cliff face and asked, "You sure you don't want to swim for it?"

Ascending into the jungle, it was Freeda's turn to carry the pack and rifle. The Lumano looked absurd walking next to her painted with mud, only his metallic cyborg eye protruding from the dull brown layer. Freeda was usually happy to be free of the constricted feeling of footwear, but she wasn't crazy about being partially barefoot in an environment in which "everything" was poisonous. When they first met, the Lumano had harped on how they stood a better chance working together, but what good was an extra set of fists when your adversary was a path covered in deadly leaves?

When they got to the top of the slope, their plan was to stay as close to the cliffs as possible and follow the coast. If they went inland, Copernicus' gyro compass could keep them traveling in the right direction, but traveling in the right direction and not being lost in the bush are not mutually exclusive. The coast as a point of reference was a welcome sight, even if it meant being close to a straight drop-off of several hundred meters.

They didn't know how long the cliffs lasted, or if the coast would ever slope down and turn into a beachline again. As they walked, Copernicus pointed out the roots and vines dangling over the edge of the cliff as a possible hideout in the event of a Galerabeast encounter, though there was no way to tell how much weight the vines would hold.

Eventually, Freeda heard an ear-shattering roar from deeper in the jungle, loud enough that flocks of nearby birds scattered upwards out of the trees. Freeda picked up the pace, and her senses sharpened. "I thought you said they don't roar."

"They don't. That was either a Galerabird or a McCallister Leopard, most likely running from a beast."

"Do I even want to know what a McCallister Leopard is?" Freeda was beginning to feel like the more she learned about this planet, the less she knew.

"The leopard was named for a scientist who was cataloguing wildlife, but he died without finishing. After his death nobody picked up where he left off, so now they just refer to every animal on the planet with the Galera prefix followed by whatever known animal it most resembles. Galerabird, for example, could be anything from an ostrich to an albatross."

"How did McCallister die?" Freeda wasn't sure she wanted to know, but she had to ask. "Poison dirt? Beast? Galeramalaria?"

Copernicus shrugged. "He got caught cheating at a card game in the city. He was shot on his way out of the casino."

At that moment a leopard burst out of the bushes, dashed between them, skidded to make the turn without flying over the cliff, and took off to the west parallel to the coast. Freeda pulled out her knife and stood her ground, but Copernicus turned and bolted, shouting, "Run, Freeda," over his shoulder.

Freeda assumed a fighting stance and prepared for the beast to emerge from between the trees. She called after the Lumano, "I don't run from the Navy, I don't run from dangerous animals, and I don't–RUN, LOOMY! RUN, NOW!"

Being the faster of the two, Freeda overtook Copernicus and was several meters ahead of him, but his camouflage worked, and the beast paid him no mind. Instead, she felt herself being yanked backwards by the shoulder straps of the backpack. She glanced upwards and backwards, and all she could make out was teeth for as far as the eye could see. Her feet lifted off the ground while she hung from the straps, trying to get an angle to take a shot with the rifle. The beast had its teeth clenched tight on her backpack, and shook her back and forth. She couldn't get a shot at its mouth, but if the beast wanted anything more than a backpack full of rations, it was going to have to open up.

Copernicus jogged to catch up, grabbed a branch, and took a couple swings at the front pair of the beast's six feet, but it bounced harmlessly off the creature's armor. "Freeda," he shouted, "let the pack go and get out of there."

"Not...a chance...Loomy," she grunted through gritted

teeth, her initial panic at seeing the size of the beast hardening into a calmer resolve. "It's...past noon and I haven't...killed anything yet today."

The creature's teeth were clenched, and it shook its head side to side, tossing her back and forth like a Galeramouse. Desperate for an idea, Freeda pulled her right arm out of the shoulder strap and twisted around to face the wall of teeth from which she dangled. The backpack was entirely in the beast's mouth, with only the straps sticking out between the massive stalagmites and stalactites of enamel. Straining to focus, Freeda caught sight of the three plasma grenades that were fastened to the side of the backpack. She reached her hand between the beast's teeth and fumbled around trying to make contact with a pin.

Just as she was giving up hope that she could maintain consciousness, Freeda felt the pin of a grenade slip perfectly around her finger. She clenched her fist, yanked her hand out from the beast's teeth as hard as she could, and slipped her left arm out from the other strap. "Grenade! Cliff!" she yelled as she hit the ground.

As Freeda flung herself over the cliff, she made eye contact with Copernicus standing dumbly in place. The light bulb in his head flickered on as the fuse on the grenade flickered off, and the Lumano jumped in time for the shock wave from the blast to float him over the edge.

The tips of Copernicus' flailing fingers brushed against a swaying vine, followed by a moment of freefall, and then a blue and orange hand reached out from oblivion and grabbed him by the wrist. The blast from above was deafening, but the hail of black flesh that went soaring out over the cliff and into the sea below was a comforting sight to the cliff danglers as they slammed into the rock face, Freeda with one hand on a vine and the other holding the Lumano.

Catching his breath, Copernicus climbed to his own adjacent vine. "Thanks," he said. "We better get moving before the mom comes to investigate."

"Wait. That was a baby?"

"Yeah. I'd say from the teeth it was probably two or three weeks old."

"THOSE TEETH GET BIGGER?"

"What? No. Those teeth are huge. Don't be silly. No, they grow more teeth. And for the love of the Statement, keep your voice down."

Freeda clenched her teeth and whispered, "More teeth? You should have killed me in my ship. Do Lumanos not believe in mercy killing?" Freeda was angry, but the Loomy was choking down laughter. Then, in spite of herself, Freeda began to giggle as well.

Their pack was gone. Their rations were gone. They were dangling helplessly from a cliff, a truth only made worse by the fact that dangling helplessly from a cliff was their current best option. At least they still had their weapons, minus a few plasma grenades. Hanging on their vines, they could feel the cliff face rumbling from the rhythmic force of footsteps that could only be mom.

Chapter 10

Copernicus climbed to the top of his vine and peered over the ledge. Freeda whispered up from below, "Well?" The look on his face said it all as he lowered himself down. They couldn't go up, and they couldn't hang on the side of a cliff forever. That left down or sideways. Sideways looked difficult, but the rocks below suggested that difficult might be the best they could hope for.

Freeda climbed down a few meters and noticed blood on a small rocky ledge. She looked closer and saw the sharp point sticking up from the ledge was not a rock, but a Galerabeast tooth with a bloody stump. It must have been from the second row of teeth, as it was small enough for Freeda to grab with one hand. While less satisfying than eating the beast's heart, it would make a good show-and-tell to accompany the retelling of her journey. With one arm she looped a lanyard around the tooth and slung it over her shoulder.

Unsure of the vines' strength, they avoided swinging too much from side to side, but there were enough roots and ledges for the climb eastward. They could hear the beast tracking their scent on the cliffs above them as they worked along the cliff face for several hours. When the sun was close to its highest point they found a small ledge, sat down, and gave their arms a break. Freeda surveyed the blue ocean. She let her gaze wander down to the rocks directly below, then began idly inspecting the cliff. Suddenly, she grabbed Copernicus' elbow, almost knocking him off the ledge, pointing frantically and gasping, "A cave!"

Almost immediately, Freeda remembered the many poisonous things that probably lived in a cave on this planet, but she was running low on alternatives. The entrance was just above sea level and slightly to the west, which meant backtracking a bit, which they did. Once inside, they searched the walls and floors for signs of life, making sure they weren't intruding on the home of some Galerabear or Galerahyena or Galeraspider colony. Happily, it turned out to be not only vacant, but pleasantly dry.

Copernicus sat on the floor of the cave and rubbed his arms. "We've been up for 17 hours," he said. "We should try to rest." He pulled his final bottle of whiskey off his belt and took a drink. Then he thought for a second and added, "You saved my life today."

"Yeah? So?"

"So, we're even now. You could kill me."

"It's not that simple, Loomy. You have no idea how honor works."

"You'll have to forgive me. In my culture we try not to overcomplicate our moral code, so we just don't kill anyone." With that he took another pull from his drink, but Freeda got up, snatched the bottle from him, and threw it against the wall of the cave. Copernicus watched the explosion of glass shards with a blank face. "That was my last bottle," he said. "Why would you do that?"

"For months my entire life goal has been to be the one who kills you."

"That's the dumbest life goal I've ever heard. You should find a better hobby."

Ignoring him, Freeda continued, "And now I see that you're nothing more than a lousy drunk. What would even be the point of killing you?"

"So leave me be, then. You didn't have to smash my bottle."

"I've got alcoholics in my family, Loomy, and I have no tolerance for it. Like it or not, we're stuck with each other, and I need you functioning. Look at you. You've already got the shakes. The Great and Powerful Monk can't go half a day without a drink. Pathetic."

"I'm not an alcoholic," protested the Lumano. "It just takes the edge off. My species, we don't usually see the horrors of war up close."

Freeda softened. "I'm sorry I smashed your bottle, but it's for your own good. But as long as we're stuck here, settle a bet for me. How did a Lumano end up as a Navy pilot, anyway?"

Copernicus shrugged. "Long story."

"Are you serious? I got nothing but time. I'm backed into a cave in a cliff on a strange planet with a vengeful momma beast the size of a battlecruiser guarding the door. And talking will do you some good and take your mind off the drink. So please, Loomy, tell me a long story. Make it as long as you can."

Copernicus raised his hands in surrender. "As you wish. As a kid I saw the war going on and daydreamed about ways to bring peace to the galaxy: diplomacy, having superpowers and going vigilante, everyone having to join together to face a bigger threat from another galaxy altogether, and any number of equally futile ideas.

"Before I joined, I worked in my family's spaceship repair shop with my brothers. We paid the rent doing repairs, but really we were inventors, always tinkering with new ways to do things. We also worked as an engineering crew for a pilot in the orbital race circuit for a while. I ended up joining the Navy as a science officer, hoping I could help develop less-than-lethal weapons so that if everyone was going to fight, at least they could do it without killing each other.

"My superior officer wanted me to stop wasting time working on non-lethals, so he ordered me to help work on better targeting systems for the Navy's regular arsenal, and I refused. He accused me of lacking empathy for our soldiers and sailors out in the field, and asked me if I liked my cushy lab job. I knew the question was rhetorical, but I admitted it had its ups and downs. He said if I wasn't going to help our boys and girls protect themselves with better tech, then I could put my own life at risk and join them on the front lines. I called his bluff.

"The next day I found myself assigned to a fighter squadron. On my first mission I got on the radio and warned my wing commander that while I would help the wing however I could, I was not willing to kill anyone. Everyone on the radio laughed at me. The wing commander was like, aren't you the Loomy that hasn't even trained as a pilot? They called me a 'silly rookie' and warned me that no one gets a kill on their first sortie, that I should just try to stay alive.

"I didn't vacuum any cockpits, but the day ended with the chief painting seven notches on the nose of my fighter. Seven. When I walked into the mess deck it went silent and everyone stared at me. I was so naive I didn't understand the significance of what I had done. After that I don't know whether the science department didn't want me back or the flight deck didn't want to let me go, but I was stuck. The mechanics chief always had my back, though. He supported the idea of a non-lethal solution, and petitioned regularly to let me go back to the science department. But the brass never listens to the chiefs, of course. If they did, probably none of us would be in this mess in the first place.

"Anyway, I'm not going back to the Navy. I must say I'm embarrassed at how long it's taken me to realize that fighting in the war is not an effective way to end it. I'll admit that violent or not, dogfighting is exhilarating. I think I got addicted to the thrill of being the top ace, and I told myself that maybe my distaste for killing would start to rub off, but sadly, even though everyone wanted to learn my tactics, it was only so that they could be better killers. Plus, they all hated me for not sharing their bloodlust, so I was never going to change their minds."

Freeda, who had been reclined against a rock, sat up straight. "Wait. Who hated you?"

"The Navy pilots. I didn't fit in."

"Wow. It never occurred to me you could be anything other than beloved by your side. Even on my side you're only mostly hated. We have a support group for pilots who have suffered the humiliation of being disabled but not killed. It's called 'Friends of the Hairless,' and they meet Tuesday nights. Your callsign is a curse word, but in group most pilots will admit that they appreciate keeping their lives."

"Are you in the group? Have I shot you down?"

"Well now, it's an anonymous group, isn't it? Hence the ambiguous name. But go on. I interrupted your story."

"Not much more to say," said Copernicus. "My brothers back home contacted me to let me know they've had a technological breakthrough, and I have to get home as soon as I can. They reckon they've devised a new approach to bring this insanity to an end, but I need to be in the city at noon tomorrow to obtain a ship so I can get home. Anyway, did you win the bet?"

"I'm sorry?"

"You said you wanted me to settle a bet. Had you bet on, 'science officer who mouthed off and got reassigned?'"

Freeda smirked. "No," she said. "I had my money on you not really being a Lumano at all. I figured you were probably two Zees, one sitting on the other's shoulders, wearing a trench coat."

Copernicus smiled and looked off into the distance. "Listen," he said. "I know you're a warrior and maybe not as obsessed with peace as I am, but you're welcome to come work with my brothers and me."

Freeda didn't answer, but she smiled at the absurdity of the offer. Fighter though she was, she felt overwhelmed at being in the confidence of the one they called The Monk. It suddenly came crashing down on her how much conviction it takes to fly into battle and refuse to kill. After all, she had been there herself, but never considered she had a choice in whether to take the lives of her foes. That's what battle was.

That's what you did. It felt surreal to share such a conversation with someone so genuinely selfless. She finally asked, "And what happens if you don't make it to the meeting?"

"Nothing huge. It will make it harder to find a ship to get off this rock, but I suppose it wouldn't set my overall plans back that far." With that, Copernicus closed his eyes and left Freeda alone with her thoughts.

Though she fell asleep second, Freeda woke up first, just at dusk. She woke up to a grumbling stomach, but tried not to think about food. At least they had fresh water. She went to the front entrance and looked out over the ocean, thinking about their next move. "Their" next move. She thought about it and tried to pinpoint the moment that she started thinking of her and the Lumano as a team. A day ago she didn't trust him at all, and maybe she still shouldn't, but for the moment they were stuck in this together.

As far as their next move, she wasn't sure. The Lumano knew a lot more than her about this planet, but she was fast becoming an expert. After all, even most of the locals had never seen one of those beasts up close, and she could now claim to have stuck her hand right into one's mouth without losing so much as a pinky finger.

Freeda looked up the cliff face. The vines meant the climb itself wouldn't be bad, but did they really want to be back at the top? Instead, she scanned the rocks. The ocean was more docile in the evening light, so the waves weren't crashing, but staying at sea level didn't appear to be a good option. There was almost no way around the rocks at the bottom of the cliff. Then she saw it. Or at least, she thought she saw it. Did she really see it?

Freeda leapt from the mouth of the cave to the first large boulder sticking out of the water. The rock came to a point at the top and lay at an angle, looking like a ship that had given way to torpedoes and was going down stern-first, its bow sticking high out of the water. She perched herself on the tip and leaned over to get a better look. The light was getting dim, but now that she knew what she was looking for it was unmistakable. There was one lone boulder, farther out from the rest, standing by itself. It was in deeper water, and even in the rough seas the waves would not crash around it as violently, which is probably why somebody at some point had thought it was a good place to tie off their fishing boat. Where that somebody was now was anybody's guess, but it was doubtful they were missing their boat.

The craft was small, but from where Freeda was perched it looked a lot more seaworthy than her inflatable raft. It was afloat, at least, and out of reach of their toothy friend at the top of the rock face. Freeda climbed back into the cave to wake up Copernicus with the good news.

"You want to steal somebody's boat?" he asked.

Freeda snorted. "You are unbelievable. You're worried about stealing right now? We can leave them a note if you like, but I think it's a safe bet that the owner isn't taking a dip. They're clearly long dead."

The two climbed out of their cave into the twilight and began hopping from rock to rock. The rocks were easy to climb on when the water was calm, but eventually they would have to swim to make it to the last one. They got as far out as they could on the boulders and took a short breather. Freeda slung the rifle over her shoulder. Copernicus took off his boots, hung them around the back of his neck, and dipped his toe timidly into the ocean. "You want to go first?" he asked.

"Not really," said Freeda, then turned and dove head-first into the water below. She resurfaced and swam hard for the boat. When she was halfway there, she flipped to her back and called out, "Better get moving. I think I'm drawing out the sea monsters right now."

Copernicus went cannonball style into the water and kicked hard.

Freeda was a stronger swimmer and made it to the boat well ahead of the Lumano. She grabbed the rail of the small fishing craft and threw herself aboard with one smooth motion, then stood at the rail and drew the rifle to her shoulder, aiming at the Lumano.

When Copernicus was close to the boat, Freeda put three shots into the water, startling him so badly that she would later claim he leapt completely out of the water. He reached the rail and Freeda pulled him aboard. As he tumbled onto the deck, he had a few choice words for her.

"Relax, Loomy," she retorted. "I saw tentacles behind you. I didn't have time to count how many." She sat down next to him and added, "Did you see the name stenciled on the stern? The Leopard. This is that zoologist's boat, McCallister. Told you no one is coming back for it."

The question with the fishing boat was whether the WID motor's power cells were any good. WID drives are efficient, but without the juice to open that first wormhole, they're not much good. Fortunately, they had a vehicle repair expert on their team. Copernicus opened up the engine compartment and had a look. There was a lot of corrosion, but there wasn't anything obviously wrong with the system.

After staring at the compartment for a few minutes, he announced, "I don't have my tools, but if I can borrow your knife, I think I can get it working." Freeda unsheathed her knife, but hesitated for a second before handing it to the Lumano. As he took hold of the Raif'yan blade he added, "Maybe once in its existence it can be used for something other than killing." Within 15 minutes he had the system powered up, and they tossed off their lines and weighed anchor to follow the coast the rest of the way to Galeria City.

Chapter 11

While organizing a fledgling government, the Kadrafians debated whether to rename themselves, but decided to keep the name as a reminder of their hard-fought freedom. Besides, everyone knew it was bad luck to rename the planet you were illegally adapted to and enslaved on.

Though the Raif'yans made it clear that they had no desire for conflict, the rest of the mining industry, particularly anyone with a financial interest in the Kadraf Mining Corporation, developed a thorough paranoia that the Kadrafians were busy in the proverbial kitchen planning a three-course meal of revenge to be served cold. The higher-ranking members of the Oligarchy, desiring to preserve the status quo, and being the empathetic and moral fellows that they were, made the difficult decision to launch a not-so-subtle propaganda campaign that would find reasons to scapegoat the Raif'yans and blame the new species for their own involuntary existence.

It didn't take long for the animosity to spread and the stereotypes to develop. The elected officials of the Oligarchy claimed publicly that they wanted only diplomacy with the Kadrafians, but they continued to build up a military presence around the Kadrafian system. Eventually the Kadrafians, motivated to keep the peace, began building up their own defenses. That was of course seen as an offensive rather than defensive move, and the Galactic Navy responded with a full-blown arms race. Anyone who's ever been in the same room as a history book could guess how it went from there. And if you're reading this, dear reader, you're in the same room as a history book right now!

-Excerpt from "For Whom the Bell Tolls: A History of Kadrafia That is Really Just, In No Way, Brief," by Brandine Lupinski

Freeda sat on the bow, facing aft, and watching for rocks

and reefs as the water parted under the hull of their small powerboat. The calm ocean and blue skies made a perfect day for a relaxing boat ride, if only she hadn't been so hungry. They searched the storage compartments when they first boarded, but their fishing boat lacked any fishing gear. Freeda walked aft and sat down across from the Lumano, The Dreaded Monk, and pondered the revelations about him from the past two days.

Her people viewed the Galactic Navy as mercenaries and bullies: a collection of young men and women of various worlds and species who'd been tricked into fighting for the benefit of the Oligarchy. The Kadrafian Combat Force, on the other hand, was made up only of Kadrafians, fighting for their home, or their people, or something. It had made so much sense when it was explained to her growing up on her home world. She couldn't help but wonder, what exactly were they fighting for, again?

Freeda had killed Navy pilots in combat. If anyone were to happen across the burned wreckage of her fighter, they'd find over two dozen tally marks painted under the gun rack. Now, riding in a "stolen" boat on an unwelcoming ocean on a foreign planet had her reflecting on those kills. Those were real people, probably with families, probably with crazy stories about having to fight off crazy creatures in crazy jungles with eccentric Loomies they'd just met.

Freeda was a warrior, and she had principles. She had shot down those enemy fighters because she believed she was standing up for her principles, but what if she was wrong? What if she had been given bad information about her enemy's desire to impede upon her principles? What if the whole thing was one giant miscommunication, and everybody was trying to stand up for the same exact ideals as everyone else, but they were all horribly, mindlessly wrong?

To be totally fair to herself, this boat ride was not the first time in her life she'd wondered about such questions, but she had never lingered on them. She was a warrior, after all. It's not like she could resign her post and take a job teaching elementary school with her orange tattoos, so it had always been in her best interest to put those questions out of her mind.

"This city," Freeda finally asked, "Raif'yans are allowed there?"

"Yeah, the merchant planets are anything goes. Interspecies trade partners are common."

"Great," said Freeda. "As long as I'm on shore leave, I may as well hit the bathhouse and then get laid. They got a Kadrafian house of free love, you think?"

"Yeah, they've got one. They've also got one that's open to all species. Like I said, the merchant planets are anything goes."

"That's tempting in a 'try anything once' kind of way, but I'm sure I'll do better among my own. The perfect symmetry of my scar tissue is rare; I'm considered quite beautiful in my culture. I had many marriage proposals from wealthy Kadrafians before I joined the combat force."

"So why did you end up joining?"

"For one thing, I had already received my tattoos. My family has been warriors for generations. Besides, there was someone else I loved, and wealthy Kadrafian men have no idea how to treat a woman."

Copernicus laughed. "I think that's true in most cultures, but I'm certainly no expert."

Freeda switched her attention to the skyline and watched Galeria City grow larger on the horizon, until finally their tiny boat pulled into the massive harbor. After tying off their craft to abandon at the dock, Freeda took the one remaining fuel cell out of the engine compartment and used it to haggle with a street cart vendor for some breakfast. They sat on the pier for a few minutes, filling their bellies.

"You know what I miss more than anything?" Freeda asked, without waiting for a reply. "The moss from home. You ever had Kadrafian moss, Loomy?"

"I tried it," Copernicus said, munching on his breakfast pie. "I'll be honest, it wasn't my favorite. It's pretty bitter."

Freeda had heard that before from off-worlders. "Oh, to our tongue it's sweeter than any pastry your bakers could ever dream of creating."

"You know, it always surprised me that you can eat the moss. The fern we share DNA with is poisonous to us. We'd have to eat a lot for it to kill us, but it's a pretty bad day if we ingest any. Gives us the shakes."

"You Loomies are weird." Freeda wiped her hands on her pants, got up, and said, "Well, it's been an interesting couple of days. I'm going to find a bathhouse. Good luck with your little plan." She started to walk away and then turned and said, "And Loomy, don't drink alone. Or at all. Don't drink at all." With that, she walked off and left Copernicus sitting on the pier.

A few hours later, Freeda emerged blinking into the daylight from the dim basement storefront of the house of free love. She stepped onto the busy city sidewalk wearing the change of clothes she had bought after the bathhouse, and she was feeling refreshed and ready to find her way back to her fleet. She slung the Galerabeast tooth over her shoulder, but when she went to attach her knife sheath to her belt it was empty. The Lumano hadn't returned her blade after he'd used it on the boat. She punched a wall in frustration, then sprinted back to the pier and asked the street cart merchant where the closest bar was. He pointed her up the block.

Copernicus was sitting in a booth by himself when Freeda entered the bar and scanned the room. The Tipsy Merchant was a standard tavern, complete with a surly group of "regulars" and plenty of dank. Its most prominent feature was the taxidermied head of a Galerabeast mounted on the wall opposite the bar. Looking at it when she walked in, a shudder ran down Freeda's spine, and she muttered to herself, "They should call it a Galera-hammerhead-landwalker." The head was not just decorative; it also served as a reminder that the owner had brought one of the beasts down by himself. The Tipsy Merchant did not require the services of a bouncer.

Freeda put her giant tooth on the floor and slid into the booth across from Copernicus, who had a collection of empty glasses in front of him. He smiled and pushed her a steaming drink, which she pushed to the side. Holding out her hand, she said, "I just came for my knife, and I'll be on my merry way."

Copernicus half opened his eyes and looked around the room. He slurred, "Hold on. I don't want to wave it around and draw attention. Let me be discreet."

He started to slide the knife across the table, but he was interrupted by a man with an athletic build, wearing a polo shirt tucked into a pair of short pants that were the color of a perfectly-cooked Galerasalmon. The man was passing by with three friends, all of whom sported spiky cyborg hair and unnaturally smooth skin. They wore matching polo shirts with their names embroidered above the pocket. The first man asked, "Hey Coper, how much for the Raif'yan?"

The Lumano replied, "About five orbits on Dakota 17 if you don't piss off, Broseph."

Freeda remained seated, but chimed in with, "Nah, he touches me, he won't live long enough to stand trial for slavery."

Four booths over, three Kadrafians sporting black merchant tattoos stopped their conversation to watch the encounter. Broseph ignored Freeda but said to Copernicus, "The new eye is looking good, my friend. No hard feelings."

Copernicus set down his glass, then rose to his feet and stumbled as he attempted to throw a punch at the large man. Broseph blocked the blow and returned a punch of his own, but he was too slow. Freeda was on her feet and caught his fist in her hand, then dropped her heel into his knee, bending it the wrong way and buckling him to the floor. Broseph's three friends, Brostopher, Brotholomew, and Chad, all moved in on Freeda. She was already spinning and caught Brostopher with a roundhouse kick to the face. Brotholomew swung and landed a punch. The three Kadrafian merchants pulled him back, and by the time the bar owner looked up from the cocktail he was pouring, the entire room was engaged in a brawl.

Freeda was connecting with a left-handed haymaker to Chad's face when an ear-shattering boom rang out across the bar. As Chad dropped, Freeda looked at her fist, confused, then looked up to see the bartender holding a WID-powered blunderbuss that he had just discharged into the ceiling.

All parties froze. A bottle rolled off a table and shattered in the sudden silence. The bartender's footsteps echoed on the wooden floor as he strolled to the epicenter of the crowd and scanned the faces. "Who started it?"

Everyone pointed in unison at Copernicus, who was sitting on the floor with his legs out in front of him. He looked up to see fingers pointing at him, then raised a finger to point at himself. "Yeah, I suppose it's probably my turn to buy a round, eh Seamus?"

Seamus the bartender frowned at Copernicus and said to the crowd, "I'll believe a Lumano threw the first punch when that beast skull over there comes alive and recites the lyrics to 'Statement Bless Galeria,' including the old super racist verse that we finally did away with."

Everyone stayed silent. After a beat Copernicus asked, "Wait, so if the skull comes alive and recites all the lyrics except for the racist verse, you still won't believe I started it?"

The bartender ignored him and waved his blunderbuss around at the crowd. "Who. Started. It."

"I started it," said Freeda, "but I was only protecting the Lumano from this scumbag." She punctuated the sentence with a kick to the ribs of the man on the ground. He let out a whimper, but did not let go of his knee.

"Fine," said the owner. "I admire your honesty." He leveled the blunderbuss at Freeda. In the same moment she picked up her Galerabeast tooth and held it in front of the gun. The bartender pulled the trigger. The molar absorbed the blast, taking no damage.

Seamus looked at the tooth and did a double take. "Is that"–

"I was about to get my Loomy...friend...out of here," Freeda explained, "as I do believe he has had his fill. But please, good sir, accept this humble gift as a token of my most heartfelt remorse for disturbing the harmonious atmosphere of your establishment." With that, she dropped the tooth at the bartender's feet with a satisfying thud. She then snatched her knife from the table, picked Copernicus up across her shoulders, and exited the bar.

Chapter 12

Opening a stable Einstein-Rosen bridge large enough for a spacecraft carrying biological matter to safely traverse the upper dimensions of space-time was much more complicated than putting a WID drive on a motor scooter or waffle iron[7]. Any school-aged child with a fission generator and half a potato at their disposal could open an unstable microscopic wormhole that would bring enough heat to burn two slices of toast. Building a hyperdimensional bridge strong enough to carry living beings safely to the other side was a much more involved process. It was easier than it had been in the early days of hyperspace travel, mind you, when space travelers had roughly only an 80% chance that they wouldn't be taking the relativity nap, but it still required a lot of precautions.

For one thing, in order to create a hyperspace bridge stable enough for solid matter to pass through, there could be no other ripples in space-time in the immediate vicinity, so it required an area clear of other wormholes. Even more importantly, wormholes cannot travel through other wormholes, so all on-board WID devices needed to be powered down before a spacecraft could make a hyperspace jump. This included the ship's artificial gravity, the ship's WID engines, and any hot plates or other such appliances in the ship's galley. All WID devices were of course equipped with fail-safes that would shut them down immediately if the absent-minded space pilot forgot to turn off his WID-powered karaoke machine prior to initiating a hyperspace jump.

In addition, passengers were required to be strapped in place for their own safety. It was one of those exciting moments in modern space travel when you felt the gravity go off, the lights went down,

---

[7]   The hyperdimensional bridge was named for two prophets of the ancient world, Alberta Einstein and Nathan Rosen. Alberta Einstein was originally known for several prophecies in the areas of physics, but she is most remembered for her correct prediction that while it had not been revealed to her with what weapons the third planetary war would be fought, the fourth would be fought with sticks and stones. Less was known about Rosen, but many historians believe he correctly prophesied that the third planetary war would be fought with sticky beads.

the cabin temperature dropped to the point where you could see your breath, and for one brief moment it actually felt like you were traveling through the vast unforgiving vacuum of outer space.

-Excerpt from "A Heartbreaking Work of Staggering Genius: Tales from Outer Space," by Brandine Lupinski

Chief Schultz looked over his shoulder as he slipped through the door to the darkened shuttle deck and picked his way through the rows of transport ships. In the far corner he turned on his flashlight and approached a shuttle with a sign that said, "Out of commission, scheduled for scrap by order of Chief Schultz." He yanked off the sign and folded it up, then checked the clock and cursed under his breath. Looking over his shoulder again, he started to climb the ladder into the shuttle when a voice called out behind him.

"Going somewhere, Chief?"

Schultz stood bolt upright on the ladder, and slowly turned to face the sound. Bear was striding toward him from the far entrance, swinging his arms far more dramatically than necessary to keep his balance. But Schultz was probably a little biased in his judgment of how much arm swinging was the necessary amount, considering he was already running late for his task.

"Planetside," the chief said. "Gotta get some ship parts from the scrap merchants. The only thing I have less of than personnel is parts."

"Mind if I tag along? I was just thinking that I need some parts, too. So many parts."

Schultz stepped down from the ladder and sighed. "Look, I'm busy. I don't have time for pilot games. What do you want, Bear?"

The pilot reached the corner of the room and stood in front of the crew chief. "I know Monk had the simulator set up to practice flying without acceleration dampers. Ain't that some kind of coincidence his ship had the same 'malfunction'?"

Schultz, who was now most definitely feeling a bias as to the lack of necessity of the air quotes, took a step up the ladder. "The question I asked was what do you want?"

"I know it wasn't a malfunction, and since you two put on your little show right before it happened, that means you know it wasn't a malfunction too. So why don't you tell me what's going on."

The chief sighed again. "I don't know what you think you know, but you don't know shit." Bear raised his eyebrows, so Schultz added, "That sounded way better in my head."

"Look, Chief, I'm sure you and Monk had your reasons, but Ashley figured it out and she's worried. We're not going to rat you out, but we want to know if Monk is alive. I think you owe us that."

Schultz really was busy, and he really didn't have time for pilot games. That part wasn't a lie. "I've been right here since he was shot down, so how would I know? Even if whatever you're accusing me of were true, that's one question I can't answer. Now if we're done here, I'd like to go get my parts so I can keep the rest of your ships running properly." Without waiting for an answer, the chief turned to climb the ladder into the shuttle, and Bear made no move to stop him.

After he parked his stolen transport on the planet, Chief Schultz jogged toward The Tipsy Merchant. He arrived to the bar to see a Kadrafian woman propping Monk on a bench out front. Monk, who was only half awake, spotted the chief approaching and called out, "You're late."

"And you're drunk," returned Schultz. "Too drunk to fly. Even for you." Then to the Kadrafian he added, "Who are you?"

The woman pulled out and displayed Monk's dog tags and said, "I'm the ace pilot who shot down The Invincible Monk."

Copernicus added, "Freeda, Chief. Chief, Freeda. She saved my life in the jungle. She killed a Galerabeast with her bare hands, so I'd show her some respect."

"You are wasted. With her bare hands? You expect me to believe that?"

"Well, with my bare hands I pulled the pin from the grenade it was chomping on, but I was just leaving. Take care of your friend, Chief."

Freeda turned to leave, but Schultz called out, "He passed out. Can you help me? I'm running very late. I ran into some complications."

"I guarantee, friend, that this Loomy's 'complications' were worse than yours, and he managed to be early."

"Freeda, please, help me get Monk up to his ship."

Freeda frowned and glanced at the Lumano, who had nodded off completely and was just beginning to snore. "First of all, he doesn't go by that anymore, Chief...?"

"Schultz."

"Chief Schultz, he doesn't go by that anymore. His name is Copernicus."

"I know what his name is. Fine. Can you help me get Copernicus up to his ship?"

"No."

Freeda turned to leave, but Schultz pleaded, "I've got a ship at pier 42. I can't take him to New Belgium myself. If you take him, you'll never see him again. If you don't, I have to take him back to the Navy and they'll make him keep flying against you."

Freeda turned back around. "Just drop him off and that's it?"

"That's it."

"Where's he gotta go?"

"His brothers have a ship repair shop."

"Why can't his brothers come pick him up?"

"Apparently they don't have any ships capable of

hyperspace jumps."

Freeda narrowed her eyes. "They own a ship repair shop, but they don't have a ship that can make a hyperspace jump?"

"They're inventors. They keep cannibalizing their own ships for parts. Apparently they don't have one running right this moment."

Freeda considered the alternatives. "You're bluffing. You wouldn't really take him back to the Navy."

Before the chief could respond, Freeda spotted one of Broseph's friends across the street talking to a pair of cops and pointing frantically in her direction. She put up a hand to silence Schultz. The body language of the cops suggested that they didn't want to be bothered with some petty bar fight, but the injured man was not dropping it. Finally, one of the cops crushed his cigarette under his shoe and turned to cross the street toward Freeda.

"Hold on," she whispered to the chief. "Help me get him up, and let's get out of here."

Together they picked Copernicus up under the shoulders and dragged him around the corner and into an alley. A few moments later the cops passed by the end of the alley without looking in.

Schultz asked, "What's that about? Are they looking for you or him?"

"Bar fight. They're probably after me, but the Loomy technically threw the first punch."

"Ha. I sincerely doubt that. So you really want to go try to find other transportation with the cops looking for you? Probably won't be hard to find the Raif'yan with the warrior tattoos. I got a ship ready. All you gotta do is drop off my boy."

"You trust me to do that? I could take him to my people for torture."

"He said himself you saved his life in the jungle. If you wanted him dead, he'd be dead."

"Maybe I want him alive."

"Do you?" asked the chief. Freeda didn't answer, so Schultz said, "See? Y'all are obsessed with honor. If you tell me you'll take him to his brothers, I know he'll get there. I've got a ship ready to go, and you've got the local constabulary unhappy with you, so now who's bluffing?"

"Fine," Freeda said, and picked the Lumano up across her shoulders. "Lead the way."

By the time they got to pier 42, Copernicus was coming around, so Schultz tried to talk to him. "Monk, your squadron figured out in less than 48 hours that this is a hoax. I can deal with them, but your plan isn't as foolproof as you think. Here's your ship, but that's all I can do for now. Promise me you'll lay low once you get home. And definitely don't try to contact me. Radio silent." Monk was already starting to nod off again, and Schultz wasn't sure he had heard any of it. "Monk? Copernicus?"

"I'll remind him when he's sober, Chief Schultz. Radio silent," said Freeda, "and he better stay 'dead' after I drop him off. When I get back to my fleet I'm reporting to my people that we will no longer be bothered by The Dreaded Monk." She sighed and added, "My people will never live down the humiliation that for over a year we were bested by this drunkard."

"If it's any consolation, he flies better when he's had a few," said the chief. "But don't worry. He never should have been part of this war in the first place. You won't be seeing him again."

Chapter 13

Bowing sat in his office and frowned at the telephone. Being at the top of his industry, Bowing was nothing short of a celebrity in the realm of weapon manufacturing and dealing. He was an intimidating man, but the telephone was unphased by his stern glare, and it continued ringing. Finally, he picked up the receiver. "Hello, dear," he said.

"Don't hello, dear, me," came the reply. Bowing slouched deeper into his chair. Being the trophy husband of the galaxy's most powerful Mafia Dawn had its moments, but it came at a price.

"Yes, Willow."

"Listen, I don't need to tell you how important this client is, so give him whatever he wants. He'll be there in ten minutes."

"But," Bowing began, before his wife cut him off.

"Don't 'but' me. I'm not in the mood. Your company is hemorrhaging money. If you want me to keep bankrolling you, you will do as I say."

Bowing rolled his eyes. "Yes, dear," he said, and hung up the phone.

Trying to play it cool, Bowing leaned back with his feet on his desk when the "client" walked in, but the sight of the giant hooded figure approaching his desk caused him to jolt backwards and take his chair with him to the floor. He got up and brushed off his pant legs.

"I have a large order to place," said the figure. "I wanted to place it in person, because this won't be billed to our normal account."

"Very good," said Bowing. "Will you be needing knives? Rifles?"

"Ships," said the figure.

"Ships, plural?"

"A fleet."

"Forming an army, then, are we?"

"Don't play coy," spat the figure. "You know very well what army this is for. I know you expect a command position in it, and I'm sure your wife will give you one, you sniveling rat. But you still won't outrank me."

Bowing cleared his throat and hunched over his computer, unable to sit on his upturned chair. "A fleet," he said. "We've been building as fast as we can in anticipation of this, but it's going to take some time. How soon are you invading?"

"We've got the army. I just need the ships. The Navy and the KCF have been killing each other off and weakening themselves for long enough. As soon as you get off your lazy ass and get a fleet together, it's time to move in and wipe them out."

"Lazy?" retorted Bowing, "Whose weapons do you think they've been killing each other with all these years."

"Whatever. Here are the numbers I need. There's schematics for one item in particular that you might want to get to work on now." With that, the figure turned and stormed out of the room, muttering under its breath.

Chapter 14

The Brothers Repair Shop was a large structure, but being located in the heart of the city, right next to the Institute of Learning, it was dwarfed by the tall spires that reached up into the sky. The city was immaculately clean, always having a look of being brand new, even though the structures were centuries old. Lumanos built to last. The Brothers Repair Shop, on the other hand, was the one dirty thing within the city limits. It was as if they had gone out of their way to build it using an ancient metallic compound capable of rusting, just to spite the perfectly reflective towers that surrounded them. If Lumanos had HOAs or golf, the HOA busybodies would be constantly coming around in a golf cart to give a friendly reminder to the brothers to relocate their spare parts bin somewhere out of sight, or the HOA would foreclose. But since the work the brothers did was appreciated planet-wide, they were able to get away with having the occasional rusted-out antique spacecraft in full public view while they restored it.

The shop had an open front with three large bays big enough to accommodate a transport craft, while the entire roof was dedicated to one single landing pad for larger ships. Next to bay number one was the cluttered office, with a ladder down to the basement laboratory, where they worked on their new innovations. The brothers were considered repair technicians first and amateur inventors second, despite the fact that they had created dozens of designs that were later implemented into regular use by the large spacecraft manufacturers. Lumanos understood PR, and it wouldn't do to admit to off-worlders that this dilapidated filling station was where some of the greatest scientific breakthroughs of this generation had taken place.

-Excerpt from "It: An Insider's Look at The Historic Brothers Repair Shop," by Brandine Lupinski

As the temperature in the cabin plummeted, Copernicus woke up and put his hands to his temples. "Ow," he muttered. "I can barely tell which way is up."

"We're about to hyperjump," said Freeda, who was sitting at the helm of the Navy transport. "The gravity is off. There is no up."

"Where are we going?" Copernicus asked.

"I'm dropping you on New Belgium."

"That's nice of you."

"I'm only doing it to keep you from getting in a Navy fighter again. It was that or kill you, and I already mentioned the whole honor thing." Freeda looked over at Copernicus to see he had already dozed off again. "Worthless Loomy," she muttered, and fired the hyperdrive.

They came out of hyperspace into an orbit over New Belgium. Freeda paused to check her navigational computer for the Brothers Repair Shop when two unmarked fighters dropped into view in front of her, face-to-face. One of the unmarked ships hailed her over the radio, and a deep voice announced, "You are harboring a traitor aboard your vessel. Surrender immediately." Before Freeda could key up the mic to respond, the radio crackled, "Too late. Prepare to be vacuumed."

A purple beam shot out from one of the hostile ship's Gatling lasers, showering the Navy transport with energy. Freeda braced herself for an untimely doom, but the cockpit remained intact. Patting herself down and checking for injury, she had not a scratch. Copernicus woke as Freeda jammed on the controls to take evasive action before the next barrage. Her ship didn't respond. She had power, life support was functioning at 100 percent, but the engines had no juice. The transport floated helplessly in orbit, and the hostile ships hung in front of them, motionless. After a second, the radio crackled again. "Well," it asked, "are you dead?"

Copernicus and Freeda looked at each other. Copernicus shrugged, and keyed up the radio mic. "No, we're not dead."

"Good," came the reply. "Then come with us."

A mag-net tow line launched from the second hostile ship and attached to the transport. The ships then began a slow descent to the planet's atmosphere. As they got lower and Copernicus realized where they were going, he relaxed and told Freeda not to worry. "That's my brothers."

After towing the transport down to the repair shop, two helmeted pilots emerged, one from each ship, and ordered Freeda and Copernicus to exit the Navy transport. As Freeda stepped down to the ground, one of the figures brandished a rifle and shouted, "Hands in the air, Kadrafian."

Copernicus stepped between the two and said, "Freeda, meet my brothers, Laneeko and Lytess."

The one carrying the rifle pointed it at Copernicus' head and shouted, "Nice try, traitor. Step back."

Copernicus walked toward the helmeted figures. "I know it's you, morons. You brought us to the shop. If you wanted to keep the prank going, you should have taken us to–" before he could finish the sentence, the figure lowered the rifle to Copernicus' torso and pulled the trigger. A stream of gray foam shot out of the rifle and encompassed Copernicus from the shoulders to the waist, hardening into a rubbery encasement and knocking him down.

Laneeko and Lytess took off their helmets and screamed with laughter. "You should have seen the look on your face," Laneeko cried. "You totally had no idea it was us." Before Copernicus could protest, Laneeko added, "You like the foam? That one's just for fun. The real deal is the Purple Inerter that we showed you in orbit. Badass, right?"

Copernicus struggled to get his arms free, but they wouldn't budge. "Yes, Laneeko. It is very badass. Now get me out of here."

"The foam will dissolve in time. You'll be able to break it in a half hour. Until then, you hang tight. Don't worry, though. Lytess has a hand truck. We'll wheel you into the shop and get you some lunch."

Copernicus continued to struggle. "Laneeko, get me out of this."

"Are you sure you want me to?"

"Yes. I'm sure."

Laneeko looked at Lytess, who nodded. "All right," he said. "You asked for it." He then flipped a switch on his foam rifle, and shot a bright blue beam at the encased Copernicus.

The foam vaporized into a puff of blue smoke, and Copernicus fell to the ground, gasping and coughing. "For science sake, Laneeko, couldn't you get it to smell any better when it vaporizes? That is disgusting."

A look of confusion crossed Laneeko's face. "You don't like it? The foam naturally has an agreeable scent. It took us a lot of work to get it to smell that bad. Just because it's non-lethal doesn't mean it should be pleasant."

Copernicus pulled himself to his feet and waved his hands in front of his face as the cloud dissipated. "We're not trying to keep people alive just so we can torture them, Laneeko," he coughed. "We're trying to end this violence altogether. You make people smell that fart-cloud and they'll go right back to killing each other."

Freeda grew agitated. She interrupted the three quarreling brothers. "What is this? I thought your whole race was supposed to be egghead scientists."

"Oh, don't worry about them," Copernicus said. "Please don't form your opinion of the Lumano species based on these maniacs. For one thing, twins are completely unheard of here. These two are an abomination, but when they put their heads together, they can do anything. Together they've saved the galaxy several times, and even most New Belgians don't know about–"

Before Copernicus could finish, a fresh burst of foam spat from Laneeko's rifle and hit him square in the mouth, silencing him. Laneeko flicked the switch on the rifle to set it to the blue beam. Copernicus started taking steps backward, shaking his head no, but it was too late. The blue beam fired from the rifle, vaporizing the foam, and sending Copernicus running into the shop holding his breath, looking for something to wash out the foul taste.

Freeda finally smiled and broke into giggles.

From inside Copernicus called out, "That went right in my mouth, you Luddite! I swear to the Statement, I will go back to the Navy right now and start inventing the most lethal weaponry you can possibly imagine, just to come back here and use it on you!"

"No he won't," Laneeko whispered to Freeda.

Lytess asked her, "Copernicus didn't mention he'd be coming with anyone. How do you know each other?"

Freeda stopped giggling. "I'm just dropping him off. I need that ship powered up so I can be on my way."

Lytess and Laneeko looked at each other. "Um, so..." Laneeko said, "That's going to take a little while. Our weapon neutralized your fuel. We'll have to flush the fuel lines and then–"

Before he could finish the sentence, Freeda was behind him with her knife to his throat. "Get. It. Working," she hissed.

"We'll get right on it," Laneeko said.

"How long?"

Laneeko closed his eyes and swallowed hard. He whispered, "First thing tomorrow morning?"

Freeda threw her knife, and the blade stuck upright in the concrete between Lytess' feet. "Not a minute past sunrise," she said, and released Laneeko, who fell panting to his knees.

Freeda climbed into the cockpit of the transport and turned

on the radio. She started to dial her fleet, but hesitated. How exactly was she going to explain that she was on the Lumano home world without giving away that The Monk was alive? It would be one thing to admit that she encountered him on the planet and let him go, but traveling with him to New Belgium would certainly raise questions about her judgment. She clicked off the radio and decided to wait until the brothers fixed the transport.

Walking into the repair shop office, Freeda found the three Lumanos lounging. "I can't help but notice you're not working on that ship," she said, her hand stroking the handle of her knife.

"We ordered a part that we need. It will be here in the morning."

"A part? I thought you just needed to flush the fuel lines."

"We thought so too. Turns out a tank full of neutralized fluids isn't super healthy for the fuel pump. We'll have it ready by noon tomorrow."

Freeda slumped her shoulders and let go of her knife. "Well, I suppose it's comforting to know mechanics are the same everywhere, even in a supposedly enlightened society."

She turned to leave, but Copernicus called out after her, "My brothers were about to show me their latest inventions. As long as you're stuck here, some of it might interest you. Come check it out."

The laboratory below the office was shiny and bright, the polar opposite of the rusted-out repair shop above, but it was far from clean. Three wide tables were set up in the center, cluttered with menacing-looking gadgets that to the untrained eye would appear to be instruments of death and destruction. The perimeter of the lab was lined with workbenches, chemistry stations, and half-eaten containers of junk food piled high on tool benches that were intended for more productive purposes than storing last night's greasy excuse for a meal. A fire-suppressant canister substituted for a stool in front of a small table. On the table was a bowl of soup that had been reheated with an open laser torch, which was lit and sitting upright, spitting its small cone of condensed energy out into the ether.

Freeda cringed at the mess in the lab. Kadrafians would never tolerate a dwelling in such condition, and Copernicus' assurance that the twins were not representative of the Lumano species as a whole was not filling her with a great deal of confidence. Still, the weapons lining the tables intrigued her, and she allowed herself a moment of optimism that they might have a test range clear of flammable piles of garbage.

Once they were down in the lab, the twins took turns showing off their breakthroughs in non-lethal weaponry. The foam gun was available in sharpshooter weapons, or lobbed in grenade form. The foam doubled as a fire-suppressant. When hardened it would last for a half hour before breaking down into the pungent vapor with the captive encased, stuck within the noxious fumes during the evaporation process. The twins assured their brother that the stench was not toxic, but Copernicus demanded that they stop using the formula that caused it to smell like the butthole of a Galeraskunk. Laneeko protested that they had already named it "Fetid Foam," a name which would make no sense if it didn't reek. And as everyone knew, it was bad luck to rename a non-lethal, weaponized foam.

They had also developed devices intended for hand-to-hand combat, which intrigued Freeda the most. One such device was a pair of forearm guards that, when used to block an incoming strike, would release a quick burst of the Fetid Foam in the direction of the assailant. Another was a padded fighting staff equipped with a WID drive capable of opening a wormhole five centimeters in diameter. The other end of the WID link connected to a point deep underwater in the oceans of the pleasure planet Hedon IV. The water pressure at that depth created a high-pressure gush of lukewarm sugar water, strong enough to knock an assailant off their feet.

Freeda picked up the staff and tested its balance before giving it a few satisfying spins and releasing a sticky spray of water at an already sticky pile of garbage. She shot an inquisitive glance at the twins and asked, "You know this is illegal, right? You can't use a wormhole to extract resources from an inhabited planet. Even the war hasn't overridden that treaty."

Lytess shrugged. "We try not to confuse morality with legality around here. You ever read the New Belgium Constitution?" Freeda shook her head. "It's a short read," Lytess said. "All it says is, 'We the People know it when we see it.' There's one amendment that says, 'So try not to be a dick.' Anyway, this is just the prototype of the fighting staff. If we ever want to license it for real, we'll change the link location."

Freeda continued to examine the staff, which came up to her shoulders when resting on the ground, and smiled to herself. "This is good quality," she admitted. "Is there a way for me to preorder one of these, be the first Raif'yan on my block to have one?"

Laneeko rubbed the spot on his neck where Freeda's knife had encouraged him to expedite her ship repairs. "You know what?" he said, "Why don't you keep that one. I think we're all better off if you're armed with something less sharp. Call it a thank you for delivering our brother." As Freeda gleefully slung the staff over her shoulder, Laneeko added, "We call that the Sugar Cane, by the way."

Freeda wandered along the workbench, looking at various other prototypes that were strewn about. She read the names aloud as she picked them up. "Itching powder grenade, whoopie cushion land mine. Are all your weapons based on childhood pranks?"

"Um, no," said Lytess.

"Yeah? Then what does this one do?" Freeda was holding a mortar round sitting next to a small launcher.

"Well, if you launch that on your enemy while they're asleep at camp, it simulates dipping their hand in warm water. Makes them wet the bed."

"That doesn't really work, you know," Freeda said, shaking her head in disappointment.

"It's worth a try," mumbled Lytess.

The pride and joy of the twins' inventions was the purple beam they had used to neutralize Copernicus' transport ship on the way in. The "Purple Inerter" they called it, partly because that's what color it was and what it did, but mostly because of the ridiculous way it rolled off the tongue. The purple beam was an energy weapon that when struck anywhere on the hull of a spacecraft that used WID technology, it rendered completely inert the fuel used to power the WID drive, but left all other systems, particularly life support, intact. It was the ultimate in non-lethal weaponry.

Copernicus and his brothers had previously been working on a similar weapon designed to stabilize time-space around an enemy craft's engines, preventing wormholes from opening. If it had worked, it would have given the same end result of incapacitating the enemy ship's WID engines, but they hadn't been having any success. This time, however, the breakthrough came while restoring a classic spacecraft for a wealthy diplomat. The old craft had been in storage for centuries, and the fuel had broken down in that time and needed to be flushed from the system. The twins realized that causing the fuel to break down would be much easier than reinforcing the fabric of space-time, so they changed course and had a working prototype in less than a month.

"I've managed to get us an appointment tomorrow to make a sales pitch to a weapons dealer," said Laneeko. "I think his name is Bolling or something like that?"

"Bowing?" asked Freeda. "You've got an appointment with Bowing? The Bowing?"

"Yeah, that sounds right," said Laneeko.

"Do you really not know who he is?" asked Freeda, her voice practically a squee. "How'd you get an appointment with him?"

"I dunno. We're charming. We looked up weapons dealers and gave him a call," Laneeko said. "He's famous or something?"

"His company makes the deadliest stuff. 'If you can't kill it with a Bowing, build it a temple.' You're meeting with him tomorrow? Can I tag along and meet him?"

Laneeko frowned. "I thought you were in a hurry to get out of here."

Freeda shrugged. "My commanding officer will understand why it took me an extra day to get back if I got to meet the guy that introduced the Widower-Makerer long-range throwing knife to the market."

Laneeko started to protest, but Copernicus cut him off. "Why don't you and I do the demo together. A Kadrafian warrior endorsing our gear could help our chances. Let us take you to dinner and we can talk about our pitch. We've got some great local cuisine on New Belgium."

"I doubt that," Freeda said. "Aren't you all vegetarians on this planet?"

"Vegans," Copernicus replied.

"Then you don't have great local cuisine, but I better eat something. I'm starving."

The three Lumanos took Freeda to their favorite restaurant, a greasy spoon that claimed to prepare tofu in a way that was indistinguishable in appearance or taste from any meat dish you requested. Freeda asked them to make her the still-beating heart of her enemies, medium-well. The server looked at Copernicus for some clue as to whether she was joking, but Copernicus just gave a subtle nod.

When the dish arrived, Freeda picked it up with one hand and took a bite. A liquid resembling blood dribbled down both sides of her mouth.

"Well?" asked Copernicus.

"Oh, wow," she said. "There's no way that's really tofu. That tastes just like the real thing."

At the shop later that night, Copernicus got drunk by himself and passed out. The twins pulled out black markers and drew on his face, giggling the whole time.

Freeda shook her head at them. "You're both imbeciles. What are you even drawing?"

Through his snickers, Laneeko whispered, "A Lumano reproduction facility."

"Huh?"

"Because, you know, there's no fun in drawing sex organs, since we don't have them."

"Imbeciles," Freeda repeated under her breath. Then out loud she said, "You know you're never going to sell any of those weapons, right?"

"Yeah, we know," answered Lytess. "We just needed to give our brother a reason to get out of the service. He didn't belong there, and it was killing him. He wants so bad to end that war, so we decided the only thing that would make him quit was telling him we had another way."

"You did all that for your brother, and now you're going to let him go in there and embarrass himself tomorrow? Then what?"

"Then we motivate him to keep working on new prototypes, keep hope alive that we can come up with something they'll buy. Tinkering with new inventions is probably the only distraction strong enough to get him sober."

Freeda mulled it over for a minute and then said, "You should get him to work on a gun that teleports your enemy's underwear to the top of a flagpole."

Laneeko guffawed. "Wait, is that a joke? Because that would be awesome. Do you think we could build that, Lytess?"

Freeda got up to leave. "Good night, Loomies."

Chapter 15

Copernicus awoke the next morning and stumbled down to the shop, where Lytess was working on flushing the transport's fuel lines, and Freeda was eating her leftover tofu heart for breakfast. Though cold and half-eaten, it thumped out a healthy rhythm. Copernicus grabbed water and a bottle of hangover pills. He wandered into the third repair bay and pulled the tarp off the hot rod.

It was a classic luxury cruiser that the twins were restoring, a two-seater capable of hyperspace jumps, but not practically intended for anything other than showing off its curves while popping out for a burger with your best gal or fella on a Friday night. The twins had painted it a sleek purple with white flames. They had modernized the engines and life support systems, but from the outside it looked the same as the day it came off the assembly line.

"We almost have the hyperdrive up and running," explained Laneeko from across the repair bay. "Finding the parts for this old bird has been particularly elusive since they used the Empirical 9th and 11th dimensions rather than the metric 5th and 10th, but we've finally tracked down a converter. As soon as it gets delivered, this baby will be ready to roll."

An hour later Copernicus was cleaned up, wearing his dressiest Hawaiian shirt, freshly pressed, and they all piled into the transport with their gear.

As the transport descended toward the landing pad on Zaibutu, Freeda leaned forward to the window to get a closer look at the bright lights and expensive cars of the overcrowded planet.

"Everything moves fast on Zaibutu," Copernicus said to her. "Even things that move slow in other places, like old people, bank lines, and justice. So what can you tell us about Bowing? Anything useful?"

"Just that his weapons are top of the line. He used to have a reality show called 'Guns and Drums,' where they'd let civilians try to fire off rocket launchers and stuff on an obstacle course, and of course they couldn't handle the recoil. They'd get tossed into the mud pit."

After they landed, the group stepped out of the rain and into the lobby of a high-rise building. They boarded the elevator with a group of Zaibutans. Laneeko pushed the button for the top floor. When the doors opened, they stepped into a room that was white from floor to ceiling. Weapons lined the walls. The north wall was dedicated to ancient hand-to-hand blades, clubs, axes, and knives, each more menacing than the last. The next wall was an array of more modern pistols, rifles, blunderbusses, and a smattering of replica ballistic weapons.

Bowing stood up from his desk when the visitors entered. His perfect hair and expensive suit should have seemed out of place among the implements of destruction that lined the room, yet something about him felt like he was in his element. Perhaps it was the confident smile and perfect teeth that would allow his tailored attire and mirror-shined shoes to be accepted anywhere, from a high-class gala to a back-alley brawl.

"What is this?" Bowing asked no one in particular. "Three Loomies and a Raif'yan? My secretary did not mention you'd all be non-humans."

"Hi, Mr. Bowing," said Freeda, blushing. "I'm a big fan of your show."

Bowing made a frown. "They have television on your planet? I thought it was all huts or whatever."

The smile on Freeda's face faded, and she looked down at her feet and mumbled something inaudible.

"Mr. Bowing," began Lytess, "we're here to offer you some technological breakthroughs that could potentially end the death rates of this war. We think you'll be impressed."

"Yes, yes," said Bowing. "I got your message about the non-lethal tech. Terrible thing, war. I hate to make my living off it, but I must put food on the table, no?"

"Perhaps we can offer a solution," said Laneeko, "in which you can put food on the table and yet sleep soundly with the knowledge that your merchandise is not making widows and orphans."

"I'm willing to have a look. If you and your assistant will step this way, our test range is through these doors."

They followed the dealer into a glass control room which overlooked a concrete firing range filled with targets and test dummies. Bowing looked at his watch and then said, "Let's try to make this quick."

Freeda walked to the center of the range with the gear and unpacked it, while the three brothers stayed with Bowing in the control room to describe the devices as Freeda showed off their capabilities. One by one, she fired the various foam guns at the targets, demonstrating the short range to the long. In the booth, Laneeko explained, "This is an exclusive offer. You would be the only one introducing these models to the marketplace."

Freeda switched to the blue beam and dissolved a block of foam, releasing the vapor. Despite being within the protection of the control booth, Bowing scrunched his nostrils and frowned. "Why does it smell like the Gomi district?" he asked.

"Yeah, we're still working on that," Lytess lied. "It just sort of naturally smells that way, but we're close to a solution."

Bowing watched Freeda's demo for a few more minutes, then put his hand to his face to cover a yawn and said, "Come on, Loomy. It's impressive, but there's no money in this. I'm a good salesman, but even I won't be able to sell non-lethal weapons to the Navy. I'd have more luck selling them white flags."

"But it's just as effective as any of the lethal options, if not more," protested Copernicus, speaking up for the first time.

"I see that it's effective, but the Navy needs show of force. If they start using this stuff, their enemies will take it as a sign of weakness. Hell, I couldn't even sell non-lethals to the cops, and they claim they don't want to kill suspects unless it's their only option. It's impressive tech, and if you put the same effort into designing marketable weapons, we could both do very well by it.

"What you have to understand is that despite what they say, people don't want weapons for protection. They want weapons that make them feel powerful. Holding a high-powered pistol makes a small man feel like he has the strength of the Statement, and he'll gaze into the mirror and fantasize about having an excuse to use it. It's psychological. Your designs are impressive, but I promise they would sit on the shelf."

Down on the range, Freeda was packing up the gear. She called up to the booth, "Mr. Bowing, would you mind if I use your practice range while you all talk? I haven't had access to a training arena this nice in quite some time."

Bowing pushed the intercom button and said, "Sure, dear. Knock yourself out."

The Kadrafian warrior stepped out into the practice arena and pulled the Sugar Cane off her back. She stepped up to a dummy and gave it a thwack on the head, testing out its resistance. Satisfied with the dummy's indifference to the blow, Freeda gave the fighting staff a few casual spins, then let out a stream of pressurized ocean at a target on one of the walls, followed by a back kick to the dummy behind her. She paused for a moment, then exploded into a full kata with her fighting staff, whaling on dummies and firing pulses of water mid-spin, timing it with such precision that only the targets were doused, and not a drop of water splashed onto the floor.

In the control room, Copernicus launched into an altruistic lecture about self-defense and the preservation of life not being mutually exclusive concepts, but Bowing was not listening. The arms dealer watched as Freeda battered and abused his test fire dummies with such fury that a dummy activist group might show up and demand the poor humanoid replicas be left alone. Copernicus was midsentence when Bowing walked out of the booth and down the metal staircase to the range to talk to Freeda.

She finished her kata and put the staff on her back, breathing heavily. Bowing gave her a slow clap and said, "Your people may be primitive, but you can certainly handle yourselves with a weapon. I have a need for someone of your abilities, and I can double whatever you're currently being paid. Work with me, and I'll get you off your shithole planet and keep you outfitted with weapons you've previously only daydreamed about."

Freeda's face darkened. "Tempting, but all I need is my knife."

"In that case, you simply must accept this as a gift," Bowing said, drawing a dagger from the inside pocket of his suit jacket. "It is not high-tech, but it comes from the ancient world. It is made out of an alloy they called 'steel,' which is a mixture of iron and carbon. It's not as strong as anything we have now, but the glint sure catches the eye."

Bowing presented the dagger to Freeda. The handle was fashioned with two ornate winged lizards spiraling around each other. "It's beautiful," agreed Freeda, "but it can't be from the ancient world. It's got Firebreathers on it, and they were only discovered 100 years ago on Planet Camelot."

"Well, you're more educated than you look," Bowing said. "The ancient world had a myth about Firebreathers. They considered them a fictional creature, and called them 'dragons.' The discovery of the Firebreathers on Planet Camelot is a bizarre coincidence, indeed, but I assure you this knife is a precious artifact from ancient days."

"Well, then of course I can't accept it, sir, but thank you."

Bowing held it out to her. "I insist. This knife deserves to be with a true warrior. Please take it. I will be terribly insulted if you refuse."

Freeda reached out tentatively and picked up the dagger. It was probably malarkey that it was from the ancient world, but it was a beautiful knife.

As they turned to leave, Copernicus tried one last time. "I hope you'll reconsider, Bowing. If you change your mind, you know where to find me."

"I most certainly do," the dealer said, and bowed as they left.

As soon as the elevator doors closed, Freeda took a deep breath and blurted out, "Well that guy is a douchebag[8] in real life."

Copernicus gave her a sympathetic look. "Never meet your heroes, I guess."

"Yeah, or your nemeses, apparently," Freeda replied. "You're a drunk, The Bowing is an asshole. I'd so much rather it was the other way around. Sorry he didn't want to buy your toy guns. What will you do now? Go into hiding as a deserter from the Navy?"

"Nah," said Copernicus. "I'll be left alone on New Belgium. Despite my dogfighting successes, I was a thorn in the Navy's side. They offered to let me out of my enlistment and be done with me."

"Wait, WHAT? Then why did you have to do the whole elaborate faking your death?"

[8] The dictionary definition of the word "douchebag" was to do with a component of a piece of drilling machinery used by the inmates of Dakota 17, but as "prison jargon" eroded its way into the mainstream vernacular, the term was adopted for popular use as a very offensive insult.

"That was our idea," offered Laneeko. "He told us he could just leave, but we wouldn't let it go. We never pass up the opportunity for a great prank."

Before the Lumanos could react, Freeda pulled the Sugar Cane off her back and wedged it horizontally under all three of their chins. With one arm she pressed them against the back wall of the elevator and lifted the trio until their feet were off the ground.

"I crashed my fighter and got lost in the jungle with this loser for a prank?" she hissed. "Do you know what I've been through the last three days, and you could have just left?"

Before Copernicus could respond that he did in fact know what she had been through, the doors opened to the lobby, and a group of Aquapersons in sharp business attire waiting to board the elevator gasped through their gills at the tableau. Freeda lowered the brothers to the floor, turned around, and smiled at the crowd. Then she picked up the bag of gear and exited the elevator.

She didn't say another word until they were aboard the transport and headed to New Belgium. "It was never going to work, you know," she finally said, sitting on the aft bench seats across from Copernicus and Lytess, while Laneeko flew. "You're missing the point. The only way you'll ever get the GNC and KCF to stop killing each other is if you give them a common enemy to fight against."

Copernicus mulled it over. "That's a terrible option. Then the killing continues but along a different set of imaginary lines. Besides, how would you even find a common enemy?"

"You get your little purple beam and a whole bunch of peace-loving Loomy pilots and you become the common enemy yourself. Then maybe they stop killing each other, and since you Loomies won't kill anyone, the war continues but nobody is dying. Well, except a bunch of Lumanos. You would all die screaming into the vacuum, of course."

"Not necessarily," mumbled Lytess.

"Freeda, that's brilliant," said Copernicus, getting excited. "That's absolutely brilliant. But we'd never get the pilots. Our people, they like to philosophize about peace and enlightenment and all that nonsense, but none of them are willing to do anything about it. They sit in their ivory towers and talk about what a shame it is that we all can't get along, but you'll notice you don't find them taking any action."

Freeda studied Copernicus' face for a moment. "So get your racing pilots or something."

The brothers exchanged a glance and then rode on in silence.

Chapter 16

I was born on the cyborg planet Titan-F411. The planet was originally colonized as a safe haven for anyone wishing to augment their bodies with technology, back when such things were controversial. Titan-F411 remained a popular destination for cyborgs and augmenters, even though by the time I was as high as my momma's knee the practice of bodily technological augmentation was no longer viewed as taboo. Sure, if you showed up to a corporate job interview with augmentations all over your face or knuckles, you had poor odds of landing the gig, but most employers stopped caring about cyborg implants as long as they could be covered by your shirtsleeves.

I left Titan-F411 when I was in my teens, and had no cyborg elements to my own classically human body. If I'm honest, I never truly cared for the culture I grew up in. I enjoyed technology when it came to fast spacecrafts roaring around a race orbit at breakneck speeds, but beyond that I am a nature lover. I lived on Paleo for a time, took on a Caveman husband, but eventually the isolationist nature of the Cavemen culture was too much for me as an outsider, and I left to pilot a big rig transport. I eventually fell in with a racing crew and ended up as a race pilot.

-Excerpt from "Me Talk Pretty One Day: A Personal Memoir of Brandine Lupinski"

When they landed and unloaded the gear, Freeda prepared to take the transport ship, but Copernicus stopped her as she climbed into the pilot seat. "Would you fly with me?" he asked.

"The common enemy thing, form a militant anti-war group with your purple beam? Oh, Statement no, Loomy. I wasn't serious about that."

"I know you weren't, but this is meant to be," Copernicus

said. "And Lumanos don't ever say stuff like that. There's gotta be a reason you didn't kill me in the jungle."

"Yeah, because I realized you're not worth it."

"Or maybe somewhere deep down you want a peaceful resolution to this conflict, too."

"No, I'm pretty sure you're just not worth it. I'm here for a ship, not to desert my people."

"Ending the war wouldn't be deserting your people. Think about it. Do you know how many Kadrafians die every year in this war?"

"I'm familiar with the numbers."

"And you don't want to change them?" Copernicus asked.

"It wouldn't work, Loomy. And I'm not selling out the KCF to fly with some pacifist on a fool's errand."

Freeda stepped into the transport, but Copernicus was getting himself wound up. "So what are you going to do? Go back and keep watching your friends die day in and day out until you're finally killed yourself, because 'honor'?"

"Yes."

"And who does that help? It's selfless, sure, but what greater good is served by your death? All the honor in the galaxy isn't going to keep your people from dying. Shouldn't 'honor' be doing what's in the best interest of your people?"

"Goodbye, Copernicus. For real this time." Freeda closed the hatch, and the transport lifted off, leaving Copernicus stuck with his thoughts.

Freeda lifted the transport out of the atmosphere and let it glide into orbit before preparing for hyperspace. She took out her knife and unscrewed the bottom of the handle. From a compartment within the grip, she pulled out a rolled-up picture of her brother, Revloo. He had spent three months in the brig for insubordination after the battle of Dealin' Dex's sales lot, then got shot down on his first mission back. Freeda was at the flight academy at the time, and almost dropped out when she received the news. Revloo was the last family Freeda had left. They came from a long line of proud warriors, all of whom had died honorably in combat.

"Us Raif'yans will never be slaves, not even to ourselves," Revloo had said. At the time she thought he was talking about disobeying a simple order, like don't break formation to save your sister, or no seconds until everyone's had firsts, but perhaps he meant it on a larger scale.

Freeda's eyes welled up looking at the picture, and she cursed quietly to herself. "I won't let you down, Rev," she said out loud.

Copernicus was standing at a desk in repair bay one, bottle of whiskey in hand, studying the chemical formula for the Fetid Foam, when Freeda landed and stepped out of the transport. "Did you forget your knife again?" he asked.

"I'm sorry I said you're not worth it," she said. "It would very much be worth my time to kill you."

"Um, thanks?" said Copernicus. "You came back just to say that?"

"I'll fly with you on two conditions, Loomy."

Copernicus' face lit up. "Name them."

"I'll agree to not kill anyone or anything if you agree to stay sober. From this point forward, not another drop."

Copernicus looked down at the bottle in his hand, and let out a long sigh. "What's the second one?" he asked.

"I'm not shooting down any KCF ships, not even with your harmless purple laser. I'll lead the squad that shoots down Navy; you lead the squad that shoots down KCF."

Copernicus hesitated, but then tossed the bottle underhand to Freeda. "We're going to change the world," he said. "I just know it."

"Most likely we're going to die together, Loomy, so let's at least make it mean something."

Back in the shop, Copernicus excitedly told his brothers about Freeda's change of heart.

"You want to raise an army?" asked Laneeko.

"A battalion to start," answered Freeda. "Enough to hold our own in a single battle."

"How many is a battalion?" asked Lytess.

"Usually around a hundred," answered Copernicus.

"One hundred pilots willing to fly into battle against both the KCF and the GNC at the same time, with the sole purpose of getting them to unite against you?"

"With the sole purpose," retorted Freeda, "of incapacitating them."

"Well," sighed Laneeko, "if you think you can find the pilots, go for it. You're going to need a lot more tech than a couple of fart rays. Once I get the hot rod up and running, you can take that to recruit pilots. Lytess and I have one more invention that will help you, but we'll need the transport to get raw materials to build more units. The parts aren't cheap."

The next day the twins got to work on their invention, and Copernicus and Freeda embarked in the hot rod to look for pilots. They hit up every pilot bar on both sides of the line, and between the two of them they made an impressive motivational speech denouncing the horrors of war and declaring how many lives could be saved every day with the use of non-lethal weaponry. After a week of giving out fliers for pilots to meet them on New Belgium, they returned to the repair shop to train their army.

Copernicus and Freeda landed the hot rod in the third bay, and stepped out. "Where are all our pilots?" Copernicus asked the twins.

"Both our pilots," said Laneeko. "Both our pilots are out back."

Copernicus sighed, and he and Freeda walked around the

building, where two pilots were lounging in the grass. The smaller one, a male, sprung to attention when Copernicus rounded the corner, but the larger woman got up and wrapped Copernicus in a tight hug.

"Well, a'll be," she shrieked. "If it ain't Coe-pernicus his same self."

"Brandine," Copernicus gasped, struggling to take in air within the hug. "It's good to have you here, but how did you know?"

"Yeah, yer brothers called me in, told me you had somethin' big and war-ending you needed some help with. I know I done said that if you ever again needed a pilot, I'd come a-running, but I was talkin' bout racing, Coper. I don't want to git involved in no fightin'."

Copernicus turned to Freeda. "Brandine, this is Freeda. Freeda, this is Brandine Lupinski. She's the orbital racing champion that my brothers and I used to pit crew for in the Galactic Racing Circuit. She's one of the best that ever was."

Brandine had light skin and naturally bright red hair, which she wore big. She was a heavier-set woman, which was a necessity in the orbital-racing circuit, where a pilot needed extra body mass to stay hydrated under the grueling conditions of a high-velocity orbital race.

"Copernicus," continued Brandine, "you know dad-gum well I'm not a fighter pilot. You need somebody to go round 'n a circle faster 'n a lizardrat with his tail on fire, I'm your pilot, but this dippin' and dodgin' nonsense, you know I cain't do all that." Finally, she turned to Freeda and added, "It's nice to meet you, dear."

"Brandine, we need you," said Copernicus. "And you've never had a problem speaking out against this war. It's not easy being anti-war in the racing circuit culture, where blind patriotism isn't just the norm, but it's built into the race-day program with the Navy flybys and the obsession with the Oligarchy anthem. But you've never been scared to go against the grain. You're exactly the kind of pilot we need right now. You have no tolerance for interspecies conflict. We've got the same goals."

"Now hon, you know I got my own reasons for disliking specism, but the war has nothing to do with my estranged husband. You're asking me to go get myself killed flying in dogfights in some ship you built from parts you pulled outta the trash."

"Ha. You won no less than three championships flying in ships I built from scrap parts, and you know it," Copernicus fired back.

"Yeah, but nobody weren't shooting at me in those. Well, except in '73, but that was over a misunderstanding involving the jukebox the previous night, and he only had a handheld photon revolver that he tried to fire out the airlock at 30 thousand orbits per day. It's not like he had a Gatling laser with a top-of-the-line targeting system mounted to his racer."

"Sister," said Copernicus, "if you can dodge a wreck at eight G's in the last lap of a 500 to win your third title back-to-back, you can fly a fighter with your eyes closed. They let kids fly these things fresh out of school. You think the mugs enlisting in the Navy have your skills? Besides," and Copernicus leaned in close to whisper, "the twins are working on an energy shield that could change everything."

Brandine shook her head. "Shoot, hon. You always did have a way with the ladies. You sure you ain't part Caveman?[9] I ain't making no promises, Sugar, but I'll check out your operation for a couple o' days. You get that shield working, maybe I'll up n' stick around a bit and a trek, but if not, I'm outta there faster 'n 50 orbits in our '74 racer."

---

[9] Brandine was not referring to the earliest evolution of humans, but rather to the residents of the Paleo star system. The Cavemen were a species of nature-loving humanoids. They had shorter legs and longer, more powerful arms than their human ancestors, and they insisted on eating a gluten-free diet. The males always wore beards, and they had a reputation of being the gentlest lovers in the galaxy.

The smaller pilot, a kid with spiky black hair, still standing at attention, asked, "You're really working on a shield?"

"Maybe," said Copernicus. "But I'm sorry, son. I'm not recruiting child warriors at this time."

"I'm not a child. I'm a Zee," replied the young-looking pilot.

"You got an ID to prove that?"

The Zees were a race of humanoids who were the result of a failed attempt at achieving everlasting youth. They spent most of their lives in puberty, all the while maintaining the appearance of a pubescent human. The Zees entered puberty at the standard age of 12 or so galactic standard years, but they didn't emerge with un-cracking voices and "hair in new places" until they were in their 60s. They then had but a few years to procreate if they cared about sustaining the population of the species.

The Zee pulled out his ID, and Freeda took it from him. "You're XxXGam3rDud3-69," she said. "The game programmer?"

"Folks call me Gam3r," he replied.

Freeda turned to Copernicus. "This guy wrote 'Blue Ace,' the game about the Kadrafian revolution. It taught me to dogfight. It won Most Pointlessly Violent Video Game of '89."

Gam3r looked at the floor. "Yeah, you know that's a joke award, right? It's not a good thing. That hurt my reputation."

"Not where I'm from," said Freeda.

"How did you get a flier?" asked Copernicus of the Zee. "We didn't recruit on the Fountain of Youth planet."

"I was off world on business and found it in the trash, if you must know," answered Gam3r. "I've wanted to be a pilot my whole life, but the Navy doesn't allow Zees. I even tried to join the Kadrafian Combat Force at one point. You can guess how that went."

"Excuse us one second," said Freeda, and took Copernicus by the arm around the building.

"A kid and a racer?" Freeda asked when she and Copernicus were assembled with the twins.

"That's all you'll need," said Lytess, beaming. "We've got something to show you." The two fighters the twins had used for their Purple Inerter prank on the transport were parked in front of the shop, and when Lytess pressed a button on a remote in his hand, they each lit up with a pink shield.

The concept of the energy shield had been just out of reach for centuries. It was attempted countless times by countless inventors, but none had ever gotten it to be stable. The idea of making the shield an energy sink rather than an energy source was a breakthrough that was unique to the twins' design. "It absorbs laser fire and uses it to recharge your life support," explained Laneeko. "You'll be practically invincible unless you come up against plasma torpedoes. We didn't want to say anything before, because if just one side or the other got that, it would be a slaughter. The death toll would triple overnight."

"And besides," chimed in Lytess, "we haven't figured out a way to get it to smell like ass yet, so we've got some work to do."

"All right," said Copernicus. "Let's go tell Brandine and the kid that they're in."

Copernicus walked around the corner, but Freeda hung back with the twins.

Lytess asked, "So, how'd he do with the alcohol withdrawal?"

"He did great," answered Freeda. "No symptoms at all. I couldn't believe it."

"Yeah, we gave him some pills before you left," explained Lytess.

"What did you give him?"

"Placebo, I think. My pills are all mixed in one bowl. It

was either a sugar pill or a strong hallucinogenic."

"Well, whatever it was, it worked."

When they were all assembled in front of the shop, Copernicus went through the plan, after which Gam3r raised his hand. "If I use my own ship, will you put a shield on it?"

"Sure," answered Lytess, glancing at Gam3r's ship parked in the front lot. "As a mechanic, I have to ask, what's that bar sticking out the top of your spaceship?"

"Oh, that's a spoiler," answered the Zee.

"Does it serve a purpose?" asked Laneeko.

"It impresses girls."

Brandine snorted. "No it doesn't, son." Then to the twins she asked, "Where will we be operating out of?"

Laneeko looked at his twin brother. "Well, since it's just the six of us, we finally have an excuse to finish building the Roid."

"The Roid?" asked Freeda.

Laneeko explained. "We've always wanted to equip a hollowed-out asteroid with a hyperdrive and WID engines and build a super secret lair inside of it, you know, for pranks. A few years back we consulted with some Cavemen about building into rock, and we picked out an asteroid and started construction, but we got distracted and never finished it. We left a locator on it, just in case. We could build it complete with a hangar for fighters and some launch tubes, and just go around the galaxy hiding in asteroid fields. We can start construction right away. Any of you ever used a laser drill before?"

"I did once," said Freeda, "in the Battle of St. Kilgore. A good warrior is a good improvisor, you know what I mean?" She put her hand up for a high five, which went unreturned. "Oh, did you mean have I used one the way it's intended?"

None of the Lumanos smiled. "Yes," said Laneeko. "I meant in the way that it's intended to be used."

"Yeah, can't say that I have, then."

Over the following days, the newly formed team of six worked tirelessly to acquire and outfit their ships and begin work on the Roid. They painted all four fighters and the transport a deep purple, along with an emblem that Lytess had fallen in love with when he found it buried in a book about the ancient world. It was a white circle with a vertical line down the center and two radius lines at downward angles. The history book claimed it had stood for peace in ancient times, and so Lytess insisted that they paint it on their crafts as a trademark.

Once they had the Roid ready to go, Copernicus hung a sign on the repair shop door that said, "Closed to Save the Galaxy (again)," and the crew headed to their super secret asteroid hideout to take on two full-sized armies with four fighters and a healthy dose of Lumano ingenuity.

END OF PART I

Part II

Chapter 17

Ashley lounged on the bleachers and frowned at the twelve rookie pilots standing at attention in the gym. Bear stood in front of them with a clipboard. He asked the group, "So, you space monkeys have applied to join India Squad?"

"Sir, yes, sir," came the reply in unison.

Ashley leaned back and pretended to inspect one of her braids, letting Bear warm up the crowd for her. Bear glanced down at his clipboard, then up at the recruits and said, "Well, for three of you, it's your lucky day. When Monk went down, Lieutenant Sokolov and I had every ace pilot on this boat up our butts to fill the empty slot in the Navy's top ace squadron, but the lieutenant has decided to make this into a training squad instead. I need Ensign Thomas Watson, Ensign Priyanka Kapoor, and Ensign Zhongwei Chen to step forward, please. The rest of you are dismissed to your current squads until these three get their asses shot off on their first mission."

Groans of disappointment emanated from the crowd, and the other rookie pilots dispersed. "Welcome to India Squad," said Bear to the three remaining. "We've read your files. The three of you have been selected because you have one thing in common: You all were on the gymnastics team in school. Lieutenant Sokolov here was a champion gymnast in her youth, and it's kept her alive in the battlefield.

"You see, rookie pilots strafe side to side in combat, because that's how they're used to moving in gravity, but a true ace feels equally comfortable moving at full speed in any direction, rotating on any axis. Our squad leader over here tumbles through the battle as though on an endless gymnastics floor, and soon you will too. Lieutenant, why don't you take it away."

Ashley stood up and sauntered over to the three pilots. She

took the clipboard from Bear and stopped in front of the first pilot, a dark-skinned human who stood almost as tall as Bear and yet as slim as the petite Ashley. "Tom Watson," Ashley read off the chart, looking up at the rookie. She didn't even come to his shoulders. "Says here you'll be flying under the ridiculous callsign of 'Wild Bill.' I almost didn't let you in this squad for that reason alone, Tom. It just says that you were a gymnast in school. It doesn't say what events you competed in."

"Well, ma'am," said Ensign Watson, "candidly, I was a, um, breakdancer. I was talked into joining the team because of the proximity it brought me to a certain female gymnast, but my tumbling is passable."

Ashley narrowed her eyes. "Your tumbling is once again going to bring you in proximity to a girl, Ensign, only this girl has two Gatling lasers mounted to her sides and an embarrassingly bad callsign stenciled on her cockpit."

"Yes, ma'am."

Ashley started to turn to the next pilot, then hesitated and returned to Watson. "Wild Bill, seriously? I mean, is your middle name Bill?"

"No, ma'am."

"Is your daddy's name Bill?"

"No, ma'am."

"You're just so incredibly wild that you can't remember your own name?"

Zhongwei let out a sharp burst of air from his nose, and Ashley turned to face him. "Is that funny, Ensign?"

"No, ma'am," said Zhongwei.

"Let's see," she said. "Ensign Zhongwei Chen, callsign 'Flare.' Looks like you were a contender on pommel horse and rings." Ashley sighed and tossed the clipboard to Bear. "Hassan, where did you find these mugs? I need tumblers to mold into deadly aces. Look at this meathead. He's all upper body. I doubt he can do a cartwheel." She turned back to the rookie pilot. "Ensign Chen, give me 50 cartwheels right now. Go."

The muscular young pilot stepped onto the mats and began counting off cartwheels. Ashley turned her attention to the third pilot, who was the shortest of the three rookies, but stood two inches higher than the squad leader. "Ensign Priyanka Kapoor, callsign 'Flips.' You have a title on the balance beam, but I noticed there was an asterisk next to it."

"It was in the cyborg league, ma'am. I have gyros and an impossibly low center of gravity."

"Gyros, eh?" Ashley looked over at Zhongwei, still counting his cartwheels. "Ensign Chen," she shouted, "get back over here. I don't care what number you're on." Flare came up from a cartwheel, turned to walk in Ashley's direction, lost his balance, and collapsed on the mat. Ashley dropped her chin to her chest and took a deep breath.

"All right, listen up," she said. "In gymnastics, we prefer backwards tumbling to forward because we can see the landing, but pilots, even ace pilots, tend to roll forwards in a scrum. I believe if we train pilots in gymnastics we'll have a huge tactical advantage. When on the defensive, most enemy pilots dodge downward and to the side, but if our squad learns to spin backwards, it brings them directly into our line of fire. I've had Lieutenant Amador here on the trampoline for the last year, and his flying has improved tenfold. And for such a giant of a man, he can land a pretty impressive layout backflip on the tramp.

"Now, tomorrow we'll be jumping to the Republic system, and I don't have much time to get the three of you trained. For those of you unfamiliar, the Republic has thirteen inhabited planets. That's more than three times any other system. The system is bordered by an asteroid belt, and just outside the belt Kadrafian forces are accumulating. They've been at a standoff with the Navy for the better half of a week, and it looks like they're gearing up for something big. We don't know exactly when it will go down, but it'll be a turning point in the war, for better or worse. Most of the Navy fleet is already in the system, preparing for the worst. I don't know how many days of training we'll get in before then, so let's begin. Ensign Kapoor, show me your floor routine."

"Right now, ma'am?"

"Yes, Ensign. Right now." Flips pulled her dark hair into a bun, took a step toward the mats, and paused. "Is there something wrong, Ensign?" Ashley asked.

"It's just, ma'am, that I don't have my music."

Ashley looked at the other two rookie pilots. "You want some music?" she asked. "Well, you're in luck, because I was just thinking Ensigns Watson and Chen here need to practice the Navy fight song, don't you, Ensigns?"

The two male pilots exchanged mortified looks, then began. They sang in unison, though not in key. "Faster," said Ashley. "Let's give Ensign Kapoor a worthwhile tempo for her routine." The two pilots doubled their tempo, and Flips stepped onto the mats wearing a face full of regret for speaking up. She focused on her feet and for a moment closed her eyes and covered her ears with her hands before finally launching into a set of back handsprings.

Flips' first pass, a roundoff and two back handsprings, was choppy and off balance. Her second pass was smoother, and she stuck the landing of her forward flip. By her third pass she was in perfect rhythm with her new squadmates' off-key singing. While Flips got into her old groove, Ashley flipped a switch, and cutouts depicting Kadrafian fighters popped up around the mats and on the ceiling high above her. Flips stuck the landing on her final double backflip, came to a salute, and held it. Ashley stepped onto the mat and gave her a slow clap. "Nicely done, Priyanka," she said. "Maybe there's hope for this squad yet. Tell me, how many Raif'yan fighters did you count while you were tumbling?"

Priyanka's mouth opened, but she hesitated. After a

second, she said, "Um, none, ma'am."

"Look behind you."

Flips turned around, and there was a cutout of an enemy fighter directly behind her, just under a meter away. Ashley shook her head and said, "That was one of the most graceful tumbling routines I've ever seen. Too bad you didn't live through it. Let's hit the trampolines."

After a few days in the gym, Ashley and Bear split the rookies' time between the simulator and going out on live patrols. It was good for Ashley to get her mind off the feeling that she had been abandoned by Monk, who was not just an ace she looked up to, but also her friend. Flying with a couple of promising rookies felt like a new beginning. Wild Bill was making impressive progress with both his tumbling and his flying, and it was improving Ashley's mood, which of course had a ripple effect throughout the entire barracks. Two weeks into their patrols, but without seeing any action, Ashley felt that they were ready. On the way out of the locker room after the gym she commented, "Nice work, Tom. You might actually live through your first dogfight."

Wild Bill nodded but didn't say anything, so Bear added, "That means she's happy to have you in our squadron. Don't worry, kid, you'll get your chance to–"

Before Bear could finish the thought, the alarm sounded for battle stations, and all five pilots broke into a sprint toward their ships. As they arrived on the flight deck, Commander Greenblatt and Chief Schultz were standing in the center, barking orders amid the chaos. The Kadrafian fleet had broken from the orbital plane and was rising above the asteroid belt. The Battle of the Republic was imminent.

Chapter 18

Kadrafian warriors who were scarred during battle would have those battle scars tattooed. They used the same color orange as their existing tattoos, but with dotted lines as a differentiator.

Early in the war, when General Dalton was a marine, any time he killed an enemy infantry he would pin down his foes and let them slash him a few times before he finished them off. Dalton rose quickly through the ranks, and his reputation for brutality, with the dashed line tattoos to prove it, helped keep the grumbling to a minimum as he passed everyone by in the ranks. In fact, General Dalton was so covered in dotted orange lines, it was hard to tell if he was blue with orange tattoos or orange with blue tattoos. What was odd was that despite his orange, General Dalton had not joined the combat force until late in life. Even so, he had risen through the ranks in record time.

-Excerpt from "Bossypants: General Dalton's War," by Brandine Lupinski

General Dalton stood on the bridge of the Kadrafian Combat Force's flagship, overseeing the fleet's preparations. Across the room, a dozen officers sat at consoles, chattering into their headsets, each preoccupied with their own specialized aspect of the battle. The only one not contributing to the din was the general, standing at parade rest in front of the window.

General Dalton had just given the order for the fleet to move their position to above the orbital plane so the asteroid belt would no longer be a barrier between the KCF and the Galactic Navy. He couldn't believe his good fortune. It had been foolish for the Navy to allow the Kadrafian forces to amass in this star system; they should have challenged him outright the very second he brought Kadrafian warships within range of this sector. Instead, they let it become a standoff.

The only one who gained from such a strategy was General Dalton, as it gave him time to bring more ships to the vicinity. Whether he won or lost the battle today didn't matter. This folly of the Navy would allow Dalton to deal them a devastating blow. Even if Kadrafian forces failed to carry the day, the psychological toll to the Navy would be worse, since the battle was happening right on the doorstep of their cultural hub. He had let the tension build long enough; it was time to make a statement.

The general put his hand proudly on the shoulder of his executive officer, Colonel Torgue, and gave the order, "Launch the fighters."

***

Ashley was determined that India Squad would suffer no casualties. In an ace squadron, the leaderboard had always been her top priority, but now that she was a squad leader, her responsibility, and therefore her focus, was to her troops. Today was going to end with a Navy victory and a healthy squadron if Ashley Sokolov had anything to say about it. She gave her fighter a few warm-up rolls and spins, and was pleased at how tight the controls felt. She and her squad formed up behind the ace squadron Delta.

"Stay tight, kids," she called out over the radio. "Follow me in, use your maneuvers, and we're going to send these miners back to planet moss."

The opposing forces were out of range but closing in fast when four unknown ships blipped onto the scanner, two closer to the Navy forces, the other two approaching the Kadrafian fleet. Ashley noticed that the unidentified ships were hailing both fleets simultaneously. Out of curiosity, she flipped open her comms. The radio crackled with a monotone voice. "This is the Pacifists. All fighters, stand down. We're ordering a cease fire." The response could not be heard, but a few seconds later the monotone voice returned. "Very well. Prepare to be pacified."

A pair of the purple ships broke formation and charged the front lines of the Navy forces, while the other two turned their tails to the Navy and faced the KCF. A barrage of purple lasers cut through Lima Squad, neutralizing that jerkoff Porter and his squadmates.

"Evasive action," cried Ashley. She jammed down on her Z axis. Her body slammed into the restraints as the G forces tried to throw her into the canopy. Purple beams streaked through the void her ship had just occupied.

Her radio crackled with panicked voices. "I can't shake it," Wild Bill cried out as he circled around.

"I got you covered," Ashley said, righting herself. She lined up the purple ship harassing her squadmate and laid into it with both guns. The ship lit up pink as her laser fire was absorbed by a translucent sphere.

"Oh my Statement," Ashley groaned, her heart sinking. "These bastards have shields."

"Orders, ma'am?" asked Flips.

"Disengage," she responded. "Keep pressing forward. Keep focus on the KCF."

The two purple ships divided their attention among the hundreds of Navy fighters, and Ashley's squad wound their way through a sea of fighters with neutralized engines, the pilots helplessly watching the battle while they floated and bumped each other like billiard balls. The radio belched angry chatter, but Ashley ignored it.

With her squad following, she danced her way toward an incapacitated Kadrafian corvette. This battle was a vital moment, interveners be damned.

She aimed for the cockpit and ordered her squad to open

fire. As she squeezed her trigger, a blinding beam of purple light flashed in her eyes. When her vision returned, an error message appeared on her dash readout. The monotone voice of the computer announced, "Engines down. Rerouting power from weapons to life support."

Ashley's craft drifted forward with a hint of a clockwise spin. She yanked on the controls. Nothing happened. A thud on the hull jerked her head upwards to see that she had collided with a disabled Kadrafian ship, canopy to canopy. The Kadrafian pilot had his helmet off and his hands pressed against the front of his cockpit. His mouth was open in what could only be a furious scream as he pounded on the glass and pointed at her. She couldn't hear him, of course, so she responded with the only form of communication available to her in the situation: a raised middle finger.

She ordered her squadron to report in. All four were in the same predicament, floating listlessly.

"For whatever it's worth," Bear's deep voice echoed over the radio, "it looks like the KCF fleet is falling back."

When the carriers stopped their advance, the four purple ships scattered and disappeared into the asteroid belt. After that, another mysterious message came over the radio. "This is the Pacifists. Each side will now send their tow vessels to recover their downed fighters. Cease fire is still in effect. We can do this all day, children."

Chapter 19

The Mesozoids were the first species evolved from a human-evolved species (Cavemen), thus furthering the evolutionary tree. The Cavemen had sought to expand their population beyond one planetary system, and colonized Mesozoa, a planet in the neighboring system. They did well for many generations, until their planet was struck by a meteor, which poisoned the atmosphere. The surviving population, loath to abandon their homes, sought out gene therapy to adapt to their planet's changed conditions. Mesozoids were more similar to humans than Cavemen in stature, but they were covered in tough scales with a greenish hue, and their movements when they were in a state of provocation were vaguely bird-like. Having been saved by genetic scientists from off-world, the Mesozoids were far less isolationist than the Cavemen, and had integrated themselves throughout the galaxy.

-Excerpt from "The Art of Racing in the Rain: The Ever-Expanding Humanoid Family Tree," by Brandine Lupinski

Out on the battlefield, Ashley had kept her cool. She was an ace, and aces survive by having poise amongst chaos. In the safety of the carrier, however, she stomped into the locker room and threw her helmet at the wall as hard as she could. It gave a nice bounce, but left her unsatisfied. She slammed open her locker hard enough that the door ricocheted shut. She slammed it open a second time, and it shut itself again. Unsure of whether the locker door understood the full gravity of the message she was sending it, she slammed it open and shut three more times, then punched the outside of the closed locker door with her fist. Finally, she gave it a scream, just to be absolutely sure the locker was fully aware of the intensity of her frustration.

Ashley turned and shouted at Bear, "What the *hell* was

that?" Bear stood quietly with his arms folded, looking annoyed yet somehow calm. He didn't respond right away, which was even worse than the response from her locker door, so she shouted again, "What the hell *was* that?"

Bear stepped to his own locker and opened it. It stayed open for him, seemingly for no reason other than to mock Ashley. Bear pretended to rummage and said quietly, "That, Lieutenant, was Monk."

Ashley's mouth dropped open. How could she have not seen it immediately? The flying styles of those purple ships had Monk's signature all over it. And who else but their former squad leader would fly into the largest battle of the century and calmly demand a cease fire? After a few beats of dumbfounded silence, she finally squeaked out a few words. "So what do we do?"

Bear shrugged. "I don't know what step four is, but I know steps one through three involve drinking heavily. I'll see you at the bar."

Ashley and Bear got a table away from the crowd, and over beers they analyzed the events of the day. They made progress on the beer, but not the situation. An hour into their rumination, a callused hand placed a round of three beers on the table, and Ashley's attention jolted upwards.

"Mind if I join you?" Chief Schultz asked.

Ashley didn't respond. The chief sat down and cleared his throat, but Ashley cut him off. "I want a rocket fighter."

"What?" exclaimed the chief and Bear in unison.

Ashley repeated herself, but this time included her partner, "*We* want rocket fighters, for the next battle. You know, non-WID fighters. Like in ancient times. They won't be affected by that purple beam."

The chief balked. "Where am I supposed to get–"

"The same place that transport disappeared to. Or should we have a talk with Greenblatt about that?" Ashley said.

Schultz gave a pleading look to Bear, who responded with an unsympathetic gaze. "Fine, Lieutenant," said the chief. "I'll personally build you rocket fighters, if that will make you happy. I know you're pissed, but ask yourself, what exactly do you have to be upset about? The Kadrafian forces retreated from the system, with no collateral damage to the civilians of the Republic. All the things we claim to be fighting for were handed to us, without a single death. Are you honestly angry that no one died today?"

Ashley listened to his speech all the way through. She knew there was a flaw in his logic somewhere, but she couldn't put her finger on it. Regardless of his motives, there was a sense of betrayal toward her former squad leader. She was mulling over a response when Bear, who'd been his usual silent self, announced in a low grumble, "Don't look now, but Delta Squad is headed our way."

The squad commander of the ace squadron Delta was a Mesozoid named Riff. His two ace wingmates, Adam and Steve, were Sheeple. They were skilled pilots and excellent wingmates who never showed the slightest hesitation in following directives. The three made an effective and deadly squad.

Riff also happened to be the pilot who had committed the painful misstep of calling Ashley Sokolov "Firecracker" to her face. The two aces respected each other, but their personalities clashed. When called in front of HR, they both swore up and down that it was just a little healthy competition.

Riff was all smiles as he approached the table, which in light of the day's events made Ashley's blood boil harder. "I finally tied you on the leaderboard, Lieutenant Sokolov! Hopefully I can keep up this streak."

Ashley stood up and took a step toward the Mesozoid, but Bear rose and stepped between them. "Come on, Riff," he pleaded, "You can't think this is funny?"

"Of course not, Bear," Riff responded. "Just trying to lighten the mood. We should be talking about this together. You don't want to leave the top ace squad out of your secret little meeting, do you?"

Bear hesitated, then said, "As a matter of fact, we don't. Chief here was just agreeing to build rocket fighters for us for the next sortie, weren't you, Chief?"

Schultz took his beer down the wrong pipe and went into a coughing fit. He managed to sputter out, "I'll see what I can do. But no promises."

Riff motioned to his squadmates to grab chairs, and they squeezed around the small table, uninvited. "Rocket fighters, eh?" he asked, turning his chair around sitting on it backwards. "You finally see where I'm coming from in supporting the sub-light movement, Lieutenant?"

Ashley scoffed. "Don't start with that. The universe is unimaginably huge. Our WID devices are poking a few pinholes in it here and there. It is downright arrogant to think that humanoid society is affecting the laws of physics of the entire ether just by heating a couple slices of toast."

Ashley was buzzed enough to get sucked in, even though she knew how much Riff enjoyed baiting her. "You're parroting the WIDCorp argument, Lieutenant," said the Mesozoid. "Look, I'm not saying we need to ban all WID devices, but we need to be conscious of our space-time footprint, keep promoting the use of renewable wormhole technology. Of course WIDCorp is going to argue that a few 'pinholes' don't make a difference. You know how much money they make off their toaster department alone? They're way too profitable to slow down their production and give an honest study to the issue."

The rest of the table knew better than to join the argument when things got political. Bear watched with folded arms, and Riff's wingmates stared awkwardly at their drinks. "I've read the studies," Ashley said. "But studies have also found that artificially-induced wormholes are having no effect on the laws of physics. Everyone knows the weak nuclear force has always naturally had periods of instability."

"Oh, come on, Lieutenant. The opposition studies are funded by the manufacturers. Of course they're finding no effects. You think WIDCorp is about to let something as trivial as the fabric of space-time stand in the way of their bottom line? They've fired up their propaganda machine to label any serious scientist raising the issue as a 'crackpot.' They may not care about leaving a livable galaxy for our kids, but I do."

"So, what? You want me to start looking for the 'Sub-light' label at the grocery store? It's a scam. Do the math, Riff. I've seen that label slapped on products that came from the NoChil system. If it came by sub-light transport from that far across the galaxy, it would have shipped centuries before WID-2's launch. They throw that label on there so they can jack up the price and rip you off."

Bear finally uncrossed his arms and spoke up. "That's enough, both of you," he said. "You've had this argument dozens of times, and this is the point where it deteriorates into name-calling. Which might at least be entertaining if you didn't use the same tired insults over and over. Let's talk about something else."

Adam looked up from staring at his drink and tried to help change the subject. "So, the Pacifists. Who do you think those guys were?"

"Extremists," answered the chief before anyone else could offer a theory. "Probably some religious cult, zealots that have suckered a couple gullible celebrities with enough money to fund the tech they have. We'll have them in custody by end of day tomorrow."

Ashley appreciated the chief's attempt to cut the discussion short, but it was folly to think the introduction of the Pacifists was not going to be the only topic of conversation on the carrier for the foreseeable future. Ashley shot the chief a glance and motioned with her eyes toward his beer, which he dutifully took a swig of. Riff, of course, had theories of his own, and so Ashley, Hassan, and Schultz sat and listened. Riff and his squadmates laid out their ideas excitedly while the three humans got slowly drunk.

When the group finally felt sufficiently tipsy and dispersed, Ashley stumbled down to the gym, tried to work on her tumbling, stopped herself from vomiting, and passed out.

When Ashley awoke on the trampoline, the morning workout crowd was already sweating away on the weights around her. Nobody had dared disturb the slumber of the Navy's current top ace, so she had the tramp to herself. Her eyes focused to see one of her hair ties lying in front of her face. She sat up and redid her double French braids.

Reverberating in Ashley's pounding head were the words of Chief Schultz: Why are you angry that no one died today? She wasn't angry at the lack of casualties. Of course she wasn't. Ashley Sokolov was no war monger. If not for this war, she'd be a teacher, gymnastics coach, something involving inspiring the youth of the galaxy to live up to their full potential.

No, Ashley Sokolov was pissed off because Monk had betrayed her. Stupid Monk in his stupid purple ships. If he had only asked her, she would have flown right alongside him in a heartbeat. But instead, he'd lied to her and left her in the lurch, so now she was going to personally shoot him down, drag him out of that ship, and slap him so hard in the face that it was going to leave confusing sexual thoughts in his prudish Lumano head.

"Good morning, ma'am."

Ashley looked up from her sitting position on the trampoline to see her three rookies standing at attention, ready for their morning workout. None of their shining faces appeared to be phased by her disheveled appearance, so she stood up to greet them. "Good morning, rookies," she replied grimly. "How can you be so chipper after what happened yesterday?"

The three looked at each other, and Flips took the lead as the spokesperson. "Are you kidding, ma'am? That was so exciting! Yesterday's battle is going down in history, and we were there for it! We happy few!" The other two nodded in agreement.

Ashley let out a long sigh. "Very well. Let's work on upper body today. I have a feeling we won't be doing much tumbling in our next dogfight. And don't let me forget, after breakfast we're hitting the simulator. We'll be learning some new settings."

Chapter 20

No one was entirely sure of the origins of the Sheeple. They were not the product of adapting human life to a hostile planet, nor were they the result of any scientific accident anyone was admitting to. It's possible they were a liberated slave race of the Kadraf Mining Corporation or another company of its ilk, but mostly they seemed to have evolved on their own, popping up simultaneously on various planets across the galaxy. Less than a century after their introduction into society, the Sheeple population of the galaxy had already surpassed the human population, and that trend never reversed.

The Sheeple looked identical to humans, except that on their heads they grew curly white hair that could only be described as wool, and in scientific testing even matched the quality of wool, hence the Sheeple's name. The Sheeple were known to be extremely talented and knowledgeable about whatever career they set their mind to, but their focus tended to remain narrowly on that task. They showed little interest in anything outside their area of expertise, and so they rarely exercised critical thinking or skepticism about any other topic.

-Excerpt from "On the Origin of Species: Debunking Common Misconceptions About the Sheeple," by Brandine Lupinski

Chief Schultz knocked on the open door to Admiral Garcia's stateroom. "You wanted to see me, Admiral?"

"Come in, Chief."

Commander Greenblatt was already present in the parlor area, sitting in a chair opposite the admiral and looking especially miserable. Admiral Garcia didn't rise from his seat on the couch, but motioned for Schultz to have a seat in the opposite chair. The suite was humbly decorated, but roomier than any other quarters on the carrier.

"Obviously we're here to address the unfortunate

development from yesterday," Garcia began. "The Republic is safe, but we've been humiliated. That's not going to stand." Schultz nodded, and the admiral continued. "I have informed high command, and they have some dedicated resources assigned to locating and neutralizing these...Pacifists. But in the meantime, the war effort continues. It's been explained to me in general terms that the weapon utilized by these guerillas renders our WID drives inoperable, and we cannot beat them in a dogfight due to their apparent energy shields. So I'm ordering you to outfit a squadron of bombers to run some long-range bombing runs against the KCF. The commander has already expressed his discomfort with the idea, but he's going to follow orders. Are you going to have any problem with that, Chief?"

Schultz hesitated, but then responded, "No, Admiral. Other than to join in expressing my discomfort, I will follow orders."

Garcia said, "For whatever it's worth, gentlemen, I'm not without discomfort either, but I don't need to remind you that we are at war, and who our enemy is. I've picked out a number of potential targets for our first long-range mission. Commander, I'd like you to have a strategic analysis of each of them on my desk in the morning, and we'll choose the first target."

Down in the hangar, Chief Schultz ordered his flight crews to begin outfitting bomber squadrons for long-range formations. There were murmurs of discontent among the older mechanics, and confusion among the younger ones.

"It's a barbaric practice, I know," the chief explained to his crew, "but we have our orders. The Pacifists can't shoot down what they can't catch. Not so long ago, we used to send bombers on long-range missions. They'll accelerate to 60% of lightspeed, make their bombing run, and pass by. It's safer for the pilots, but we have to send a large formation of bombers dropping a lot of bombs, because at that speed it's hard to get your payload right in the pickle barrel. The pilots will wear Doppler goggles to account for the distortion of the incoming light waves, otherwise they will 'see' heat and radio waves."

"Why'd they stop doing it this way?" asked a mechanic.

"A couple reasons. One, the inaccuracy means there is collateral damage to civilians, but mostly because both sides set up a crap-ton of minefields. At 60% of lightspeed, there's not much you can do about a minefield other than take it on the nose. That's why we switched to the more maneuverable bomber formations."

"Won't it take days to accelerate to 60% under humanoid tolerances?" asked a voice from the back of the pack.

"That's where we come in," answered Schultz. "The pilots will be wearing G suits, but we also need to outfit these cockpits with WID-powered gravity distortion fields. If we rig them right, we can get the acceleration time down to a few hours. Here's a copy of the plans. We need to get to work on this on the double."

The chief then broadcast a message to the deck chiefs of the other carriers in the fleet, letting them know to begin the same prep work. He expected he'd receive an immediate reprimand from some of the more pedantic chiefs for sending such a message using the lowest encryption level, but no one seemed to notice.

Chapter 21

*There were several noteworthy things about the phenomenon
that was the Zees. The original name of the species was simply the
Kidz, spelled with a Z, but that proved to be confusing. When
referring to the species, a speaker would have to clarify by saying,
"Kidz with a Z," so eventually it was shortened to "Zees."*

*The Zees' ancestors were wealthy humans who'd been duped by
a pair of con artists known as the Immortality Brothers. The humans
paid top dollar to be a part of an experimental process that promised
to bring them eternal youth. By the time the scam was discovered,
the Immortality Brothers could not be located, but they likely didn't
get away with the money, either, considering many of the clients they
had scammed were well connected Mafia Dawns.*

*-Excerpt from "The Great Gatsby: Why Money Can't Buy Me
Youth," by Brandine Lupinski*

The morning after their first official mission, Freeda walked
into the common room to find the other Pacifists lounging
around the mismatched couches and cushioned chairs
Laneeko cannibalized from the waiting room of their repair
shop. Gam3r had also donated the gaming table from his
dorm to the cause, much to the chagrin of his old roommates.

Copernicus sat in the corner with a small toolset and a rag,
doing maintenance on his artificial eye, while all around him
the other five Pacifists engaged in rowdy revelry. The twins
took turns describing how the battle had looked from their
vantage point on the bridge of the Roid, while Brandine and
Gam3r remarked on how different a real battlefield was from
their expectations, this being their first launch as fighter pilots.
Freeda taught the group the Kadrafian fight song that was
popular among the warriors on her home planet, after which
Gam3r rewrote the lyrics to fit the Pacifists' cause.

One by one, everyone dispersed. Freeda was the last to go. She wandered up to the bridge, where Brandine was monitoring the Navy patrols that were searching the asteroid field for the Pacifists.

"Think they'll find us?" Freeda asked.

"Well," said Brandine, "The Navy will know those fighters we were flying would need a carrier to get out of the system, and they'll probably guess that it's hiding in the asteroid belt. The question is, will they guess that we're in a rock, or will they scoot right by us like a herd on a stampede? I tell you what, though, I am still so amped up from being subjected to live fire, I can barely get my nerves to calm down..."

Freeda had grown to enjoy the sounds of Brandine rattling on at 300 words per minute. There was an innocence about her cadence and goofy phrases that were comforting. She reminded Freeda of the moss farmers with their red tattoos and delicious baked goods.

"...that was the real deal, Shoog. They were kneeslapping me from all angles, but that shield held stronger'n a raceway guardrail. And the way that you're protective of Copernicus, is just a-DORE-able. Not only is he the Navy's top ace of, like, all of time, but you know he's got himself one of them fancy pink shields, and yet you're out there picking bogies off his tailside like you're actually worried about him. Don't think I didn't notice that..."

Freeda was watching a Navy patrol pass from asteroid to asteroid, working its way closer to them.

"...and that Gam3r, I tell you what, he was having himself a grand ol' time, weren't he? Whoopin' and hollerin' and carryin' on. That boy may play too many of them vidja games, but they sure do make his senses sharp. I think he cleared out his quadrant faster'n the rest of us combined, I do..."

Freeda put up a hand to silence Brandine. "I know we're concealed very well, but this whole concept of hiding puts me on edge." She whispered it, in spite of the thick rock walls and meters of vacuum that separated them from the patrol. "I'm used to charging straight ahead with my knife in my hand and a battle cry on my lips."

Freeda moved her hand to the control panel, preparing to let loose a burst of Purple Inerter blasts from the Roid if the patrol got too close. As the Navy fighters floated between the Roid and its nearest asteroid neighbor, one of the ships turned and faced directly toward the window of the bridge. Freeda could make out the facial features of the Mesozoid pilot, helmet off, peering through the asteroid belt. For an instant Freeda swore he was looking right at her. Her finger stayed on the button, but didn't twitch. The pilot spun his ship, and the patrol continued on their way. Freeda relaxed her hand and turned her attention to Brandine. "Go on, my friend. You were saying?"

A few hours later, Freeda was teaching self-defense tactics to Gam3r and Brandine in the small gym they had set up in one corner of the flight deck, when Copernicus sprinted into the room.

"Laneeko! Lytess! Laneeko! Lytess! La–" He was panting by the time he reached the far side of the hangar. "I just intercepted a radio transmission. The Navy is going to make long-range bombing runs to avoid the Inerter! We've gotta figure something out, and fast."

The group gathered into a circle and waited while Copernicus caught his breath. "Let's think it through," said Laneeko. "How do we shoot down a bomber traveling at 60% of lightspeed?"

"They're WID engines," said Copernicus. "There's nothing stopping us from using the Inerter if we can match speeds with them. The problem is if you disable their engines at that speed, they can't slow down. They would keep coasting at 60% off into deep space."

"We could use the repair shop's tow line to slow them down after we disable them," offered Lytess.

Copernicus shook his head. "There will be three dozen bombers in formation. You can't tow them all at once, and you can't slow one down and then catch up with the others. Besides, you don't just pull up alongside a formation of long-range bombers at 60% of lightspeed like you're merging into the shipping lane."

Freeda spoke up. "Could you put the magnet-tow in mine form, and then build a minefield, deploy it ahead of them to slow them down?"

Copernicus looked at Freeda and remembered their fateful collision. "That would work," he said. "If anyone made it through, though, we'd be the direct cause of their death. I'll use the tow rig, just in case any stray bombers miss the minefield. The rest of you will be deploying the mines."

Freeda balked. "You're not going into a dogfight in a tow rig without fighter cover. I'm going with you."

Now Brandine puffed out her chest and spoke up. "Hode up, hode up, hode up. Y'all got a mission where the main skill you need is to withstand major acceleration forces, y'all need an orbit racing champ."

Freeda scowled. "We need to shoot down three dozen bombers in under 30 seconds. You need a fighter ace. I'll be fine withstanding the G-forces. I'm a Kadrafian warrior."

Brandine was getting excited. "I know you can withstand those forces, honey, but can Coper?" Brandine jiggled her ample lower torso and asked, "Copernicus may have the head of a raging bull, but does he have the belly of one?"

Copernicus hesitated, and Lytess urged him, "We can rig a magnet-mine launcher on your fighter so you can hit them with mines from behind, but it's your call, little brother. Don't go five-percenter on us."

Copernicus nodded, and spoke authoritatively. "Gam3r, you'll be with me in the transport deploying the minefield.

Freeda, you better get Brandine to the simulator and neither of you sleeps until she can take down 18 bombers in 27 seconds. Laneeko, Lytess, get to work building some mag-tow mines that are strong enough for the job. Let's get moving."

Brandine, swept up in the excitement of the moment, sang their new fight song as she headed toward the simulator in the far corner of the flight deck.

Lytess looked inquisitively at Laneeko and asked, "Isn't she the one we were barely able to convince to sign up for this?"

Laneeko smiled broadly and turned toward the lab, joining in the song on his way out.

Chapter 22

Ashley stood with her squad on the flight deck of the *Centauri*, waiting for Commander Greenblatt to call the deck to attention. Greenblatt stepped up to the podium and paused for the din to die down, then stepped aside so that Admiral Garcia could address the crew.

"Pilots of the *Centauri*," the admiral began, "as you know, we were recently attacked by a group of terrorists calling themselves the Pacifists. We are working to identify them and their whereabouts, but first we're going to hit the Raif'yans hard and show them we're not distracted. To ensure our mission today is not disrupted by these beatniks, we'll be targeting the Kadrafian military installation orbiting the NoChil star system, using long-range bombers."

Murmurs rippled across the flight deck until Commander Greenblatt shouted out, "Silence, space monkeys! Your admiral is addressing you!"

The admiral continued, "The dilemmas of long-range bombers are not lost on me, so no one is being ordered on today's mission. Chief Schultz has outfitted three dozen bombers for a long-range sortie. I'm asking for 72 volunteers to step forward and report to Commander Greenblatt for briefing; 36 pilots and 36 pilots willing to fly as bombardiers, preference given to seniority. We need experienced pilots who have done this before. This is a dangerous mission, and if you've never trained in high-speed ordnance drops, I'd rather you sit this one out. Launch is in one hour."

The deck was silent for a minute as everyone looked around to see who was volunteering. A few squad leaders stepped forward, followed by their squads. Flips, Flare, and Wild Bill turned and looked toward Bear and Ashley. Ashley shook her head no, and the rookies stayed put. Within two minutes, the flight deck deteriorated into chaos. Volunteers were being assigned to ships; those who hadn't volunteered were discussing why. Some non-volunteers tried to talk their friends out of participating. Eventually, Greenblatt returned to the podium to order the flight deck cleared of all personnel who would not play a role in the mission. Ashley and her squad turned to exit, but the chief emerged from the crowd to stop her.

"Sokolov! I have your ships ready, but I'm begging you not to do this. Your squad has been training on rockets for a single week. In the ancient times, pilots trained their whole lives to fly rocket-powered fighters. You know what their life expectancy was in a battle, Lieutenant? Eight minutes. And I don't know if a single one of these birds ever got shot down. They usually just crashed into each other. Don't do this."

"Thank you, Chief," she replied, "but we're going to give these bombers some fighter cover."

One hour later, India Squad was lined up in front of the three rocket fighters the chief had specially prepared. Ashley paced in front of her squad. "First off, this mission is volunteer only. I hate everything about these death traps, but it's the best I can come up with to counter that purple beam. I should probably just fly this one on my own." Ashley looked at her squad, but none of them budged. "Very well," she said. "We've got three of these birds. I'll be flying the small one solo. Hassan, you'll be flying the second, with Tom in the top turret." Bear and Wild Bill nodded. "Priyanka, you'll be flying the third with Zhongwei in the turret. You all sure you want to do this?"

"Yes, ma'am," they said in unison.

"We obviously won't be able to keep up with the bomber formation to give them cover, but these ancient birds are capable of hyperspace jumps, so we'll be scouting out ahead of the bombers and looking for trouble. We'll start at the midpoint of their route and go from there. Remember what you learned in the simulator. You can't spin, and you can't strafe. We move in giant sweeping arcs, so be patient. Lining up your target requires a lot more finesse than a twitch of the controls. If flying a WID fighter is akin to gymnastics, this is going to be like that gameshow on Zaibutu where they make the convicted criminals run the obstacle course with all the gruesome death traps."

"You mean Probation Revocation, ma'am?" asked Priyanka.

"I love that show," said Wild Bill. "But why don't they ever run out of willing contestants?"

"I suppose anything is better than Dakota 17."

"We're getting off track, Priyanka," said Ashley. "There's a kind of sacred reverence for the ancient pilots that flew in these ridiculous contraptions, but now that we're about to climb into them ourselves I have mixed feelings about that. Should we respect their fearlessness, or should we scoff at their stupidity for captaining these un-steerable baskets of fuel?" Bear started to answer, then thought better of it. Ashley continued, "Either way, I suppose we're about to join them in both their audacity and their obtuseness. Hopefully history will be kind to us. India Squad, let's load up."

***

An exhausted Freeda was sitting in front of a box of magnet-mine parts, screwing them together and tossing the assembled mines into a second box. They'd worked nonstop for 12 hours to prepare for the Navy bombers. "Lytess, where are we, again?"

"Orbiting NoChil(8)," Lytess answered. "It's not the best hiding spot for a giant asteroid, but no one will be coming this way anyway. All the good brunch places in this system are on Planet NoChil(1)."

"Did I hear you say earlier this used to be the Anchilio

System?" Freeda asked.

"It was. NoChil is condensed from North Anchilio."

"Anchilio used to be a Kadrafian system. I didn't know we'd lost it."

"You technically didn't. The Kadrafian military outposts are all still in the outermost orbit of this system, but the inner orbits are cheap real estate. It's a hotspot for young 'entrepreneurs' who run small companies with unsustainable business models so they can feel important while living off their parents' money. They give the neighborhood a cute nickname and suddenly the property value skyrockets, a bunch of microbreweries open up, and Kadrafians get priced out of the area. That's why the Navy is launching their bombing mission from here. They can safely park their carrier near the center of the system and then fly their bombers toward the Raif'yan outposts in the outer orbit."

"NoChil," Freeda muttered under her breath, "what a stupid name."

The mine she was working on slipped out of her hand and went skidding across the floor. She got up with eyes half closed to get it, when over the intercom Gam3r announced, "Bombers are launching from the carrier. Everybody suit up. I'll have their trajectory as soon as they're in formation."

Freeda grabbed the box of completed mines. "This doesn't look like it's going to be enough," she said to Lytess.

"Well, it's gonna have to be."

Freeda ran down to the hangar to find Brandine already halfway into her G suit. "Boy howdy," she said to Freeda. "Do I look sexy in this thing or what?"

Freeda didn't respond. She pulled her own suit off its hanger and stepped into it. "These are really going to work?" she asked.

"Dunno. But the twins ain't never let me down yet, love. Ready when you are."

The two pilots climbed into their fighters, raced through their preflight checks, and shot out the launch tubes. Minutes later, they accelerated along vectors the twins fed them over the radio.

For the first two hours of their chase, Freeda and Brandine chatted over the radio to keep each other awake. They were up to 45% of lightspeed and closing fast on the bomber formation when Copernicus' voice came over the radio.

"Brandine, come in," Copernicus called out over the comms. "We've got a problem."

"Go ahead, darling," Brandine radioed back. "We've had problems before. We always get through them."

"Gam3r and I are in position to lay down our magnet mines, but somebody beat us to it by several decades. There's already a lethal minefield here, a relic from the days of the massive long-range bombing. It's huge. We're pretty sure it forms a sphere around the entire system, so you're completely surrounded. You can't get around it, and you won't be able to stop the bombers before they hit it. You need to abort."

There was a pause, and then Brandine asked, "Can we hail the bomber pilots and warn them, love?"

"Believe me, I'm trying," said Copernicus. "They weren't in the mood to take my call, unsurprisingly. I don't know if it's a good idea for us to make it our role to tell either side information about the other, anyway. Listen, there's no risk of civilian deaths on this one. I'll keep trying to warn them, but we've gotta call this one a wash. It's the only wise choice."

The normal cheerfulness was gone from Brandine's voice in her reply, "Did I win all those championships by doing the wise thing, Copernicus? Or did I do it by forging ahead against your overcautious advice?"

"Freeda," Copernicus said, "I'm not losing two of my four pilots on our second mission. Can you talk some sense into your wingmate, please?"

Freeda's response was as unwavering as Brandine's. "Don't

worry, Copernicus. We'll stop them."

Chapter 23

As the bomber formation came into view ahead of her, Brandine adjusted her Doppler goggles and scanned the new additions to her dashboard. The twins had equipped both fighters with a mag tow line that could latch on to another craft. The bomber formation was spread out, however, and Brandine and Freeda wouldn't be able to snag all 36 or even 18 at the same time, nor could they take a couple at once and come back for the rest.

"Gam3r and Copernicus won't be able to stop these bombers in time with their magnet mines," she said to Freeda over the radio. "It's going to be up to you and me to stop them before all of us go blazin' into that minefield and light up the night sky of NoChil like a Zaibutu new year celebration."

"How do we stop them?" Freeda asked.

"You ever watch the races, love?"

"I went to one once as a kid."

"We have a saying that rubbin's racin'. We're gonna do it like the cowgirls, darlin'. Y'all got cowgirls on Raif'ya, right?"

"Um, no. Cows can't survive the Kadrafian conditions. We just have a whole lot of moss. But I'll follow your lead, and we can do it like the cowgirls."

As Brandine and Freeda inched their way up behind the bomber squadron, Laneeko's impatient comments arrived via wormhole to Brandine's WID radio. "We're calculating how much time you have before you can no longer stop the bombers. The time dilation is making the calculations difficult, but you are out of time. You need to break off and begin decelerating now."

Brandine had no intention of breaking off pursuit and leaving the bomber pilots to be swallowed by the minefield ahead. She pressed the radio button and mimicked the sound of static in response. "Roger shhh Laneek shhh bomb shhh we'll keep shhh pursuing." Laneeko responded in a panic, but Freeda and Brandine ignored him. Instead, she leaned back in her seat and took in the beauty of deep space for possibly the last time. Though Brandine had spent years of her life racing at these speeds, she never got over how fascinating the galaxy looked when it got stretchy and distorted and the stars became short lines in her goggles.

The two Pacifist pilots came into range of the bombers, and Brandine checked on Freeda over the radio. "How you doing with the G forces, darlin'? You gonna pass out on me?"

"I'm awake. The kadrafalene is kicking in right now. I'll be fine as soon as I get to start shooting things."

"Kadrafalene?" asked Brandine.

"Is that not common knowledge among Yoomies? It's our version of adrenaline, but three times as potent. Unscrupulous Raif'yans harvest it from their own bodies and sell it to other species as a drug."

"Well I'll be," mused Brandine, and began spinning up her Purple Inerter. "It takes all kinds, I s'pose."

While the star field appeared blurred and elongated, the bombers hung in front of them in perfect clarity as Brandine and Freeda matched speeds to the formation.

"Don't forget to lead your targets," Freeda reminded. "Our lasers aren't instantaneous at this speed. Looks like we have three clusters of 12 each. I'll take the left flank, you take the right, and then we can meet in the center."

The radio crackled with Laneeko's voice, still agitated. "Ladies, I'm sorry, but let the bombers go, or you're going to be gentrifying that minefield."

"With you in a second, love," said Brandine, and squeezed her trigger to put Inerter fire into the 12 bombers in front of her. Satisfied with her efficiency, she turned to the center group only to see that Freeda had already disabled them. The Kadrafian was a good shot, but it was time to herd these ships into a giant ball, and that was Brandine's time to shine. She told Freeda to watch her technique, and then brought her ship alongside the outermost bomber and gave it a healthy bump. The bomber soared toward the center of the formation, knocking into another disabled ship. Brandine bumped two more bombers toward the middle and a clear cluster began to form.

Laneeko's voice came over the speakers again, more frantic. "Ladies, now. There's no sense in dying alongside those bombers."

"Too late," said Freeda. "We knocked their engines out. If we leave them now we're murderers."

Freeda attempted to follow Brandine's cowgirl method. On her first try, she whiffed entirely. She got up next to the bomber and tried again. On her second attempt she clipped the ship's engines, sending it into a brutal spin. Freeda recovered and locked her engines against the bomber's, stabilizing it. "Don't think I didn't see that, darlin'," Brandine called out, calm as ever.

"I'm better at shooting things than ramming them."

"Copernicus might disagree with you there," Brandine snorted, then added, "Sorry. Couldn't help myself."

On her third attempt Freeda sent the bomber coasting perfectly toward the center of the formation.

Brandine had all 12 bombers from the left flank bounced into the center group of 12, and was working on making the center into a more orderly ball of spaceships. Freeda made up for lost time by lining the bombers up and pushing them three at a time toward the center of the group. As Freeda pushed the right flank into position, Brandine came around to jam the whole group into one tight ball. She had to be careful not to bump them together in a way that would transfer the energy and have another bomber come shooting out the other side like a marble.

Brandine came over the radio with her final instructions to Freeda. "All right, darlin'. When we decelerate, spin your ship around to face backwards, then jam forward on the accelerator, rather than hitting the brakes. If you hit it backwards, you'll pass out for sure, because the gravity field in your cockpit will be hurting rather than helping you. We're going to do this here thing in series, not in parallel. You're going to snag me with your tow line, and I'm going to hit them with mine. Then we'll slam them brakes for all we're worth. After that, all we can do is sit back and hope them twins got their numbers wrong.

"Why not in parallel?"

"Because trust me, that's why. I've hauled every kind of weird cargo there is." Brandine fired two magnet mines at the center of the bomber cluster and watched as the loose ball of ships crunched together into a tight bundle.

Freeda fired her tow line at Brandine's ship and asked, "Ever hauled 72 unconscious Navy pilots before?"

"More times than I can count, shoog." Brandine fired a third mine at the bombers just to be sure, and then hit them with her tow line. "Punch it."

Freeda's tow line went taught, and Brandine jammed hard on her throttle. Her ship lurched and decelerated at a rate only a three-time orbit racing champion would have the tolerance to withstand. The twins had done the math and assured them that while the Navy pilots were sure to lose consciousness, they would survive the trip.

"How we doin', Lytess?" Brandine asked.

"You needed to begin your deceleration eight minutes ago."

"Our time or yours?"

"Does it matter?"

"Guess not. We'll have to make up for lost time and really put these G suits to the test, eh?"

Since there was nothing left but the waiting to see if their bundle stopped successfully before the lethal Kadrafian minefield, Brandine put on some music and tried to relax and not think about her bladder. After an hour of in-cockpit time, she checked her dashboard readout and saw that they were down to under 40% of lightspeed. She checked in with the twins, who were continuing to map her progress.

"It's a funny feeling, isn't it?" asked Brandine. "We're in this intense fight against time, yet all we can do is sit here and wait a couple hours and see if we die or not. At least the fear of death is keeping me awake." Brandine watched Freeda's ship ahead of her out the windshield (or technically behind her, for the pedants). "How you holding up, Freeda? That kadrafalene doing the trick?"

The radio was quiet for a few moments, and then came the groggy reply. "I'll be ready when the ready is ready. Don't worry about the ready."

"One more time, darlin'?"

"The old one. You know, the old one? We gotta go back to the old one."

Brandine had plenty of experience with the effects of sustained G forces. In the races, pilots would succumb to them and lose consciousness, which would result in crashing their ship in a glorious fireball. Though few would admit to it, most orbital race fans only watched for the crashes. In the races, the ships maintained a constant speed, but due to the race track's orbital nature, the acceleration vector would be toward the center of the orbit, resulting in the large G forces that were the demise of many a rookie competitor.

"Freeda, come back."

No response.

"Freeda, you got your ears on, good buddy?"

No response.

"And that's why we didn't do this in parallel," Brandine

muttered to herself.

Chapter 24

India Squad set coordinates for a hyperjump and arrived at the midpoint of the bomber formation's planned route. Seeing nothing there, they jumped ahead. Still nothing but deep space. Since they were well ahead of the bomber wing, it was a good time to practice a few maneuvers. Ashley ordered her squad to follow her through some tactical routes.

After a few sloppy drills, Ashley clicked on her radio in frustration. "This may have been a mistake, Hassan."

"Oh, it was definitely a mistake, Lieutenant."

"I'm serious," said Ashley. "My left hand keeps reaching for my directional input, but there's nothing there. All that's over there is this worthless throttle. I mean, the difference between all the way forward and all the way back on this speed control is painfully unnoticeable. You try to line up a target, but as soon as it's in range you go whizzing past it and all you can do is pound your dashboard in a blind rage while you let it sink in that it's going to take the better half of ten minutes to arc this damn fighter around and get another shot."

"I know," said Bear. "And the visibility is garbage. Why did they ever think that sitting all the way forward on this long-ass dart was a good idea? I can't see my stern; I can barely see 45 degrees to the sides. Explain to me again why we have such a romantic respect for the ancient pilots?"

Ashley ignored the question. "How are you holding up, Priyanka?" she asked.

"Ok, ma'am," said Flips. "What's getting to me is the vibration from the rocket engines. The whole cockpit is bouncing around like a cart with square wheels. There's no way you could ever line up a clean shot in your gunsights."

Before Ashley could respond, there was a blip on their scanners that the whole squad noticed in unison. Ashley veered her fighter into a pursuit, and her squad fell in behind her. Zhongwei used his turret scope to zoom in for a visual. "It's a purple ship, ma'am, but it's not one of those fighters. It's a Navy transport design. How do you suppose the terrorists managed to steal a Navy transport?"

Ashley thought about it for a few seconds. "Hassan, you remember a while back when we caught Chee...someone borrowing a transport to take AWOL shore leave on Galeria? We didn't think to check to see if he came back in the same ship he left in."

Hassan mulled it over. "And why would we have? We couldn't have known he was going to...lose...a Navy transport ship. Sneaky bastard."

"The rest of you disregard that," ordered Ashley. "Hassan and I will deal with that later."

"Affirmative, ma'am," said Priyanka.

"Disregard what?" added Wild Bill.

As they approached the purple transport, Ashley gave the order to fire at will. Before the mission, Hassan had demanded that the chief outfit the rocket fighters not with the standard Gatling lasers, but with the mass driver cannons that were used on these ancient ships back in their heyday. Bear guessed the energy shields used by the Pacifists were calibrated to combat laser frequency, but the shields would be useless against solid projectiles.

Ashley, Hassan, and Flips lined up their sights, but the vibration in the cockpit from the massive rocket engines sent the fire from their railguns flying harmlessly off into the distance as the fighter formation went hurtling past the purple transport. Wild Bill and Flare lay on the triggers of their turrets as they passed, but the vibration was just as bad for them, and they missed just as wide.

Ashley pushed forward on the throttle to speed up and give herself room to come around for a second pass, and her squad followed. As the transport came into view she pulled back on the throttle, but the purple ship took evasive action, and Ashley's guns unloaded into deep space, missing again. As she sped by the transport and pushed forward on the throttle to get ready to make another pass, she noticed the terrorist ship was hailing her on the radio. After hesitating for a second, Ashley decided she had nothing better to do for the next few minutes while her slow-turning fighter came back around, so she pushed the comm button.

"Sokolov," the radio crackled, "do not speed up. You're heading straight for a Kadrafian minefield. You need to drop your throttle and bank as hard as you can right now."

Ashley had no reason to take at his word the pilot of a stolen Navy transport ship whom she was currently attempting to shoot down. If she had believed the message to be coming from anyone other than her former squad leader, she would have jammed forward on the throttle as hard as she could. Monk may have betrayed her, but if there was one thing he cared about, it was preserving life. After another moment's hesitation, she pulled back on the throttle and pushed forward on her joystick, sending her fighter into a hard downward arc. She ordered her squad to follow.

The three Navy rocket fighters arced downwards in front of the minefield, and sure enough, there was a grid of small dots above them, consistent with mines. Wild Bill and Flare let loose a few volleys of turret fire toward the grid, and they were met with an impressive fireworks display as their projectiles collided with the mines.

Bear lost no time calling the *Centauri* over the radio to warn them, but the carrier had lost contact with the bomber formation. Before anyone could say anything, Flare picked up a strange reading on his turret sensors. "We've got something big coming our way, ma'am."

"I'm getting it too," said Wild Bill. "It's huge. What in the ever-loving Statement is that?"

"I've got a visual on it, ma'am," Flare responded. "I'm zooming in. It's our bombers. They're clumped together, and they're dragging two of the purple ships with them. Looks like the bastards got caught in their own trap. They're all headed straight for the minefield, ma'am."

Ashley was too busy flying to get a good readout on her own sensors. "Tom, can you confirm that?" she asked.

"Roger, ma'am. The bombers are clumped together in a tight ball. They're dragging two Pacifist ships. They're headed our way, but their speed is dropping fast."

"How fast?"

"Um, faster than is healthy, ma'am."

Bear's voice chimed in. "Ha. They're not dragging the Pacifist ships. The Pacifist ships are dragging them. They're trying to keep the bombers from hitting the minefield. What do you think, Lieutenant?"

"It does look that way. Hold fire. If we succeed in shooting down those purple derelicts, we'll be dooming our own pilots. Hassan, I need you to call the situation in to the *Centauri*. Stand by."

Ashley switched her radio from her squad channel to the transport ship. "Ace, I know that's you," she said, "but how did you know it was me?"

"Who else is crazy enough to fly into a combat zone sitting on top of eight kilotons of volatile rocket fuel, Lieutenant?" came the reply.

Ashley tried desperately to stop herself from smiling under her helmet, but failed. Through tears, she replied, "So you are alive. Just because I'm happy about that doesn't mean I won't still kill you, Copernicus."

"Noted, Lieutenant."

***

At 15% of lightspeed, Brandine was groggy but functioning. Laneeko was explaining something to her over the radio, but she wasn't quite getting it. "We're calling it how close, Laneeko?"

"At this rate, too close. Lytess was just saying that you're coming up on some rocket-powered fighters giving Coper and Gam3r a hassle."

"Ah, shoot," said Brandine. "I thought I was keeping it together under these acceleration forces, but now I know I'm losing it. It sounded like you said something about rocket-powered fighters. Nobody is that crazy."

"Brandine, you need to increase your deceleration, or you're going to hit the minefield."

"I'll try, Laneeko, but I'm at my limit here. This straight line nonsense ain't for me."

As their speed ticked down toward zero, Brandine removed her Doppler goggles. She checked her dash and through blurred vision noticed that she was picking up the transport and the three Navy fighters on her sensor.

Just as she was close enough to make a visual on the minefield, Brandine and her bundle of bombers finally came to a crawl, then a stop. She waited until they were beginning to move back in the opposite direction, just to make double sure that the bombers would be floating away from the mines when she disengaged. Though Freeda was unconscious, her ship was pulling hard on its tow line, so Brandine brought her Purple Inerter up to full spin. Her ship's computer announced, "forward guns, three-round burst." With one last effort Brandine squeezed the trigger and held it down, and three rounds of purple sank themselves into Freeda's ship.

Brandine disengaged her tow line from the bombers, but stayed connected to Freeda. She yanked her friend's disabled ship out of the path of the approaching rocket fighters, then switched her acceleration dampers on. The Navy pilots would be calling to the fleet for a rescue for the unconscious bomber pilots, but the three Pacifist ships would be long gone before the Navy backup arrived. Brandine had already arranged with the twins to be picked up in the Roid at the outer edge of the star system.

Chapter 25

The land masses of Kadrafia

Are purply-blue

They're covered by moss

That gives them that hue

'Twas the blue moss of the planet

That the scientists used

To change human genes

And fill Kadrafians' shoes

It protects from conditions

And helps them survive

On the cloudy blue planet

The moss keeps them alive

They are safe from the elements

Through thick and through thin

With this moss in their beautiful, splotchy blue skin

-Excerpt from "Oh the Places You'll Go: A Children's Book of the Planets," by Brandine Lupinski

The mood on the Roid was not celebratory like it had been after their first mission. The crew sat together in the common room to decompress, but after a day and a half of nonstop prep followed by a mission that pushed them to their limits, they were too exhausted to engage in any rowdiness. Copernicus had locked himself in the lab and asked to be left alone, so after Freeda checked the room for any hidden containers of alcohol, the remaining members plopped themselves on the couches and chairs in the common area and tried to de-stress. The twins had managed to get their hands on some of the most popular microbrews from NoChil on their last supply run, as well as some brunch takeout.

The crew picked lackadaisically at their eggs Benedict. Freeda nursed her hazelnut-infused hot chocolate. She was still feeling a bit woozy from her blackout during the mission. She knew she shouldn't be having caffeine, but it tasted like hipness and warmed her trachea. She finally broke the silence with a question directed at Laneeko and Lytess. "So, what's the deal with you two anyway? How did they end up with twins just this one time? Was somebody in genetics playing a prank, and that's why you two are such pranksters yourselves, because you are a prank?"

Laneeko snickered into his mimosa, and Lytess answered. "We don't know. The fertilization process is randomized, but it's not conducive to twins. Our labs are forbidden from doing any genetic engineering. We value science and learning, but if we engineered it so that every baby was a science prodigy, we'd have no one working in the trades, and our society would crumble. We need diversity."

Gam3r coughed into his oatmeal stout. "But you two are science prodigies, and you work in the trades," he pointed out.

Laneeko responded, "Yeah, but we're the exception to every rule. We figured out the trades are where the money is, and we have to fund our various scientific exploits, saving the galaxy and all that."

Gam3r didn't want to let it go. "But you've been in the trades since way before you were saving the galaxy."

The twins giggled. "You sure about that?" asked Lytess. Laneeko stopped giggling and gave Lytess a serious look, then subtly shook his head no.

"What's that supposed to mean?" asked Gam3r.

"Don't worry about it," pleaded Laneeko. "Just drop it. It's not a big deal."

"Drop it? I think that ship has left orbit, Laneeko. You just confessed that you have 'saved the galaxy' before. There's no secrets among the Pacifists, are there?"

Laneeko shrugged. "Fine. Tell them," he said. "But this doesn't leave this deck."

Lytess explained that as youths, the three brothers did an experiment that proved that as insufferable as the sub-light activists could be, they were correct about the overuse of WID technology destroying the building blocks of space-time. The three brothers knew, however, that having scientific proof of something carried no weight in the political spheres, where influence matters more than facts.

The young Lumanos, instead of wasting time publishing their findings, took it upon themselves to find a solution. They worked tirelessly to invent a device capable of reversing the local effects of WID damage.

The "scrubbers" they came up with worked like an exhaust vent, allowing the built-up unbalance of WID byproducts–gravity waves, antimatter, misguided angst–to flow back to the depleted areas of the galaxy, restoring the solar ecosystem to balance.

The scrubbers were expensive to build, and the brothers had to install one in each populated star system. Fortunately for the three young mechanic-scientists, they had any number of inventions that could make them a lot of money very quickly. They determined that the biggest, quickest, and least scrutinized money-making scheme was in the racing circuits, which is how three altruistic Loomies ended up in the less-than-intellectually-stimulating world of spaceship orbital racing.

They won purse after purse and series after series with their ship designs, working up from the minor leagues to the majors, where the real money was. In the off season they traveled the galaxy setting up scrubbers in every populated star system, unbeknownst even to the rest of their racing crew, who assumed they were spending their vacation on New Belgium doing weird nonsexual Loomy stuff. After just over a decade they had the scrubbers in place, and retired from racing without ceremony and with little more money than they started with, despite their well-earned place in the record books. The scrubbers were a temporary solution, but with the galaxy at least in less imminent danger, the brothers returned home to work in their shop and lead a carefree life.

But the war raged on in the galaxy, and as they matured the three brothers felt more and more like their obligation to society was unfulfilled. Just because they had prevented the Milky Way from turning into one giant Milky Black Hole didn't mean their work was done forever. Surely every thinking being in our universe has an obligation to do their part for peace, do they not? And so the trio went back to work, this time looking for a solution to war.

What the brothers learned, sadly enough, is that reversing the effects of centuries of tearing holes in the fabric of space-time is child's play compared to the task of getting the various tribes of the galaxy to stop killing each other for virtually no reason at all.

Freeda was aghast. "Why did you need to race? You could have sold the scrubbers themselves to pay for the cost of production. You know, like how literally every business in the galaxy works?"

Lytess sighed. "Perhaps. We worried that if we went public with the invention, the Oligarchy would have taken control of the patent and therefore the profits. They would have installed the scrubbers but then charged rent for them on a continuous basis to further control the galaxy and widen the wealth gap even further. We'd solve one problem but contribute to another.

"Anyway, we were attempting to use the same concept for our Inerter weapon, a hyperdimensional vent to stabilize space-time in a small area and thus trigger the fail-safes on any nearby WID drives. If their WID drives couldn't open any wormholes, it would render fighter engines inert. We weren't having any luck with that approach, but then Laneeko found a way to render the fuel inert with the Purple Inerter. Pretty brilliant, if I haven't said so already."

"Like all of the greatest inventions," mused Laneeko, "I discovered it quite by accident while working on something else. Still, when you have an accident like that, you need a trained focus to understand the implications. It pains me to think of how many brilliant ideas have gone undiscovered because the person who happened upon it didn't know what it meant, cursed their bad luck at having a bathtub full of a delicious gelatinous dessert instead of an industrial adhesive, and moved on with their lives without ever knowing that they had stumbled into something magnificent."

A few minutes passed in silence while the crew contemplated the revelation. Then Freeda had a morbid thought. "I know you guys won't kill to save these people, but would you die for it?"

Neither brother hesitated. "Of course," they answered in unison.

"But they're not even your people! The Lumanos are the one species in this galaxy unaffected by the war. Why make it your problem?"

Laneeko looked lost in thought for a second, then offered, "In the ancient world they had a saying that the definition of 'insanity' is doing the same thing twice and expecting a different result."

Freeda was confused. "I'm not sure I follow how that

relates to this."

Laneeko snapped back to the present. "Oh, it doesn't. I was just thinking of it because in New Belgium we have a saying that the definition of 'insanity' is tribalism. No good ever comes of it."

"That seems like a pretty narrow definition of insanity, if you ask me," mumbled Freeda, with her eyes down. She was looking at the back of her hands and examining her tattoos.

Lytess offered, "It's meant as intentional hyperbole. The point is that New Belgium is one of the only cultures that doesn't outright celebrate tribalism. It solves nothing. It starts at the top and trickles down to the smallest factions. The Navy hates the KCF, but the Navy is made up of a bunch of species that, when the KCF isn't around to unite against, fight with each other. Those species are united among themselves if there's other species around, but they otherwise identify only with their speciesmates who hail from the same planet. Then the same region. Then with fans of the same grav-ball team. Then with alumnus of the same school. The only time any two factions aren't fighting with each other is when there's a faction in a larger category for them to unite against. How is that not insanity?"

Lytess trailed off, and Laneeko continued, "On New Belgium, even the citizens who aren't Lumanos have embraced a less tribalistic attitude. I'm pretty sure it's that single aspect of our culture that has made our planet so prosperous. The consensus among outsiders seems to be that we succeed because Lumanos are smart, but that's not it. If Lumanos were as tribalistic as everyone else, we'd be no better off than the factions of Octobrox."

Freeda made a face. "You can just keep the ancient definition of insanity, though, since yours fits under it. Tribalism has been tried countless times, and it's never yielded a different result. Besides, it sounds to me like you're claiming that your lack of tribalism is what separates you from all the other tribes, eh? Makes your tribe superior to theirs? Maybe y'all are no better off than Octobrox." The twins looked at her confused until she burst into laughter, adding, "Oh, come on. I'm joking."

Lytess said, "That's just one of many misconceptions about us. There's misconceptions about every culture."

"You have no idea," said Gam3r, without looking up from his game. "Try being straight-up fetishized, and I don't even mean sexually. Marketers cater to Zees because they think everyone wants to be a Zee. People can't seriously think it's a preferable thing to be a kid forever, can they? Does no one remember what puberty was like? Everything, and I mean everything, is the end of the world. Yoomies who survive puberty seriously fantasize about recapturing that feeling? Right now we are laboring to end a galaxy-wide war, but you know what's pissing me off at this moment?"

He didn't answer his own question because he was leaning forward in his seat and tapping furiously at his game. After a second he threw his keypad onto the table and sighed, "This boss on level 21. I can't get past him, and it is consuming me. I didn't tell anyone this, but yesterday I had to get a med wrap for my hand after I punched the bathroom wall over this level. Do I know that's a stupid thing to get upset over? Yes, I do. Can I stop myself? No. Because my body has been saturated with puberty hormones for 20 years straight."

Gam3r picked the keypad up and restarted the level. Without looking up he added, "But I have to focus on trying to beat this boss, because three days ago Freeda's breast brushed against my thigh when she was training me in self-defense moves, and I haven't slept a wink since. And yet everywhere I go people tell me they wish they could be young again, and how great it must be to be a Zee. They have no idea how stupid they sound. And when I tell them how stupid they sound, they just blow me off, because nobody listens to a Zee." After a second he added, "Except all of you."

Brandine sighed. "I always thought it would be nice to continue to think you're invincible for your whole life, though. I do miss that about being young."

Gam3r laughed. "Ha. Yeah, that's fair. That's probably why I kept wanting to join the Navy so bad. I want to go out in a blaze of glory, a hero's death in battle. We don't have a ton to look forward to, as Zees. 40 years of teenage angst, then we get to become sexually active for, what? A couple dozen times, and then just like that, it's over. Doesn't seem worth waiting all that time for. Going down in battle and leaving some kind of hero's legacy is way cooler."

Freeda shuddered. "You know not of what you speak. That's exactly what I wanted when I was younger, but I've watched plenty of shipmates get their hero's death. The older I get, I don't know why that ever sounded like a good option. Who cares about coolness if you're dead?"

"Well, Zees care about coolness more than we care about life itself, if you believe the stereotypes about us, which most people do."

Freeda didn't want to let it go. "What about the survival of your species?"

Gam3r laughed out loud. "Think back to when you were in puberty. Did you care about things like the survival of your species?"

"No, I guess not," Freeda admitted.

"I'm so sick of stereotypes," chimed in Brandine in her trademark way of being a half-topic behind the conversation. "People write me off because of the way I talk. It's like, just 'cause I like my vehicles and I use some colorful language, I must be stupid or somethin'. I wrote a book chroniclin' how we became the race champs racin' with homemade rigs that y'all slapped together usin' junkyard parts, and every slack-jaw I run into assumes it was ghost written. I'm like, ghost written? Just because I don't pronunciate the letter G don't mean I can't be findin' it on no keyboard, I tell you what.

"Someday I'm gonna get back to writin'. You know what I'd love to write? A history book. I think it would be so fun to do the research and put it together." Brandine paused for a minute, then looked at Freeda, who had resumed studying the tattoos on the backs of her hands. "What about you, darlin'? Surely there's a freighter fleet full o' misconceptions about your folks?"

Freeda looked up from her hands. She felt generally comfortable in this group, but suddenly all eyes were on her, and it made her shift in her chair. "Everyone thinks we're all warriors," she offered. "Which doesn't bother me, because I happen to be a warrior, but it's not true. Just like everyone else, our warriors are ruthless, our poets are gentle, our politicians are corrupt, and our masses are gullible. I think the rest of the galaxy forgets that pretty easily because you only ever see our Combat Force. I'm a warrior, but I'm fighting to protect a rich culture on my home world."

She paused, then added, "When I was young I was with a musician. He wrote the most beautiful songs and had the most vibrant yellow tattoos. We loved each other, but his family were vehemently against him being with a soldier. He tried to join the Combat Force to escape his family and be with me, but he didn't fit in. He stood out horribly in the KCF with his artist's yellow. We love and respect our artists, but we don't feel comfortable relying on them in the chaos of a battle, so they kicked him out in basic training.

"Kadrafians are tied to the fate of our choices when we go through our rite of passage. The bright colors of our tattoos are supposed to symbolize our freedom, but I'm realizing it limits our options in life. We call ourselves free, yet we give ourselves no opportunity to change our destinies. Anyway, he's doing well with his music. He wrote a couple songs for me a few years ago. I used to play them in my fighter on the way into battle."

"Can we hear them?" asked Gam3r.

"You a big fan of Kadrafian music, are you?"

"Actually, I am. My roommates got me into it. One of them was learning to play the Kadrafian squeezebox. He's terrible. But we're super into Stenothraxica, and not just because she's hot. I used her song 'Mossi, Mossdi, Mosschee' in my last racing game."

"Fair enough," conceded Freeda. "I've got it at my bunk. His name is Treshler. It's acoustic folk, a lot tamer than Stenothraxica, but I'll put it on if you want." Freeda loaded the album on the common room sound system, and everyone listened and relaxed. When it ended, everyone else headed for their bunks, but Gam3r set it to repeat and dozed off on the couch in the common room.

Chapter 26

The Conspiracy Theorists of Planet Skepton were a humanoid species of competing hive minds. The first hive to colonize the planet was a group of humans from Planet Orb, which they insisted was flat. Professional skeptics, The Flat Orbers had contrary beliefs for everything from the presence of government mind control substances in drinking water to whether humans had ever really traveled to outer space. After years of ridicule, the Flat Orbers got so sick of being mocked for their beliefs that they decided to leave altogether and travel through outer space to colonize a new planet, which they could believe, in peace, was flat. Over time, more and more queens developed competing hives, and Planet Skepton was plunged into a perpetual power struggle.

Excerpt from "Cloud Atlas: True Tales of the Flat Planet," by Brandine Lupinski

Greenblatt was tapping his fingers on the table. "Well, Lieutenant?"

India Squad sat around the conference table for their mission debrief. Ashley slouched in her chair, playing with her braids. "It was the Pacifists, sir. We gave chase, but they escaped."

"And my bomber pilots that don't remember anything?"

"They're alive, sir."

"They're alive," Greenblatt echoed. "That's it? A few of the bomber pilots remember that these terrorists tried to contact them over the radio, but they ignored them."

Ashley raised an eyebrow. "So?"

"Well, did they contact your squad during the scrum?"

Ashley glanced at her squadmates, then brought her eyes back to Greenblatt. "No, sir."

The commander looked at the other four pilots. "Anybody have anything to add?" he asked.

"No, sir," the squad said in unison.

Though it was midnight when they got out of the debrief, Ashley took a walk by herself through the mess deck in hopes of finding the chief. She knew she wouldn't be interrupted by Riff this time, since he was in the med bay sleeping off a deceleration hangover. Sure enough, Chief Schultz was sitting in a booth by himself enjoying his midrats, probably on a short break while working straight through the night. Ashley plopped her tray down across the table from him. "I thought I might find you here."

Schultz failed to conceal his smirk. "I heard about your mission, Lieutenant."

"Already?"

"Of course. News like that travels way faster than 60% of lightspeed. How'd you like those rocket fighters?"

"Very funny, Chief. I don't even want to get into why you would let me do something as stupid as flying into battle in one of those things. Copernicus saved my life tonight, Chief. Though I think you already know that."

"You know I can't comment on that, Lieutenant."

"No, you can. Listen, Chief, I don't know how involved you are, but after today I'm a true believer. Ace and his Peacelovers or whatever they are saved over 70 lives today. Every single one of those bomber pilots would be dead right now if that motherfalsing Lumano hadn't been there, and so would my squad. I can't be pissed at him for that. You don't have to tell me anything, but I want you to know, if you need my help with anything, you've got it. Just don't ever let me fly in one of those ancient phalluses ever again. That was the dumbest thing I've done in a while."

Schultz smiled. "I heard you did pretty good. And I thank you for not crashing those birds. They're antiques. They'll pull in a good price in the collectors' market."

Ashley ignored him. "There's something that's bugging

me, Chief. I know you were a marine before, and a decorated one. What made you go so soft that you would participate in some Lumano civil disobedience war protest? I just don't get it."

"First of all, Lieutenant, I'm as frustrated as you are by the Lumano war protest. I wasn't in on that, and I didn't know I was going to be spending my days flushing fuel lines like some common grease monkey, but as far as losing my taste for blood, it's a long story. I did two tours as a marine, and I was in the shit the whole time. I saw some horrible things–nothing you haven't heard before. The real problems started when I got home and tried to transition to civilian life. People always talk about the nightmares, but I was grateful for those. If I'm having nightmares, it means I actually fell asleep in the first place. In the civilian world, my relationship fell apart, my friendships fell apart, and within a year I was reenlisting to escape life in the real world. Things just make more sense to me in the service. I'm focused and I'm stable. But I didn't want to go into the shit again, so this time around I became a mechanic.

"Anyway, it's a confusing spot to be in. I hate the war, because it's the thing that messed me up so badly, but I'm also dependent on it at this point. It may be too late for me, but I'd like to see peace in my lifetime so that the younger generation doesn't get sucked into the same cycle. We're in a stalemate with the KCF. This war is going to require some bold gambits. As annoying as it is, Monk's little antics are reducing the death count. I gotta appreciate him for that."

Ashley saw that the chief had finished his chocolate pudding, a coveted item at midrats, so she slid her untouched bowl over to his tray. "Thank you, Chief. You should try to get some sleep. It's late, and I'm sure we'll have a full day tomorrow when the admiral has some new bright idea."

***

Over the next few months, the war ground on, and things settled into a new routine. The Pacifists made guerilla runs against both sides as often as they could, but the GNC and the KCF knew the purple nuisances couldn't be everywhere at once. With no large battles for the Pacifists to interrupt, all they could do was knock out a few patrols or bombing runs every couple of days. They were an annoyance to both armies, but they were far from forcing any sort of peace treaty.

The news about the Battle of the Republic, however, spread throughout the galaxy and caused a sensation. Factual reports about the Pacifists turned into rumor, conjecture, speculation, approval, disapproval, miscomprehension, outrage, and all other manner of opinion that arises when people think they know everything about a topic they found out about mere minutes ago. If nothing else, it was something new for the public to obsess over, so anyone who wanted to keep up with the conversation in the break room at work had to stay up to date on where and how the Pacifists had struck their latest blow.

With the exception of the Conspiracy Theorists of Planet Skepton, who were sure the Pacifists were up to something sinister, polls found the general population viewed the group favorably. Suddenly it became okay to publicly question whether a war that drags on for decades was any kind of solution to the conflict between the Kadrafian government and the Galactic Naval Corporation. Previously, any suggestion that the war was not 100% necessary to the stability of the Oligarchy was unquestioningly seen as unpatriotic and insulting to "the troops," but after a month of the Pacifists being at the top of the news cycle, peace-minded citizens grew bolder in their opinions. A few small anti-war protests turned into a few large anti-war demonstrations that also made the news.

Other than their standard warning of "Prepare to be

pacified" before unleashing their barrage of Purple Inerters on military vessels, the Pacifists themselves made no public statements, nor released any manifestos. The galaxy was left to wonder: Who were these guys? Where had they come from? What was their end game? Hoaxes claiming to have those answers gave a few pranksters their 15 minutes of fame, and shady entrepreneurs sold T-shirts and toy fighter ships with the Pacifist logo, falsely claiming the proceeds supported the cause for peace.

On board the Roid, there was growing doubt that they were accomplishing anything, but Copernicus remained confident. He scanned the news feeds every day to monitor the changing tide of public opinion about the war, and talked about the possibility of trying again to recruit more pilots to their cause. They fell into a routine where Brandine would plop her bare feet up onto the gaming table in the common room and complain about her "tired dogs." Copernicus would say something like, "Now Brandine, we have to stay the course." To which she would reply something like, "You got a map of this course?" And he would maintain that if the war protests continued to gain momentum, the tipping point was closer than they thought, and the politicians of both sides would have to negotiate peace if they wanted to maintain their offices.

Two months passed, then three. The Pacifists were flying missions every couple of days, knocking out a few Kadrafian bombers here, a succession of Navy patrols there. They had been motivated in the beginning, but they were getting run down, exhausted. Copernicus was hanging up photos of war protests from around the galaxy to try to keep them focused, but it was having little effect on morale. And then, early in the morning on the Roid, while Freeda was out on patrol and Gam3r was on watch, the simmering cauldron boiled over, and Copernicus got his tipping point.

Chapter 27

Nightmare 13 was originally colonized by a group of mixed species who believed themselves to be vampires, lycanthropes, and sorceresses. They chose Nightmare 13 not because of its abundant resources (it had very few), nor because of its temperate climate (it was cold and foggy), but because of its two large moons that occupied opposite points in the same orbit, and the fact that the planet did not spin in relationship to its star. This meant that in one hemisphere of the planet, it was always nighttime, and at least one moon was always up, and, thanks to a little "magic," full.

The settlers of Nightmare 13 were not actually vampires or werewolves, and they possessed no magical powers. They were regular humanoids infatuated with the macabre. They didn't need a planet on which it was always nighttime; what they needed was a place to settle where everyone would leave them alone and stop pedantically pointing out that magic isn't real, so off to a new world they went.

To an uninitiated visitor, there was no reason to doubt that Thirteenians were supernatural beings in possession of magical powers, because most of them used cyborg augmentation to give themselves exactly that. To say that through scientific method humanoids disproved the existence of magic is only one way of looking at the matter. Another way to look at it would be to say that science and technology were able to invent magic. After all, what fictional magical spell in myth didn't become attainable through technology? A potion to heal? Try a medical wrap. A spell of levitation? Get yourself a WID-backpack and some stabilizer boots. A charm to make the object of your desire fall hopelessly in love with you? Go to a life coach. The Thirteenians may not have had anything supernatural about their genetic makeup, but who's to say they weren't real conjurers?

Excerpt from "A People's History of the United States," by Howard Zinn

Bowing, the arms dealer, was sitting in his office, leaning back in his chair with his feet up on the desk. He held an ancient steel katana, inspecting its craftwork for the hundredth time. The steel was sharpened to the limits of the ancient material. It was almost as sharp as a modern Kadrafian combat knife, though it wouldn't hold its edge as long.

Bowing was waiting for a radio call from his contact. His wife set up the deal, but Bowing was determined to make it a successful one. For years he had begged his wife to let him in on bigger deals, let him prove that he was more than a pretty face and a chiseled body, but she always blew him off. This time, however, Bowing finally had leverage. He had something everyone wanted, and he could name his price. His price wasn't going to be money, of course. He already got a reasonable allowance from his Mafia Dawn wife. No, this time his price would be a position of power in the new world order, which seemed only fair. Bowing could remove an obstacle to achieving the new world order, because he knew how to find the Pacifists, and the Pacifists had shields.

The radio buzzed. Bowing clicked it on. "Who's this?" he asked in an overly pleasant tone.

"You know who it is. Do you have the coordinates?"

"I have them. You've got 24 hours before they expire. Your team is assembled?"

"You mean your team. This isn't the crew I'd choose, and you know it."

Bowing smiled to himself and ran his fingertip along the blade of the katana, feeling its sharpness. Toward the hilt he sliced his finger, drawing blood. He opened his mouth in a silent shout, but with the radio active, he prevented himself from making an audible yelp. "Semantics," he retorted to the radio. "That's the deal we had. My prisoner, my team. You bring me the Lumano, and I will make sure you get access to my genetic reassignment lab."

"You mean your wife's genetic lab."

Bowing frowned at the jab, but reminded himself that soon he would be seen as more than a mere trophy husband with a reality show. "Again, semantics," he said. "You'll be back to your old self in time for your fleet of ships to be ready, and we'll both get our command positions in the army. Rendezvous is at 1800 hours. Stand by to receive coordinates."

***

The Night Before:

Out the window of the Roid, Freeda remarked at the beauty of the gas giant Frankenstein in the Nightmare system. The Roid was orbiting Frankenstein, parked in its rings. On Nightmare 13, the next planet over, Nightmare Festival was in full swing, and the twins were insisting on going planetside for a night of relaxing.

They all piled into the transport and went right in their purple jumpsuits, hiding in plain sight under the guise that their Pacifist uniforms were a playful costume. Much to Gam3r's chagrin, but everyone else's delight, they found themselves to be in good company. Pacifist-themed costumes were the single most popular costume at the festival that year. No one else had purple jumpsuits, since no one else had seen the Pacifists out of their ships, but there were all manner of interpretations. A group of young men painted themselves purple with white tiger stripes, a girl wore a tight purple dress with two white circular Pacifist logos over her breasts, and many people had made themselves bulky costumes in the shape of the Pacifist fighter craft. One festival-goer had even outfitted his costume complete with a set of guns that put on a purple laser-light show when he pulled the trigger.

Brandine, Freeda, and the Lumanos were thrilled to see how popular they'd become, and flattered any time anyone complimented their "costumes," but Gam3r was miserable. To a Zee, individuality is tantamount, and Nightmare Festival is all about having the most original costume. That they were there in the trendiest disguise of the year was devastating to Gam3r. He kept his flight helmet on to hide his face until he could duck into a shop and buy some makeup so he could at least be the only "zombie" Pacifist for the rest of the night, but he didn't stop complaining about their costumes.

Freeda, on the other hand, had a ball. She got the most compliments, as all night long the festival-goers debated whether she was really a Raif'yan, or if her interpretation that the Pacifists could possibly include a Raif'yan member was brilliant or culturally insensitive. The twins had tried to talk her out of bringing weapons to Nightmare Festival, but the Sugar Cane slung over her shoulder and the knife on her waist served only to draw in more positive feedback. A group in their twenties stopped to compliment Freeda and give drunken high fives to the entire group. A girl among them wore a Tautologist school uniform that showed entirely too much of her thighs to ever be welcome on any real school campus. She turned to Gam3r and held out a pumpkin-shaped bucket full of chocolate treats. "Here you go, young fella," she said. "Happy Nightmare Fest!" Gam3r rolled his eyes, but took the pumpkin.

The six weary team members strolled down the main street, happy to feel like regular citizens far removed from the war, if only briefly. Vendors and carnival games lined the thoroughfare, and all night long (and all day long, if you want to get technical, since it was always night on Nightmare 13) creatures of all species paraded up and down in their costumes of varying levels of cleverness and originality. The streetlights were decorated with scary apparitions, and brass bands on balconies played upbeat jazz music.

They stopped to watch a human street magician with a small crowd gathered around him. He had a long, dark mustache that stuck straight out to the sides, and he wore a head-wrap with a jewel in the center. He was finishing a card trick when they joined the circle, and something about Copernicus drew his attention. "My Loomy friend," he called out, "you must volunteer for my next trick. Step right up and be amazed by The Astonishing Stanley."

As Copernicus stepped forward, the magician joked, "I love your purple uniform, by the way." Then he snapped his fingers, and Copernicus' uniform changed color to the bright red of a GNC flight suit. The crowd gasped, then applauded. "But you are a Pacifist, so you don't side with the Navy, of course." The illusionist snapped his fingers again, and Copernicus' uniform changed to the dark blue worn by the KCF.

This time the crowd laughed, and Freeda stepped forward, drew her knife, and held it to the magician's throat. "Change it back, Yoomy," she demanded.

The Astonishing Stanley was an old salt. He had dealt with hecklers before, and he knew how to keep it from derailing his show. He grinned wide enough to let the audience wonder whether this was in fact a scripted portion of the show. "Of course, my lady," he said, and touched his finger to Freeda's knife. In the same instant Copernicus' uniform changed to a rainbow tie dye, and Freeda's knife disappeared from her hand.

The crowd went wild, and Copernicus took a bow to play along, then winked at Freeda to let her know it was all in good fun. As Freeda blushed and stepped to the edge of the circle, Stanley announced to her, "My Lady, if you would like to retrieve your instrument of pacification, you must visit my wife, Madame Soofeeth. Her fortune teller's tent is at the end of this block." The crowd applauded politely, and the magician grinned with the satisfaction that he had just doubled his tips for the evening.

Copernicus stayed to play along as a volunteer for the original trick the magician had intended, at the end of which his uniform was restored to purple, to the delight of the audience.

Brandine walked with Freeda to the end of the block to retrieve the knife, stopping along the way to watch a three-card monte dealer run his timeless scam. He was an Aquaperson from the ocean planet Tridens, and his webbed fingers made him particularly good at concealing the cards. Brandine's orbital racing reflexes, however, made her the bane of even the most seasoned monte dealer. She took a unique joy in giving them their comeuppance whenever she saw them hustling their con. The dealers never paid her the money she rightfully won, which, in her mind, further exposed their fraud to any lookers-on, and added to the deserved humiliation of the scam artist.

Leaving Brandine to her card game, Freeda ducked under the low-hanging curtains and into the fortune teller's tent, and waited for her eyes to adjust to the dim candle lighting. After a few seconds everything came into focus and she let out a gasp.

"You're a Raif'yan!" Freeda exclaimed.

"And so are you," retorted Madame Soofeeth. Madame Soofeeth sat on a pillow in front of a standard crystal ball, and on the pillow opposite her lay Freeda's knife. "My dear Freeda," continued the fortune teller, "You do know you're supposed to wear a costume to Nightmare Fest, do you not?"

Freeda sat down and returned her knife to its sheath. "You're good," she admitted. "Are you really married to that cyborg magician?"

The fortune teller gave a knowing smile. "The Astonishing Stanley. Yes, my dear. For 23 wonderful years and counting."

"Do you not face... prejudices here?"

"Of course, occasionally. But I just remind people that our governments are at war, not our species."

"Your tattoos," said Freeda. "Red and white. I've never seen dashed lines before."

Madame Soofeeth smiled again, as if she knew the question was coming. "Yes, my child. I was a farmer before I left Raif'ya. I added the white dashes when I came here to pursue my gift. As the only Raif'yan fortune teller, I got to choose the colors for such a career. Freeda, do you not sometimes feel that we Raif'yans have bound ourselves to our tattoos? It's a willing sacrifice of our freedom, in many ways. The irony for me is that as a fortune teller, I know that we cannot change our fate, and yet here I am, the only Raif'yan I know of to have changed my tattoos. Do you understand?"

"I understand."

"Very good. I can see that you, too, are capable of great change. Once a proud warrior, your Lumano friend has shown to you that war is as pointless as arguing philosophy with a Tautologist. Now, Freeda, may I read your fortune?"

Freeda nodded, and dropped some coins into the fee jar to her right. "I should warn you that I don't believe in this stuff. I'm guessing you know my name through information that came here from your husband outside, likely the same route as my knife. But honestly, it's just kind of nice to see another Raif'yan. I mean, I love the people I'm traveling with right now, but..."

Freeda trailed off as she realized she was giving away too much information to a woman whose entire scam was to glean things from unsuspecting rubes. In her head she cursed herself for not insisting that she was in costume. It also crossed her mind that Madame Soofeeth might not be a Kadrafian at all. She could be using her husband's color-changing trick to match species with whomever walked into her tent.

Madame Soofeeth made the standard show of looking into

Freeda's eyes. She then scattered a handful of trinkets on the floor in between them, followed by closing her eyes in a show of trance-like concentration. After a few minutes, she bestowed her sage advice.

"You hide within the rocks of space,
but malicious forces have found your place.
Lost in the void, the storm you'll weather,
You'll end up in a place of pleasure.
So far already, you have come,
Yet you must return to where you're from.
For so many years, our people beguiled,
Saved by the one they call a child.
When it's all done, the statements willing,
It's up to you to end the killing."

Madame Soofeeth's eyes then shot open in a dramatic gesture, as though she had seen something shocking. All part of the show, of course. She paused, then added, "And Freeda, tomorrow morning, you must be on the lookout. They are coming." The fortune teller then collapsed backwards into her pillows in a theatrical display of exhaustion.

As she got up to leave, Freeda had a thought that might test whether Madame Soofeeth was a true Kadrafian or not. "Madame," she asked, "I don't suppose you have any moss? I've been traveling, and I haven't tasted it in quite some time. I do miss it so."

A devilish grin came across Madame Soofeeth's face. "I keep some on hand, and I must admit it's not as enjoyable when I'm surrounded by those who do not appreciate its sweetness. Come, share some with me." She went to a pantry and produced a jar, and the two women each took a helping. Freeda savored her own bite, watching Madame Soofeeth closely as the fortune teller bit into a piece. Freeda thanked her for her kindness and left the tent satisfied with the fortune teller's identity, if not with her vague and unhelpful fortune.

When Freeda emerged from the tent, Brandine was engaged in a heated shouting match with the three-card monte dealer. The small crowd of onlookers sided with Brandine and grew belligerent toward the dealer as he angrily packed up his table. Freeda pulled her Sugar Cane off her back and prepared to come to her friend's aid, but as she came up next to Brandine the dealer was already storming off with his table under his arm.

"What happened?" Freeda asked.

"Oh, the usual, hon. He asked me where the lady was, and I said, 'You mean the one in your shirt sleeve? Cause she sure as sugar ain't one of the three cards on this here table.' And he tried to deny it, but then I flicked his breast pocket and what don't come sailin' on up outta the fabric but her majesty the queen o' hearts her same self. You saw the rest. You get your fortune told, darlin'?"

"I did. By a Kadrafian fortune teller, if you'll believe that."

"Prob'ly in costume, deary. Let me guess. You've gotta do some things what you might not want to do, but you should persevere the best that you can, 'cause a journey of a million lightyears starts with but a single hyperspace jump? Somethin' like that?"

Freeda smiled. "Yeah, something like that. It rhymed, at least."

They met up with the rest of the group, and as they strolled up the street, the twins took the fun out of the magic trick by explaining that it was most likely a holopaint generator. "We invented those," Lytess announced. Gam3r gave him a skeptical look, so he told the story of the time they were in school, and they used their newly invented holographic paint generator to make their dorm building appear to be a daycare, a Navy outpost, and finally a "Lumano House of Free Love." They had kept the prank up for a full two weeks before the dean figured out where they concealed the generator.

At the conclusion of the story, Laneeko turned to Gam3r. "You see, Gam3r, the concept of a Lumano House of Free Love is a hilarious absurdity because–"

"I get it, Laneeko. I am a Zee, not a child. We've been through this." Laneeko smiled wide, patted Gam3r on the head, and dropped some candy into his pumpkin.

***

The next morning Freeda awoke before the rest of the crew, donned her flight suit, reminded herself that she was not superstitious and that Madame Soofeeth was nothing more than a very charismatic scam artist, and launched her fighter to patrol Frankenstein's rings.

Chapter 28

Freeda was in her fighter, cruising through one of the denser sections of the planet's rings. She had been enjoying the silence, but then her radio lit up. "Freeda, come in."

"Morning, Gam3rDud3. I woke up early, so I decided to run a quick patrol."

"Next time leave a note or something. We weren't sure where you went."

"Yes, mom."

"Funny."

Freeda weaved her way through the dust and chunks of ice, unsure of what she was looking for. Just as she was deciding to head in, something in the corner of her eye caught her attention, but when she turned to look it was gone. Nothing to see but space debris. Then she swore she saw movement in the corner of her other eye, so she turned back. Still nothing but dust. She turned her ship toward the Roid, when she saw it. There was one ice-covered boulder the size of a transport ship that wasn't flowing right. It was drifting upstream, leaving a subtle wake in the dust. Freeda darted her ship toward it and fired a few purple beams, causing it to turn and dodge sideways.

"Gam3r, I got something. Make sure everyone is up."

"Roger."

Freeda chased the rogue space rock and put more fire into it, but her Inerter had no effect. Taking off upstream toward the Pacifist base, the berserk rock ducked and dipped through the debris in an attempt to shake Freeda off.

Finally, the intruder circled around a behemoth and into a small cluster of ice, joining the flow of the ring. Freeda came hurtling around the corner and came to a stop. Her eyes darted back and forth, but all she could see was jagged edges. She hadn't memorized the particular shape of her target during the chase in anticipation of standing in a dark room behind the one-way mirror as one by one, various street-hardened and menacing-looking space rocks would be asked by the bored space rock police officer to step forward and recite the line printed on the index card.

Freeda got in close and squinted at the cluster, looking for any signs that one of the chunks didn't belong–wrong amount of spin, fluctuations in speed, or even just putting off a subtle vibe that was a little too smug for her liking. And then there it was. One of the rocks in the cluster had a laser drill mounted on it. If she didn't know better, she'd suspect someone was planning on using that drill to lay siege to a super secret asteroid base, if it happened to come upon any.

Freeda clicked on her radio to warn Gam3r, but when she looked up again the rock was gone from the cluster. Spinning her ship around to look for it, she caught a glimpse of her target a moment too late. The rock smashed into her head on, pushing her into a cluster of debris. Her head slammed into the seat, and everything went dark.

***

When Gam3r lost contact with Freeda, he ran to alert everyone. "Freeda was racing through the belt like a maniac," he panted, "but there's nothing else on the sensors. Then I lost her."

As Gam3r finished his sentence, the Roid shook with the thud of a collision, and everyone sprinted to the bridge. "We're being boarded," said Lytess, checking a sensor. "By an asteroid ship. Bastards stole our idea. They're trying to dig through our hull."

"Where are they?" asked Gam3r.

"Directly above the flight deck. They'll come down right into the hangar."

"We could launch in the fighters and transport, abandon

ship," said Brandine.

"What about Freeda, though?" asked Copernicus. "Besides, I'm sure what they really want are the shield generators, now that they know we have them. If they get their hands on those, they can reverse engineer them."

"Well, I doubt that," said Laneeko, strapping himself into the seat next to Gam3r, who had taken the helm of the Roid. "We built so many dummy circuits into those things, if anyone tries to copy our design they'll end up opening a wormhole that connects to the fart cloud nebula."

Gam3r ignored the conversation while he powered up the manual steering mechanism. "Everybody strap in," he shouted. "Ima shake 'em." Without waiting for his crewmates to take their seats, Gam3r spun the Roid around and surged it forward into the denser portion of the gas giant's rings, toward where he lost contact with Freeda. The base came hard against a large rock, flicking the siege ship from its surface like a bug. As the rogue asteroid ship righted itself and came at the Pacifist base, Gam3r charged through the dust, dancing his giant rock through the maze of debris.

Brandine was unstrapped, and her body struck the bulkhead with a thunk. "Nice flying, son," she said, pulling herself into a seat. "You should make this your next game. Call it Roid Race."

"If we survive this, I will do just that. Everybody hang on, I think I'm coming up on Freeda's ship." Before Gam3r could locate his friend, however, an explosion shook the Roid. Gam3r groaned and rubbed his head for a moment before putting his hands back on the helm to resume his race. "Controls aren't responding," he cried, drowned out by the siege ship violently reattaching to their surface.

Almost instantly, they could hear a laser drill plunging its way into the Roid's hull toward the hangar deck, the hardest section of the Roid to defend, what with its open area and lack of good choke points.

Gam3r stayed at the helm while Brandine and the Lumanos went to set up shields and barricades around the hangar entrance. Brandine briefly swore at Copernicus that this was not what she signed up for, but then resigned to her fate and set up with her Fetid Foam rifle behind a shielded barricade. Under her breath she hummed to herself Freeda's Kadrafian fight song that they had rewritten what now felt like an eternity ago.

Gam3r struggled to get the controls working until Lytess called out to him that the breach was imminent. The Zee grabbed his rifle and sprinted down to his defensive position, waiting for the boarding party to blast through the final layer of the Roid's hull.

Chapter 29

The intruders pressure-sealed the top of their drill-hole, then used breaching charges to blast through the last few meters of rock into the flight deck. A hailstorm of rocks and smoke rained down into the open chamber. The Pacifists were poised at the two doors to the room, each of which connected to the same hallway that led to the other areas of the base. Copernicus had given the order to hold fire until his command. Rappel lines dropped in, and as the first two sets of boots appeared, Copernicus used a remote to click off the Roid's gravity. Two commandos drifted into the exposed hangar, helpless to speed up their descent toward the cover below.

Brandine and the twins opened fire, encasing both intruders in a puff of rubbery Fetid Foam. Copernicus then clicked the gravity on, and the commandos dangled on their lines.

Reacting to the zero gravity, the next pair of commandos had already come head first into the chamber without their rappel lines. When the gravity reengaged, they tumbled to the floor. Before they could roll onto their feet, they too were trapped in foam.

The next thing to come through the hole was not a commando, but a bouquet of stun grenades. Copernicus shouted to take cover, and the commandos dropped in a dozen troops and set up behind cover. The leader of the siege team dropped in last, wearing a visored flight helmet that covered his or her face.

"All-black uniforms," Brandine whispered to Copernicus. "Are those Navy?"

"Not one that I've seen. They're special forces, but they must be mercs."

The boarding party launched barrages of laser fire into the shields, which absorbed the volley with its signature thudding sound. The Pacifists returned fire with their foam guns, their shots splatting on the various tool carts and ship parts that the commandos had taken cover behind. Laneeko used his blue laser to sublimate a blob of foam into the foul-smelling gas. The commandos coughed and donned gasmasks off their belts. For two long minutes, the situation was a stalemate, both sides pinned down.

Finally, the leader shouted his demands at the Pacifists. "All right, listen up. We're here for the Monk. The only way out of here is your ships, and you'll have to go through us to get to them. You've got nowhere to go. Give us the Monk, and the rest of you live. Otherwise we're blowing this whole rock to dust."

Copernicus started to get up, but Laneeko and Lytess held him down. Lytess whispered to him, "You're not going out there. I'll foam you if I have to."

The leader called out again, "I know your little shield here doesn't work against solid matter, so I brought along plenty of grenades. You wanna try me?"

Copernicus tried to stand up again, but the twins held him. "He's bluffing," said Laneeko. "He wants you alive, or he'd have already tossed those grenades."

The floor began to rattle as Freeda's damaged fighter banged its way down the launch tube. The commandos turned their guns upward. There was a grinding noise, but the fighter did not appear. A second later Freeda came hurtling downward out of the tube, still in her flight suit and helmet, but waving her Sugar Cane in front of her and knocking three commandos off their feet as she doused them with sticky water. She landed knee-first on top of a merc, swinging her staff at another, then rolled to dodge the laser fire. The rest of her team unleashed a torrent of foam from behind their shield cover.

The merc leader moved in on Freeda from behind and swept her legs before she could scramble to cover. She tried to roll to her feet, but the visored commando had his rifle barrel against her chin. He again called out to Copernicus. "I want the Monk out here right now, or this one dies."

The twins turned to grab Copernicus, but they were too late. Their little brother had moved out in front of the shields. He dropped his rifle and raised his hands.

Freeda screamed in anger. "Don't do it, Copernicus. He'll kill us no matter what. Let us fight to the death." She rolled and grabbed her Sugar Cane, an instant too slow. The merc leader grabbed her by the upper arm and threw her effortlessly toward the Pacifist barricades, while one of the commandos got Copernicus by the collar and dragged him toward the breach hole. It was over as quickly as it started.

"Kill them," ordered the visored commando, and the mercs tossed grenades through the shielded doorways. All five remaining Pacifists took off at a full sprint down the hallway. They fell on top of each other as they were pushed forward by the blast, which caved in the corridor.

The commandos placed demolition charges around the hangar, loaded Copernicus up the hole and into their asteroid ship, and detonated the charges as they took off.

Freeda was the last one up the ladder to the bridge, and as she was climbing the top rung the entire room shook. The instruments went haywire, and the gravity disengaged. Gam3r pulled himself to a screen and began calling out which systems were failing. "WID drives are down," he shouted. "Life support is at 20%. Hyperspace has power, but the navigation system is out. Our current trajectory is...directly toward the planet. We're entering the atmosphere in one minute. It's about to get hot in here."

The hangar was blown open, and their ships were turned to mangled space debris, cluttering up the otherwise pristine ring of dust. Though the corridor was caved in, oxygen hemorrhaged from what was left of the Roid. Lytess ordered everyone into their flight suits, a task made difficult by the spin of the base as it hurtled into the planet's atmosphere. Freeda already had her suit on, so she turned to head toward the lab.

Once they donned their suits and helmets, Brandine picked her way down the corridor. It was blocked off, so she sealed the rubble in Fetid Foam to slow down the loss of pressure. They could only access the bridge and the lab; even the common room was caved in. The WID drives of the Roid were not only down, but inaccessible. That left the hyperspace drive as their most promising form of escape. Without a navigation system, however, a hyperspace jump would at best take them somewhere equally as hopeless as their present location, and at worst take them to instantaneous doom.

Lytess floated himself down to the navigation core to see if they could Lumano-rig it, while Laneeko stayed on the bridge and manned the navigational console. Having no luck, Lytess retreated to the bridge. The window was beginning to get a noticeable orange hue to it as the Roid plummeted into the outermost layer of the gas giant.

Gam3r yanked on the unresponsive steering controls, desperate for an idea. "It's now or never, kids. We may as well fire the hyperdrive at random," he said. "Deep space is better than getting eaten by Frankenstein."

"I've got it," said Laneeko. "What if we take the nav chip out of another WID device and hardwire it to the main drive, bypass the navigation computer?"

"Oh, sure," Lytess spouted. "Let me go grab the chip out of the toaster, and we can hyperjump to the center of a small star. Every WID chip we have links to either a black hole or a supernova. Would you prefer to be crushed to death, or vaporized?" He paused, then added, "Copernicus would know what to do. I thought you had ahold of him."

Laneeko looked across the dark room at his twin brother. "I thought you had ahold of him!" he shouted. "I was trying to give Freeda some covering fire."

The orange glow from the window was getting ever brighter, and the temperature sweltered, but neither brother took notice. Lytess pushed off the wall toward his brother. Laneeko saw him coming and pushed off his own wall. The two came together and struggled in a zero G wrestling match until Gam3r dove in to separate them. A loose pole floated across the cabin, which Gam3r grabbed with one hand and jammed between the twins for leverage. Laneeko saw it and let go of his brother. "Freeda," he panted, excited but no longer combative, "I need her Sugar Cane."

"So you can assault your brother some more?" asked Gam3r. "What would that accomplish?"

"No," said Laneeko, gasping. "The nav chip in the Cane's WID drive. It links to Hedon. I could use a quick stop at the galaxy's finest pleasure planet, couldn't you?"

Gam3r blurted out, "False Statement above, that's it!"

"Hold on," Lytess said. "That links to the bottom of the ocean. That's only marginally better than a black hole. Do you know how deep we had to link that Sugar Cane to get strong enough water pressure?"

Gam3r's optimism in the idea was unshaken. "How deep, Lytess?"

"I don't remember, but, like, deep. So we arrive at the bottom of the Hedon ocean traveling in an actual rock. How do you propose we make it to shore?"

"Look out the damn window," insisted Gam3r. "Unless you got a better idea, I vote for Hedon. Always wanted to go. Zees aren't granted travel there. Let's get Freeda's chip and get working on this. Hey, where is Freeda, anyway?"

Lytess found Freeda in the lab by herself. "Freeda, we

gotta go. What are you doing down here?"

"I dunno," she answered. "I wasn't any use on the bridge. I thought maybe I could find something helpful down here."

"Listen," said Lytess, "we need your Sugar Cane. We're going for a swim."

Freeda didn't say anything, but floated the staff toward Lytess.

Lytess came forward to catch the Sugar Cane, but something caught his eye and he grabbed for Freeda's pack instead. "I just remembered something that gives me an idea," he said. "Get your staff up to the bridge for Laneeko. We're out of time."

Freeda nodded and pulled herself out of the room, while Lytess grabbed a video screen out of the pack.

A few minutes later Lytess came to the bridge, where the rest were scrambling to repair the hyperdrive. "I got somethin' you should see," he said.

"Lytess, this isn't the time," said Laneeko, with his head fully inside the navigation console.

"Yeah, it's probably not," admitted Lytess, "but since we might be dead soon, I figured I might as well tell you. I remembered the code, so I'm connected to a live video feed from Copernicus' cyborg eye. We don't have the equipment to track its location, but we can see in the first person view where he's being taken."

Chapter 30

Laneeko didn't stop working, but Brandine and Gam3r stared at Lytess. "You can connect to his feed?" asked Gam3r.

Lytess cleared his throat. "Well, we hacked it when he first got it, left ourselves a back door, but we swore we'd never use it again."

"Copernicus still doesn't know it," said Laneeko, from inside the console. "Freeda, hand me the Sugar Cane and a knife, please."

"Hacking his eye was our most elaborate prank ever," Lytess continued. "If we live, I'll tell you about it."

Freeda pulled a knife out of her bag and placed it in Laneeko's hand. The orange glow out the window made it easier to see, but in exchange she was drenched in sweat from the rising temperature. She handed the fighting staff to Laneeko and asked, "Wait. What are we doing?"

Laneeko sighed. "We're going to use the nav chip in there to make a hyperspace jump to Hedon, where we will then be stuck at the bottom of the ocean until someone has a brilliant idea about how to reach the surface."

Freeda thought for a second. "Does that foam float?"

Gam3r slapped her on the back, a little harder than he meant to, and hooted. "Freeda FTW."

Lytess frowned. "FTW?"

"For the win."

Lytess shook his head. "Gam3r, it takes more time to say 'FTW' than it does to say 'for the win.' I just don't understand Zees today."

Freeda avoided glancing at the orange glow of the window as the Roid continued its descent into the gas giant. She tried not to listen to the sound of crackling as the outer layers of rock gave way to the friction of the atmosphere. To distract herself, she picked up the video screen with the live feed from

Copernicus' cyborg eye. He was alive, at least, sitting down
with a commando pointing a rifle at him. Just then the video
went black as one of the commandos put a cloth bag over
Copernicus' head.

"I think I've got it," announced Laneeko. "There's still the
problem of depressurization. We're in space suits, not deep-
sea suits. This will push them to the limit."

"Well, I'd rather be sick than dead," said Brandine. "We'll
pressurize them with every last molecule of atmosphere we
have left before we open the door. As soon as we're out of
hyperspace we'll rig together some balloons and start filling
them with what foam we have left. It's going to stink like a
boss when we hit the surface."

"I'm sending a mayday communication to Hedon," Gam3r
added. "I gave them the coordinates. We'll be picked up by
the authorities and arrested, but at least we won't be stranded
at sea."

Laneeko ordered everyone to strap in and double check
their helmets. Looking at the glowing window, Freeda chided
him, "Any time now."

Laneeko looked from person to person. "Strap in, kids," he
said. "It's about to get wet and sticky." Brandine and Gam3r
giggled in spite of themselves. Laneeko ignored them and
gave a dramatic countdown from three, then slapped his hand
down on the button to engage the hyperdrive. The drive
made a sputtering sound.

"I said, strap in, kids," Laneeko repeated, and slapped the
button again, harder. This time nothing happened. "I said,
strap" – Laneeko raised his arm to deliver a monster slap to
the button, but before he could finish his sentence, the drive
tore a Roid-sized hole through the ether, and the bridge and
its occupants dissolved into the upper dimensions of space-
time.

END OF PART II

Part III

Chapter 31

The world hung upside down in front of Ashley. Her squad was the only thing right-side up as they kept falling and crashing into the ceiling, exhausted. They were in the gym, where Ashley had been making the squad hold handstands for 20 minutes straight. As he collapsed once more to the mat, Wild Bill spoke up. "How is this helping us again, ma'am? Tumbling makes sense in the field, but we've been stationary here for almost a half hour. How do we use that in battle?"

"Because, Tom," Ashley replied, balancing perfectly on her hands, her short braids dangling toward the floor, "this is teaching you to be comfortable seeing your surroundings from a counterintuitive angle. Get used to letting your brain correct the angle that your eyes are seeing, and you can respond to any threat in a battle, whatever direction it comes from."

Flips let out a faint moan. Her gyros kept her in balance, but her arms were shaking. "Couldn't we accomplish the same thing in the zero-grav chamber, ma'am? That's, like, the whole point of ZG exercises."

"No, Priyanka, we could not accomplish the same thing in the zero-grav chamber. In ZG all you have to focus on is your orientation. I want you to concentrate on reorienting over top of fatigue. That is a direct skill you will need in the field." As she finished saying it, Ashley stepped gracefully out of her handstand and added, "I can see you've all had enough. Let's hit the tramp." Her squad groaned as they dragged themselves to their feet and trudged in the direction of the trampolines.

As exhausted as they were, they kept their complaints to a minimum. They'd been through several skirmishes as a squadron, and Ashley's leadership kept them alive. There were days their training squadron put up better numbers on the leaderboards than the veteran squads, so if their squad leader wanted them to do layout backflips on the trampoline until their muscles gave out and they toppled into the bleachers, grounding them for weeks with a concussion...well, surely she had a good reason for it.

Ashley had been working her squad in the gym nonstop, and her motivations were twofold. First, she cared about them becoming skilled pilots who would have the best chance of survival in a battle. But also, once her squad started outperforming the veterans often enough to not be a fluke, Ashley wanted them to have a constant visual presence working on gymnastics. She wanted everyone on the carrier to understand exactly why her particular rookies were finding success.

The ploy worked, too. Within two months, the trampolines had seen a spike in popularity. Pilots challenged each other to pull off bigger and bigger tricks. A game was devised in which targets were set up around the trampolines, and a jumper held two training pistols while jumping on the tramp, scoring points on the targets while upside down. The statistics in the simulators saw an undeniable improvement with the popularity of "tramp-shooting," and Admiral Garcia finally approached Lieutenant Sokolov about the possibility of initiating a program at the academy. It was what she had wanted for a while, but Ashley told the admiral that for the time being, she felt needed in the fleet.

Feeling confident that her squad's high score in tramp-shooting would go unbeaten for the rest of the day, and when they seemed satisfactorily exhausted, Ashley released them for the rest of the afternoon. Then Ashley and Bear went to meet the chief for lunch, as had become their custom. Bear wasn't technically required to participate in Ashley's gym regimen, but he dutifully showed up and suffered through it. Officially, he claimed it was to set a good example for the three young pilots, but mostly he was afraid that with Ashley's expert training, the rookies would surpass him in skill. He was, after all, seeing a noticeable improvement in his own stats.

Ashley and Bear had become close with Chief Schultz now that they shared his secret, but they never spoke of their missing shipmate. They had bonded in their own right, spurred on by the new routines that came about as the culture on the *Centauri* shifted following the departure of the Lumano ace. This day, however, the chief did mention the Pacifist leader, and had a favor to ask.

The three sat in their normal corner of the mess hall, where the rest of the *Centauri* crew had learned to leave their favorite table vacant. As they finished their lunch, Schultz leaned over his tray and broached the subject. "So, you probably noticed you've been off the patrol rotation this week."

Ashley sensed they were about to be asked for a quid pro quo, but Bear was grateful. "Yeah, Chief," he said. "You had something to do with that? We've been going nonstop. This break is much needed."

Schultz cut him off, "I need you to do something for me."

Bear frowned. "Oh, right. Should have seen that coming. The blood is still not redistributed from my head. What do you need?"

"While I've already admitted that I respect the work Monk is doing, I do feel he owes us some penance for attacking us after I helped him out, but I've been swamped in the repair bay. I can't get a minute to myself. I want to know how those shield generators work, so I need you to go to Monk's repair shop and look for anything useful."

"Like schematics?" asked Ashley.

"I mean, that would be wonderful, but I doubt they'd leave that lying around," mused the chief. "See if they've got a stockpile of raw material or something. If I could at least know what it's made out of, I could work it out. Or if you can find a working unit, I can reverse engineer it. I don't know what they look like, but I have a feeling I'd know it when I saw it."

"So, you'd know it if you saw it. Will we know it when we see it?" asked Bear.

"I don't rightly know. Hopefully. I'll be in the repair bay with my headset on, so if you get stumped, radio me on the secure line. Your squad won't mind a day off from the monkey bars tomorrow, will they?"

"Uneven bars," Ashley said flatly. "And just because I won't be here doesn't mean they're getting a day off."

The next morning Ashley gave her squad a set of tumbling routines to work on while she was gone, which the rookies blew off and spent the day challenging other squads to tramp-shooting.

Ashley and Bear arrived to the Brothers Repair Shop in the late morning. The shop was empty, but the door was unlocked. The waiting room was gutted of furniture, Ashley assumed by squatters, and the repair bays were vacant except for one ship in the third bay with a tarp over it. Ashley pulled off the tarp and let out a low whistle at the classic hot rod restored to shiny perfection. In the age of WID drives, when every vessel had the same acceleration and top-speed capabilities, ships had lost their flair and panache, but the hot rod just looked fast.

"We're looking for schematics," Bear reminded her.

"Or a working unit," retorted Ashley. "If you had both this beautiful machine and access to a shield, surely you would protect the former with the latter. I think we should check out the cockpit, see if we can find anything. And if not, maybe take it for a spin to clear our heads while we brainstorm."

Bear opened his mouth in protest, but Ashley had already

opened the hatch and was climbing into the cockpit. He shrugged and followed her. The interior was as much a work of art as the body of the ship. Ashley lowered herself into the pilot chair and looked around. "Now this is luxury," she cooed. "The chief can have his shield blueprints as penance. I think we should take this puppy."

They looked around the cockpit, but located nothing useful, so they were forced to admit that it probably wasn't in the hot rod. They exited the craft, pulled the tarp over top of it, and continued their search.

Eventually Bear discovered the hatch in the office of the shop and opened it to reveal the entrance to the brothers' laboratory. Thinking he had cracked the case, he hurried down the ladder only to discover the messy and disorganized lab. He called Ashley down to join him, and the two began picking through piles of tools, ship parts, and good old-fashioned garbage.

Frustrated, Bear picked up a bowl full of stale pretzels and scoffed at it. "This is disgusting. I thought these Lumanos were some kind of enlightened geniuses. This is squalor. Or is this some kind of science experiment, see who can create the most foul-smelling living quarters in the galaxy?"

Ashley was inspecting the underside of a landmine. "I might have something," she said. She pressed a button and it let out a loud, sustained sound of flatulence. "Yeah, I don't think that's it," she admitted. "Let's keep looking."

Chapter 32

The Zees' youthful appearance required them to always carry proof of Zeehood when off planet, to prevent being mistaken for a child lacking adult supervision, and subsequently kidnapped by the roving nuns of the Tautologist Orphanage of Dakota 16. Counterfeit Zee ID passes were coveted among human teenagers. Planet FOY was fantasized as a paradise among human youths, who could pass easily as adults there; and human perverts, for obvious reasons. As a result, obtaining travel permission to Planet FOY as a non-Zee was almost impossible.

Despite their closed borders and small population compared to the other species of the galaxy, the Zees were considered to be the most important consumer market, and most products were marketed specifically to the Zees. It was widely understood in the business world that if the product you were backing didn't sell well on FOY, that investment was going in your books as a loss.

There were myriad assumptions about the Zees that were popular around the galaxy. Humans loved to stereotype them as being lazy, apathetic thugs. Each generation of Zees was deemed to be lazier than the last by the human cynics. It didn't matter that the hard statistics about them suggested otherwise–that they worked longer hours, accomplished more noteworthy innovations, were more politically active, and their teen pregnancy rate was nonexistent. Cliches are, after all, so much easier to remember than real statistics.

-Excerpt from "Pride and Prejudice: Comparing Common Beliefs with Real Statistics," by Brandine Lupinski

The Roid dropped out of its wormhole and settled itself on the ocean floor of Hedon IV. The Pacifists glanced at each other amidst a chorus of bulkhead seams straining under the pressure. As soon as the base came to a rest, they unstrapped and sprang into action, heading for the bunk room to tear bed sheets into parachutes and fill them with foam. Laneeko pulled out the knife he had used on his hyperdrive fix and tossed it to Gam3r to use on a sheet.

Gam3r caught it and froze. "Where did you get this?" he asked.

"Bowing gave it to Freeda when we tried to sell him weapons," said Laneeko.

Freeda added, "Apparently it's some ancient artifact."

"Well, it is steel," said Gam3r, "but I doubt it's ancient. I don't think the ancients usually embedded last year's model of tracking chip into the handles of their weapons, but I've been wrong before." As he said it, Gam3r pried the chip out of the knife handle and smashed it under his heel.

Freeda punched the nearest bed frame and cursed. "He's known where we were all along," she said.

"Nothing we can do about that now," said Brandine, lugging two tanks of foam ammunition toward the bridge. "Let's load up whatever we can and get going."

They assembled on the bridge, each grabbing a bundle of foam wrapped in a bedsheet, and tying the draw line around their waists. With the corridors to the hangar deck collapsed, their only way out of the Roid was through the windshield, which was already showing cracks under the pressure of the ocean.

They lined up against the outer bulkhead on either side of the window, out of the way of the imminent water flow. Freeda kicked open the panel to the navigation system and ducked into it to retrieve the chip for her fighting staff. Lytess called out to her, "Freeda, just leave it. Hurry up and get up here."

Freeda already had the chip in her hand. She held it up to show Lytess, then stuck it in her pocket. She picked up the bag she had packed from the lab and slung it over her back, and finally brought her foam flotation device over to the bulkhead. The tortuous sound of the window cracking continued, but the glass held. The crew stood against the bulkhead, afraid to move.

They waited in silence, expecting the glass to break at any moment, but it didn't. After a minute the silence turned from anticipatory to awkward. Gam3r started to whistle, but Freeda shushed him. Growing impatient, she gave her staff a full-length swing toward the window, which shattered into tiny rainbows and gave way to the luxurious waters of the Hedon IV ocean.

While the water gushed in, they stayed braced against the bulkhead next to the window until the air bubble was gone from the bridge. Then, one by one, with Laneeko using hand signals to keep an orderly egress, they shoved their flotation devices out the opening and began their ascent. Gam3r went first and misjudged the force with which his ball of foam would rise. He was facing down when the rope jerked taught and pulled him upwards from the waist. After a minute of struggling, he got his feet below him and leaned into the rope in a sitting position. The rest learned from his mistake and held on tight as they were yanked upwards.

They started deep, but the rise was fast. It took ten minutes of hanging uncomfortably to their ropes and breathing shallowly with the anxiety of whether their suits would shield them from the rapid drop in pressure. All five of the weary Pacifists were feeling the pressure of the morning in more ways than one.

Their balls of foam breached the ocean surface with a series of splashes, and they crawled awkwardly onto their flotation devices. Brandine signaled that she would be the first to release the pressure on her suit. She unlatched her helmet, and it was met with a slow hiss. The other four braced themselves for the worst, but Brandine gave a thumbs up and pulled her helmet completely off. The others followed, then tossed their lines back and forth to tie their foam rigs into one big raft, and pulled themselves up out of the water.

The Pacifists sat atop their floating ball of Fetid Foam, greedily inhaling the sweet-smelling Hedon air. In ten minutes, the foam would begin dissolving into the foul-smelling gas, and they'd have to either tolerate the stench or start swimming.

While they waited, Freeda pulled out the video screen with the feed from Copernicus' eye. The screen was still black, but it reminded Brandine to ask the twins how and why they had first hacked into Copernicus' cyborg component.

"You remember shortly after you took him to Titan to get the eye," started Lytess, "he thought he was hallucinating and almost checked himself into the hospital?"

"Yes."

"Yeah, well, that was us. After we realized we could hack into his eye, we went to the flatlands and built a life-sized replica of the shop and surrounding area. Then, since we're twins, we set it up so in his right eye he was seeing Laneeko in the real world, and in his left eye he was seeing me in the replica. We completely choreographed our movements so he couldn't tell the difference from eye to eye, and we could add in whatever extras we wanted in his left eye. We were sure he'd figure out the gag right away, but it worked too well. He thought he was losing it."

"So we shut it down but never told him," added Laneeko.

Freeda asked, "How did he lose his eye in the first place?"

"If you can believe this," answered Brandine, "Way back in the day he and I were out drinking after a race. This Galerian parts supplier says some offensive things about my honor, and Coper was drunk and stepped in. The guy ends up stabbing Coper in the eye, so I took him to Titan to get a cyborg replacement. I got him the top of the line model, with all the bells and whistles–microphone, HUD display, closed captioning, everything. Bet you'd never hear about a Loomy starting a bar fight, eh?"

"What happened to the Galerian?" asked Freeda.

"Oh, him? I think he did five orbits on Dakota 17. He's probably out by now."

Before Freeda could say anything else, Gam3r squinted into the daylight and called out, "Looks like they got our distress signal. A boat, due east, heading our way."

The boat was not an official rescue craft, but a party boat full of three dozen naked vacationers of various species, all with skin far too fair to be fully exposed to the hot sun of Hedon. As the craft pulled up next to the stranded crew, the driver/tour guide playfully announced over his PA system, "Folks, if you look to your starboard–that's this side over here for you landlubbers–you will see, THE PACIFISTS!" The crowd broke into a wild applause, jumping up and down on the deck of the boat. Lytess tried to cover Gam3r's eyes, but Gam3r gave him a shove, and the Lumano lost his balance and tumbled into the water.

As the Pacifists climbed aboard the party boat, they received pats on the back and cheers from the partiers. One Mesozoid woman saw Gam3r and instinctively grabbed a towel to wrap around herself. Gam3r noticed, and announced, "Oh, I'm not a child. I'm a Zee, and I could care less about your unadornment." The statement placated the Mesozoid woman and dispelled the awkwardness with the rest of the crowd, though Gam3r did little else to conceal his glances at the females on the boat.

The very physically fit "captain" sat at the helm wearing a necklace made of the teeth of various predators from the Hedon ocean, a straw hat, and nothing else. Though they were only a few feet away, he held his conversation with the refugees through his PA microphone. "G'day, Pacifists. How ya going? Welcome abo'd the good ship Celebration. We were in the neighborhood, heard about ya troubles, fig'yad we'd swing by an' give ya a lift."

Laneeko kneeled down beside the helm where the captain

was sitting, and whispered, "Listen, Captain...?"

"Mick."

"Captain Mick, we appreciate the rescue. We're hoping to be a little bit discreet when we arrive ashore. I doubt the authorities share your favorable view of our work."

"Oh, don't you's worry about a thing, mate," came the reply. "Discreet is what we're best at in the Hedon system. I've already gotten word from the blokes in charge. They ain't unfriendly to your cause. You'll see when we get there, she'll be apples."

Laneeko breathed a sigh of relief and accepted the beverage full of fruit and strong liquor that was offered to him.

When they arrived at the pier, a crowd was cheering and chanting "Pacifists" as the boat docked. "Like I said, mate, discreet is what we're best at," Captain Mick said with a wink. "Oh, don't look at me like that. These are friends. You blokes are in no danger on Hedon IV. The rescue call that went out assured me that you'll be given an audience with the gov'ner, and he can personally guarantee ya safety."

As the Pacifists stepped off the boat, they were surrounded by naked vacationers giving them hugs and high fives. Freeda was overwhelmed with emotion that she received just as much attention and affection as the rest of the crew. No one said a word about her being a Kadrafian.

What Freeda didn't know was that it was a perfectly common trend throughout the ever-repeating cycle of history that during the victory parade, soldiers of every color, creed, and species are cheered with the same vigor. It's after the war, when the veteran soldier attempts to move into the neighborhood where people don't look or feel the same, suddenly the neighbors have forgotten how loudly they cheered his or her heroic efforts during the conflict. But perhaps this time it would be different. This crowd, after all, was not cheering for a war victory, but for peace. Maybe these vacationing naturists would be the ones to finally break the cycle.

True to Captain Mick's word, the governor of Hedon IV was among the ranks of unclad celebrators on the pier. He stood out with a superior physique and less pasty thighs than the rest of the crowd. After the five clothed refugees worked their way through the throng, Governor Dusty Cheeks greeted them with the million-dollar smile that facilitated his reelection, and ushered them toward his office on the beach-side capitol building before discussing any business.

The capitol stood in a town square filled with lounge chairs, lined by surf shops, and with a pool that wove itself around the downtown area like a canal, but a canal with a series of swim-up bars so you could get nice and blasted while your cargo ship traversed the locks. A blue half-tube of a waterslide originated at the upper floor of the capitol building, wound around the square, and ended in the pool.

The Pacifists filed into the governor's office, an open room with surf boards and old fishing nets lining the walls, and laid-back surf guitar playing over the speakers. The governor donned a light beach robe that came to just below his buttocks. He tied the belt around his waist and motioned to Gam3r to shut the office door behind them.

"Listen, bros," he began. "I understand that technically there are warrants for your arrests, and technically, as an elected official within the ranks of the Oligarchy, I am technically obligated to turn you in, but I am technically not going to do that. I need to be an ear to my people, and the very beautiful people of my planet appreciate your efforts.

"You have to understand, my dudes, tourism is one of the few industries that does not benefit from a wartime economy. We're missing out on an entire demographic of customers here because of this gnarly conflict. I've arranged transport for you tomorrow. They can get you wherever you need to go. For the rest of today, relax, join the party, have a drink or seven.

"There's no cameras allowed on Hedon, by the way, so you don't have to worry about your visit appearing on every newsfeed in the galaxy. Our official rescue crews are patrolling an area of ocean ten clicks from where you surfaced, pretending to look extra hard for you. That's why we had you picked up by the party boat. In three days we'll call off the search, and you'll be long gone.

"We've got a bungalow reserved for you for tonight. You're gonna love it. It's right on the beach, fully stocked bar, hot tub, the works. I'm billing it to our diplomatic account. It's free of charge, as long as you promise to be at our lip sync battle tonight in the town square."

Brandine spoke for the group. "I'm terribly sorry, Governor, but we just narrowly escaped death, and we're missing one of our crew–our leader, in fact. I don't think we're up for a party."

The governor had a soothing and very influential tone, almost hypnotic, that served him well in his position. The sweet-smelling air of Hedon had a compounding effect on the governor's speech that put their minds further at ease. As he spoke, they could feel their muscles relaxing. "Listen, bros, if I have an opportunity to have the one and only Pacifists present at our nightly lip sync battle, and I miss that once-in-a-lifetime, my people will, like, try me for treason or something. You gotta be there. We can't get you off this rock until tomorrow morning, so there's nothing you can do tonight anyway. You may as well relax. I know my Z-man here wants to see the sights of Hedon, since that's a damn special privilege. Don't leave me hanging, bra." The governor held his hand up for a high five, and Gam3r returned it.

Brandine caved. "All right. Wouldn't miss it. Thank you for your kindness, Governor."

"Please, call me Dusty."

Freeda skipped the festivities. Instead she sat in the bungalow with the monitor for Copernicus' cyborg eye on her lap. She barely noticed the loud music and chatter blaring outside the thin bungalow walls. The display was black, but she refused to let it out of her line of sight. So she waited, passing the time chatting with the host assigned to their bungalow, a youngish-looking Sheeple named Meadow. Meadow, who wore her wooly hair in long white dreadlocks, sported a dark tan and rambled incessantly about her sub-light activism, but Freeda was glad for the distraction.

At one point while Meadow was off on a long sub-light tangent, Freeda zoned out to think about Copernicus and how they were going to find him. Freeda realized with a start that Meadow was asking a question. "I'm sorry. What was that?"

"So, do you ever, like, get bored with the orange? Don't you ever, like, want to just do rainbow or something?"

"You mean my tattoos?" Freeda asked. Meadow nodded. "Rainbow, huh? That would certainly turn some heads. But the orange means I'm a warrior. I'm very proud of that, in fact."

Meadow had a childlike expression of wonder on her face. "Wow, man. A warrior. But, like, aren't you some kind of anti-war chick? I thought you guys were, like, against war."

"We are. I guess it's a confusing thing. The proudest day of my life was the day I got these tattoos, but maybe I need to rethink that."

Meadow got excited. "Yeah, man. I'm super proud of my ink too. Check out this one on my ankle. It's like a she-wolf, howling at the moon, yo. Because that's like me, man. The she-wolf is me."

Freeda smiled politely and changed the subject. "I'm confused about the sub-light thing. Your whole economy is based on tourism. If we stop using hyperspace travel, won't your planet be in trouble?"

"Nah, man. We'd like, live off the land and stuff. Did you know there's berries that you can eat right off the bush? They don't even have to be in like a fruit salad or anything. It's, like, wild, man."

Freeda had to admit, though not out loud, that living off the grid on a luxury planet with an ocean of sugar water sounded pretty good to her. Maybe if the war ever ended, Treshler's band could get a standing gig playing the nightly Hedon beach party, and they could settle down together right in this very bungalow.

Chapter 33

*Unbound from the distractions of reproductive hormones, the
Lumano youths of New Belgium spent their formative years
developing an appreciation of scientific education as well as a sense
of community and enlightenment. The rest of the galaxy spent their
young adulthood staring at their WID-phones, awkwardly exploring
their bodies, and obsessing over the boy/girl in their class who they
would surely love forever, only to discover weeks later what a loser
that boy/girl was, and moving on to obsess over the next classmate.
Meanwhile, the deadline for their science project was fast
approaching, until finally, the night before the science project was
due, while devastated because their newest crush didn't know they
existed, they'd slap together a poorly-made scale model of their local
star system made of Styrofoam balls and pretend they learned
something about science that semester.*

*-Excerpt from "The Poisonwood Bible: How to Science Like a
Lumano," by Brandine Lupinski*

It wasn't until after midnight that the screen went live
again. A commando pulled the hood off Monk's head and hit
him in the face with a rifle butt to wake him. The blow left a
crack on the lens of his eye implant, which now showed on
Freeda's screen. She sat bolt upright in bed and seethed at the
image.

On the screen, the visored leader struck the commando
with the back of his hand. "Did you just hit him in the head?"
he roared. "This Lumano has a price on him because of what's
in that hairless head. If you damage my merchandise I will
personally escort you out the airlock."

Freeda glanced around, but she was alone. The screen was
set to record; she'd show everyone in the morning.
Unblinking, she watched as Copernicus was dragged by the
collar with a gloved hand, and stopped in front of a small

entourage of men at the head of a hangar bay. Copernicus' camera was sideways as he lay on the ground, so Freeda turned her handheld screen ninety degrees.

***

"Hello, Monk," said the man at the center of the entourage. "Welcome to the new world order."

Copernicus blinked repeatedly, hoping it might help the blob in front of him solidify from a fuzzy blur into a real person. The crack in the lens gave his vision a reddish tint, but the cyborg camera was otherwise working. He could see from the HUD that he was at 1.2x zoom, night vision was on 10%, hence the redness, but there was also a blinking green icon in the corner that he didn't recognize. What was that? A person with ridiculously large ears? A painter's easel during a groundquake? It must be an error indicating damage to the unit, but before he could figure it out the autofocus activated, and the blur dissipated into a baby-smooth face and a perfect haircut. "Bowing?" Copernicus mumbled.

"So nice to see you again," said the arms dealer. "Wish it were under different circumstances." He was wearing an all-white uniform with admiral insignia on the cuffs and shoulders, but it didn't belong to any military entity Copernicus had seen before. The other men in the entourage also wore white uniforms with officer bars on their sleeves.

Copernicus rolled up to his knees and glanced at the commandos still standing behind him. Bowing addressed them. "You can be dismissed. We'll be in touch as soon as we deal with the Republic." Copernicus looked down at the gloved hand of the merc leader, still holding him by the collar. The hand released him, and the commandos departed.

Armed guards in white uniforms came to the side of Copernicus, and Bowing continued. "You were holding out on me when you were hocking those silly toy guns. If you'd told me you had energy shields, I would have bought all that other junk as a bundle just to get them. Give me the plans, and as soon as I confirm they work, I'll let you go. I won't turn you in to the Navy. You can go right back to pounding out dents on New Belgium."

Copernicus, still on his knees, looked at the floor. "You had my brothers killed. They're the ones who designed it. You captured the wrong Loomy."

"Yeah, I thought you'd say that, but that's ok. We've got plenty of time. My Purist army is just now beginning to mobilize. We were going to let the Navy and the KCF kill each other for a bit longer before we stepped into the fray, but because of you and your obnoxious friends, it's time for us to finish what we've started. But if you'll give me those shields, we can exert our power in a way that I can make sure you'll be preventing an all-out genocide."

Copernicus looked around the spotless hangar deck of the Purist carrier. In each stall stood a shiny silver ship, fighters and bombers, all brand new. The Purists were ready for war.

Bowing had a satisfied smile as he watched Copernicus assessing the hangar. "Monk, I know you want to stop the killing. We want the same thing. If you give me those shield designs, this war will be over in a matter of days. No one else will have to die. Without those shields, I'll have to do it the old-fashioned way."

Copernicus shook his head. "You think I don't know that the end game of the Purists is genocide? I would have to be a special kind of savant to be smart enough to design a shield for you and dumb enough to think that would end the killing."

"Oh, poor, innocent Monk," sighed Bowing. "My wife is the Purist in the family. I don't care what species someone is. Don't you see? The puries are as much a pawn in this game as the KCF or GNC. They're useful because their prejudices make them easy to manipulate. An arms race is far more profitable than a full-blown war. I just need tension, not death. And I don't care if the galaxy threatens to tear itself apart because of interspecies conflict or because of religious conflict or because of each other's taste in music, as long as they do it with my weapons."

The last comment drew Copernicus' attention to a Mobius strip, the symbol of Tautologism, hanging on a chain around Bowing's neck. For all that was going on, seeing a religious necklace on a man threatening to mass murder millions of innocent people distracted Copernicus. He raised his head halfway and asked, "Wait, you're a Tautologist?"

Bowing looked down at his necklace. "Yes, of course I am. My faith is largely what drives me to strive for personal success. This statement is, after all, false. But you science-loving Lumanos have no moral compass, so what would you know about it?"

Copernicus scoffed. He knew better than to argue with a Tautologist, but he'd had a very, very bad day, and he gave in to the temptation. "Manipulating the galaxy into violence is in direct contradiction with Tautologism. You can't seriously not see that. I may not be a believer, but I've read your scriptures."

Bowing's face grew grim. "I am a devout man of faith," he said. "I will not stand here and have my beliefs insulted by a Statement-less Lumano. There are no contradictions if you don't want there to be. It's faith. If you believe that this statement is false, then the Statement is false. But I wouldn't expect some Paradoxist to understand that."

Copernicus, kneeling on the floor with his hands bound behind his back practically forgot where he was. "I'm not a Paradoxist. I'm not saying the Statement cannot be false. The Statement could be false, but how can we ever know? I just think if the Statement were really false, it would reveal itself to be false. I mean, if this statement is false, then why do bad things happen to good people? And don't get me started on your ridiculous quarrel with Versimilitudism[10]."

Bowing gritted his teeth at the mention. "They have no faith. They believe in two interconnected Statements. Every true believer knows that there is only one Statement. And my faith that this statement is false is exactly what makes the Statement false."

"No, Bowing. That makes the Statement true, which it can't be. How can you not see that?"

Bowing rubbed a finger over his necklace, then let go. "Have it your way, Monk. In two days this fleet will travel to the Republic, where you will see killing like you've never seen before. If you want to stop it, give me the designs. Otherwise, you can sit in your cell and watch it happen. Get him out of here."

Copernicus didn't resist as he was dragged down white corridors and thrown into a small cell with a single bed. The front of the cell was an open wall laced with white laser beams in a horizontal grid. A single guard sat at a white desk outside of the brig. Copernicus slumped onto the bunk and closed his eyes.

$$***$$

Freeda broke into a cold sweat the second she heard the words "Purist army." At first she tried to convince herself she hadn't heard it correctly, that she was groggy from the late hour and her prolonged state of exhaustion. When the feed went dark again, Freeda went through the video and saved a

[10]   Versimilitudists were the second largest religion in the galaxy. They had a holy scripture known as The Vox Dicitur. On one side of The Vox Dicitur was printed, "The statement on the other side of this scripture is true," and on the opposite side was printed, "The statement on the other side of this scripture is false." The origins and theologies of the Tautologists and Versimilitudists were largely overlapping, and yet the two sects each believed the other to be the work of pure evil. The bloodiest, most gruesome wars in the history books were all fought between the Tautologists and the Versimilitudists for virtually no reason whatsoever.

separate file with the relevant clips, then paced around the bungalow waiting for her friends to return. Fifteen minutes later she was out of patience, and she headed to the town square to look for the twins.

Freeda got to the beach party just as Gam3r was climbing to the stage to receive his trophy. That's when it started. All she could hear was the roar of the crowd when his name was announced as the winner for his lip sync of Stenothraxica's song, "The Monk." Freeda called out to Gam3r, but in his drunken state he was oblivious that the booming clangor could be anything other than his overexcited fans. Suddenly, Oligarchy law enforcement ships descended on the party, sending drunken, unclad vacationers scattering in every direction. Freeda charged the platform and tackled Gam3r to the ground as a shell from an Oligarchy ship whistled by her ear and obliterated the stage.

Governor Dusty Cheeks threw on his beach robe and pushed his way through the crowd toward Freeda, just as Brandine and the twins converged on the crater where the stage had been.

"We gotta get you out of here," Dusty shouted over the commotion. "I can't help but feel like maybe inviting you to a very public party right now wasn't my best decision as governor. Fall back to my office in the capitol building. I'll stall them as long as I can. Go!"

Brandine, Gam3r, Freeda, and the twins got low and snuck through the crowd toward the tall stone steps of the capitol. A black Oligarchy ship landed over top of the pool, splashing the governor with a wave and dousing his perfect hair. Cheeks stood steadfast, tightening the belt on his robe and straightening his shoulders to approach the SWAT commander, who was emerging from the ship followed by three goons on either side.

"Governor Dusty Cheeks, we have information that you are

harboring terrorists in your jurisdiction. I'm ordering you to turn over the Pacifists to us right now," said the SWAT commander.

Cheeks attempted to hand the commander a beverage in a red plastic cup, but she didn't reach for it, so he took a sip himself. "I don't know what you're talking about, Betty. Ain't no terrorists here. Everyone here is, like, suuuuuper chill. Why don't you relax and catch a buzz?"

The SWAT leader was stone faced. "Governor, the punishment for treason is death." She turned to the soldiers next to her and said, "Kill this traitor."

They raised their guns, but Cheeks rolled to the side and took off running up the steps to the capitol building. At the top of the steps he took cover behind a large stone pillar and waited for a wave of laser fire to blow by, singeing his robe. He then sprinted through the doors to the capitol and called out over his shoulder, "You'll never take me alive, posers."

The commander put her face in her palm and muttered to herself, "We're not... we're not trying to."

Inside the capitol building, Cheeks ran up the stairs and into his office, slamming the door. The Pacifists were already inside, and Brandine and Freeda overturned the governor's desk and barricaded it against the door. SWAT officers pounded on the door with battering rams.

"Listen," said the governor, pulling his surfboard off the wall, "I know I said before I want this bogus war to be over because of, like, the economy or whatever? It's more than that, bros. I'd be joining up and flying with you dudes if I could, but instead I'm going to hold these killjoys off so you can get out of here. Get to the shuttle port. My pilot will know what to do."

"What are you going to do?" asked Freeda.

Cheeks winked. "The only thing I'm truly good at." With that, he yanked open a hidden door that revealed a staircase, and said, "You dudes better get going." Then, readying his board, he took a running start and threw himself onto the waterslide that led from his second-story window. He stood up on the board, tossed his beach robe to the wind, and carved his way around the curves of the waterslide, heading downtown one last time.

The Pacifists filed down the hidden staircase. Freeda went last and took a final look at the chiseled public servant. Though laser fire was raining down around him, the elusive governor was rock-steady on his longboard, high on the curves and low on the straightaways. At the end of the run, Dusty Cheeks came splashing with perfect form into the pool and stood up in the water, where he was promptly cut down by laser fire[11].

The staircase led to an underground tunnel with a ladder at the end that opened up into a small clearing outside the downtown area. Freeda was first up the ladder. In the distance, she could see the town square flashing bright with laser fire, and could hear the shouting of the troops laying siege to the capitol building.

The group jogged along the boardwalk toward the shuttle port. While they ran, Freeda described what she had seen on the video feed.

"Purists," whispered Gam3r. "I knew it. I've been saying for years that there's Purists in all levels of government, but nobody ever wants to believe me. I knew they were behind this whole war. I saw a documentary about it. They want to get rid of all other humanoid species, but they can't take them all on at once, so what do they do? Set them against each other. Haven't I been saying this, Laneeko?"

"Yes, Gam3r. And of course you know that and I know that, but nobody wants to believe it. It's humanoid

---

[11]   Years later, this heroic last ride would be immortalized in the square with a statue of Cheeks standing triumphant on his longboard. In deference to his sacrifice, the sculptor was particularly generous in the depiction of the governor's manliness.

psychology: If you acknowledge it, you have to do something about it."

"A whole army," said Brandine. "They must have more control of the government than any of us want to admit."

"I could have told you that," Freeda said, and all eyes turned to her. "As an outsider to your government, it's obviously controlled by puries. My people have known that since before the war. Take us and the Mesozoids, for example. Before the war, we were both being oppressed. We should have joined together to fight for our rights, but your Oligarchy played us against each other. They granted insignificant rights to the Mesozoids but not the Kadrafians, and it was enough to make my people bitter and the Mesozoids defensive, and next thing you know the Mezzies are enlisting in the Navy in droves, ready to fight us and die on behalf of a government that despises them."

Everyone was silent, except Gam3r, who pointed at her and said, "Thank you, Freeda. I've been trying to tell people that for years, and no one ever sees it." He looked around and added, "Present company excluded."

"Well, we believe you, of course," said Lytess. "Lumanos have been spared from this war, but a Purist army won't let us get away with that much longer, since we're not human either. We've had that poem hanging in the shop for years, the one about 'First they came for the cyborgs.' That was one of the inspirations that got us involved in this whole ordeal."

The shuttle port turned out to be not a structure, but rather an open field with transport ships parked haphazardly, with no rhyme or reason. Freeda halted the group just outside the perimeter, under cover of foliage, and assessed the situation. An Oligarchy ship flew over, shining its spotlight into the trees, and they dropped to the ground to take cover.

"That must be our pilot," Brandine said, pointing to a woman standing outside of a transport ship with government markings. The bay door was open, and the pilot was motioning to them to hurry.

Freeda waited for the spotlight of the Oligarchy ship to swing the other way. When it had, she whispered, "Move, now." The group charged into the clearing and piled into the ship. Freeda was the last in, but she dropped her screen with Copernicus' feed on it. When she turned to retrieve it, a SWAT team was coming over the hill on the far side of the clearing. They opened fire, missing Freeda as she dove into cover behind a cargo bin on the launch pad. The pilot had the ship powered up and was lifting off with the bay door still open. Freeda rolled out of cover and grabbed the screen. She then leapt for the transport, catching it with one hand and pulling herself in.

"Glad you made it, Freeda," said the pilot, without turning around.

"Meadow?" asked Freeda. "You're a pilot?"

"I told you I was the she-wolf," Meadow replied, jerking on the transport controls to take evasive action from an Oligarchy assault ship.

Gam3r was climbing into the co-pilot seat. "Wait," he said, "this thing isn't sub-light, is it? I don't know how much of our discussion you overheard, but we don't have several million years to get to New Belgium."

Meadow took one hand off the controls and pulled her helmet over her dreadlocks, clicking it into place. "Be there in a jiff," she replied, while simultaneously taking defensive maneuvers and bringing the vessel into orbit. "I do want a sub-light world," she explained, "but in the meantime, like, a girl's gotta pay the rent, doesn't she?"

As they rose above the atmosphere and into orbit, leaving the Oligarchy ships in their wake, Meadow added, "I mean, technically my parents pay my rent through my trust fund, but like, I still need money for booze or whatever, and shuttle piloting is good money. Seatbelts, everyone." Gam3r was about to respond, but Meadow shut off the lights and gravity and announced, "Next stop, New Belgium," and her ship tore a hypocritical hole through the space-time continuum.

Chapter 34

*Because the Lumanos did not love romantically, the rest of the
humanoid species looked down on them as inferior. After all, the
ability to love was what set the humanoids apart from the animals, at
least according to the pop songs, rom-coms, and Tautologist
preachers. The Lumanos would have argued that there are so many
other kinds of love aside from romantic love, and that they actually
had a heightened sense of empathy compared to species who were
obsessed with any number of weird sexual fetishes. They would have
argued that, except that they didn't really care what the rest of the
galaxy thought of them, so they didn't bother to argue about it at all.*

*-Excerpt from "Love in the Time of Cholera: Debunking
Stereotypes of the Species," by Brandine Lupinski*

Meadow dropped the Pacifists at the Brothers Repair Shop
and flew off. They had invited her to stay and help with their
preparations, but she claimed that all the WID technology on
New Belgium was giving her a wormhole headache. The
twins assured her that's not a thing, but she left anyway.

The twins, Brandine, and Gam3r went into the repair bays
to power up the radio and attempt to contact Chief Schultz
and warn him of the new developments. Freeda wanted to
reinstall the nav chip on her Sugar Cane, so she headed for the
lab. When Freeda came down the ladder, two humans were
standing at the workbench at the center of the room,
rummaging through boxes of gadgets.

For a moment, there was a silent, frozen tableau as the three
exchanged confused looks. Then the female human gasped,
"A Kadrafian? What in the–how do you know about this
place? Have you hurt him?"

Copernicus had told Freeda about his squadmates being a
petite woman and a giant of a man, so it didn't take much of a
leap to work out who the two strangers snooping around his

lab must be. "You're Copernicus' squadmates," she announced. "I'm a friend. I've been working with your Monk."

The female human's face changed, and she shouted, "Ace is working with a RAIF'YAN?" The Navy lieutenant reached for her rifle, and Freeda's warrior instincts kicked in. She hissed and put her hand on her knife. The humans both raised their weapons towards Freeda. As the salvo of rifle fire tore through the lab, igniting a pile of garbage, Freeda dove under the workbench and called out, "I don't want to hurt you, Yoomies!"

Freeda remembered her oath and sheathed her knife. She readied her fighting staff, then vaulted over the table. She delivered a simultaneous blow with opposite ends of the cane to the female's stomach and the back of the giant male's head, landing behind them. Then with her left foot she kicked the woman's rifle from her hands.

Freeda turned and aimed the staff at the male, but when she activated it, only a few drops of sugary water came dripping out the end. The giant dropped his shoulder and charged, but she blocked with her forearm gauntlets and sent him rolling in a net of Fetid Foam.

The woman did a forward roll toward her rifle, grabbing the handle with her right hand and landing on her back, but Freeda came down on top of her. Freeda's knee pinned the rifle, and she brought her Sugar Cane across the woman's throat, applying just enough pressure so the Navy lieutenant knew that her state of consciousness depended entirely upon the Kadrafian's mood over the next few seconds.

The woman loosened her grip on her rifle and yielded, breathing furiously through her nose, but stayed quiet.

"Now, if you humans are ready to listen," Freeda said, "I am not your enemy. Your Monk is trying to end this war, but he's been captured and is in great danger. There is a Purist army mobilizing toward the Republic. If you want to rescue your Monk, you're going to have to trust me."

The female turned her head to the side and spat, but the male spoke up. "What my partner is trying to say," he said, while struggling in his cocoon of foam, "is that there's no possible way we can trust a Kadrafian warrior just at the moment."

Freeda countered, "Then there is no possible way you can get your Monk back. I'll just have to do it myself."

Freeda picked up a foam gun to encase the female human while figuring out what to do with them, but the Navy pilot put up her arms and cried out, "Wait!" Freeda lowered the weapon and looked it over, noticing its seemingly lethal design. "We'll help," the woman said, "but if you're lying, Statement help me, I will rearrange your perfectly symmetrical face tattoos."

The Kadrafian smiled and winked, then turned her rifle toward the burning pile of garbage and fired a round of foam at it, extinguishing the flames.

The others heard the commotion and came scrambling down the ladder to find Freeda standing over the two humans with her foam rifle. Freeda looked over to see the twins, then turned to Lieutenant Sokolov and asked, "See, that wasn't so hard, was it? I'm Freeda. This is Laneeko, Lytess, Brandine, and Gam3r. You probably know us as the Pacifists."

"Yeah, I got that." The woman sat up and rested her elbows on her knees, but didn't get off the floor. She looked down and took a few deep breaths. Finally, she looked up at the two Lumanos, avoiding eye contact with Freeda. "I'm Ashley. This is Hassan."

"Everyone calls me Bear."

"First of all," Ashley continued, "which one of y'all saved my bomber pilots outside of NoChil?" Brandine raised her hand and pointed to Freeda. Ashley still wouldn't look at Freeda, but she continued. "Well, thank you for that. That was the day I changed my mind about vacuuming every last one of you derelicts. You say there's a Purist army forming? Remains to be seen whether that's our problem or not, but we'll help get our wing leader out of a rut if we can. What do you need?"

Freeda answered, "We need ships."

"I look like Dealin' Dex to you?"

"Ask your Chief Schultz," said Freeda. "Tell him the Kadrafian named Freeda needs ships."

Ashley gave Freeda a side-eyed glance, but pulled out her radio and dialed up her secure connection to Schultz. "Chief, Hassan and I are at Ace's lab. We haven't found your data, but we got a problem. Belay that. We got several problems. Big ones."

"Give me the smallest one first," came the reply.

"So, I got a Kadrafian here, calls herself Freeda. She says Copernicus is in trouble, and she needs ships. You wouldn't know anything about that, would you?"

The radio was silent for a few seconds. Finally, the reply came, "What happened to the one I already gave her?" Ashley shot another angry glance at Freeda, but then looked away and held out the radio.

Freeda took the radio and held it to her ear. "Chief Schultz, this is Freeda. We met on Galeria?"

"I remember," said the chief.

"We were attacked and lost our ships, but listen. There's a Purist army that is going to attack the planets of the Republic. You need to alert the Navy to this."

There was another silence on the radio, followed by, "Can you prove that?"

"As a matter of fact, Chief Schultz, I can. We have a video from Copernicus. He has been captured by the Purists."

"Thank you, Freeda. Can you put Lieutenant Sokolov on, please."

Ashley waved her hand. "That's me," she said. Ashley

took the radio and walked over into a corner to discuss logistics with the chief. After a few minutes she walked back to the group. "All right," she said. "Hassan and I are going to meet the *Centauri* in the Republic, and I've been ordered to bring you with us. You two, Loomies, how many of those shield devices you got?"

Laneeko and Lytess looked at each other. Lytess said, "None. Our shield generators are vacationing on Hedon right now. And before you ask, we have neither the raw materials nor the time to build any more before the attack. We just want to find our brother. If you're saying you'll help us with that, we'll come willingly."

"Fine," said Ashley. "Now, can you get my wingmate out of this foam, please?"

"Sure," said Freeda, switching on the blue beam, "but you might want to clear to the far corner of the room before I do."

"Wait. Why?" asked Bear. Ashley shot an inquisitive glance at Freeda, who only smirked. "Why do you need her to clear out?" asked Bear again.

Ashley turned and followed the other Pacifists to the far side of the room. Freeda vaporized the foam encasing Bear, and the room was filled with a floral aroma with hints of lavender. The twins shrugged. "Must have been an old batch," said Laneeko.

One by one, everyone climbed the ladder to board the transport ship. Freeda hung back and leaned against the workbench. She pulled out Copernicus' Navy dog tags, which she had carried with her since the jungle, and turned them over in her hands. She wasn't thrilled at the idea of going aboard a Navy carrier, but she didn't have any better ideas. Still holding Copernicus' eye display, she could see that he was sitting alone in his cell, leaning against the wall and staring at his feet.

Ashley was the second last to go up the ladder. She

climbed up the first rung, hesitated, then stepped down and faced Freeda. "I'm sorry I shot at you," she said.

"No hard feelings, Navy. I've been shot at many times."

"The chief told me you saved Ace's life."

"Your Monk and I have each saved the other more than once, Ms. Ashley. Your Monk is a true warrior."

"It's just Monk."

"I'm sorry?"

"It's just Monk. He's not my Monk. He's not the Monk. He's just Monk. And I don't even call him that. I'm not big on nicknames. Anyway, thanks for looking out for him. He means a lot to me."

Ashley turned and climbed the ladder, leaving Freeda a moment alone with her thoughts. Freeda looked down and continued turning Monk's dog tags over in her hands, muttering to herself the words "The Monk." After a minute, her head shot up, and she tore up the ladder, taking three rungs at a time. "I know who that was," she blurted out, blowing past everyone upstairs in the shop. "I know who took The Monk," she yelled.

"Yeah. Bowing," said Lytess. "But we don't know how to find him."

"No, before that," panted Freeda. She was throwing things into her pack. "I know who the commando was. He kept saying he wanted The Monk to surrender." She brought up the video of the night Copernicus was handed off to Bowing. Advancing one frame at a time, she stopped it at the moment Copernicus was released by the gloved hand. In one single frame there was a separation between the glove and the sleeve of the commando leader. As plain as day they could see two centimeters of blue skin covered with a blur of dotted orange lines going in every direction.

"Right there," Freeda proclaimed with a gasp. "That's General Dalton." Freeda pulled up a picture of Dalton on the screen, so everyone could see his extensive amount of battle scar tattoos. "He was the commander of the carrier group I flew on."

Everyone looked at each other, one to the next, in confusion. Laneeko finally asked, "A Kadrafian? But how could he work with..."

"Purists?" finished Lytess. "That doesn't make any sense."

"There's a lot about General Dalton that suddenly doesn't make sense," snarled Freeda. "I never in a million years would have thought he was a traitor. I must confront him." Freeda put down the display and was pulling on her flight suit as she talked. "He might know where Copernicus is. I have to go now."

Freeda took two steps toward the third repair bay where the twins' restored hot rod was parked, and everyone leapt in front of her, the two Navy pilots included. "You're doing no such thing, darlin'," announced Brandine. "Where exactly are you going? You don't know where that general's fleet is at this doggone moment. You just gonna fly around lookin' for him? We know we'll find them in the Republic soon. We need to stick together and make a plan."

Freeda took another step forward, and the group moved with her. "I'm not waiting around for them to kill him. I'm going to Kadrafia. I can log in to the fleet network from there."

"Freeda," pleaded Laneeko, "if you find him, what are you going to do? Beat the information out of him? We saw you go up against this guy on the Roid. He's twice your size. He tossed you like the gravity was off."

The Kadrafian took two more steps forward, moving to the center of the crowd. Her gaze was on the tarp that covered the hot rod. "If I can prove he's a traitor, I may not have to fight him alone this time. I'm sorry, friends, but I'm going."

She pushed Brandine aside and pulled the tarp off the classic purple ship. The group stared at her. Ashley took another step forward, but Brandine whispered to her, "She's determined. To stop her now, you'll have to fight her, and we need our extremities in working condition."

"And who knows," added Lytess. "It may be worth it to let her try." Freeda closed the hatch on the hot rod, and everyone watched silently as she took off out of the repair bay.

Everyone but Gam3r, that is.

Chapter 35

There was a faint, nagging voice in Freeda's head telling her that she hadn't thought this through, that she should talk this over with her fellow Pacifists, but she'd long ago trained herself to ignore the voice in her head. Freeda was a warrior, and warriors act on instinct. If she listened to self-doubt, she would have parted ways with Copernicus on Galeria, returned to her post at the KCF, and would currently be unwittingly serving under the command of a traitor to her tribe who was plotting with a Purist army. That voice in her head may have sounded like the voice of wisdom, but it had a history of being the voice of folly.

Not knowing how else to locate the general's fleet, Freeda plotted a course to her home planet. From there, she'd have access to a network of information not available anywhere else in the galaxy. She'd powered down the hot rod's WID drives, preparing for the hyperspace jump, when from behind the passenger seat someone yelled out, "Wait! I need to strap in!"

Freeda jerked her head around to see Gam3r climbing out from behind the shotgun seat. "Gam3r, what are you doing? You just cost me an hour's time. Now I need to take you back before I can go on."

"No, you don't. I'm coming with you."

"I'm going to Kadrafia. You can't go there. Even if you could survive on my planet, you won't make it through security."

"Um, neither will you," retorted Gam3r. "You think you're going to tell them you're Treshler's girlfriend and they'll just wave you through? Your ID belongs to a pilot who was logged as MIA months ago. You were able to go places like Nightmare and Zaibutu because security on those planets is pure garbage. Wartime security on your planet is, I dare say, a little tighter."

Freeda let out a heavy exhale and watched the moisture in her breath dissipate in the dark cockpit. "Fine. I'll just have to tell them I was stranded on Galeria for the last six months, and I've just now worked my way home. Either way, I have to take you back. You can't go to Kadrafia."

"Freeda, that would be a terrible idea. Your only proof about the general reveals that you've been working with a terrorist group, so you can't present it, and instead you'll be sent to debriefing and medical evals. You won't get anywhere near your general for weeks. You're going to need me to come along. I can get you there."

"Yeah, right. You?"

"Yes, me. I used to run a fake ID operation out of my dorm. I'm well respected in the fake ID industry, which is a legitimate career on FOY. Here," he said, handing her a small card. "I already made you one. The credentials will check out if they run it. Raif'yan ID's are among the hardest to rig, but it's not the first one I've done. I did a couple back in the day to get me and my friends into a Kadrafian music festival."

Freeda frowned, looking over the card. "What is this?"

"It's your ID."

"This is not a Raif'yan name."

"Yeah, I know. But it's an awesome name."

"I don't care if it's an awesome name. I need a Kadrafian name. You literally just said yourself that planetary security is wartime tight. If I try to gain entrance to the planet with an ID that claims my name is Sculpted_A55, we will be arrested immediately."

Gam3r mumbled, "It's pronounced Sculpted Ass."

"It's pronounced what?"

"Sculpted Ass. It's an awesome name."

"I don't care if it's pronounced, 'I am not a traitor to my people,' Gam3r. This ID will get us locked in a military prison. Change it."

"Fine. It was meant as a compliment, though."

Freeda relaxed her furrowed eyebrows. "Well, thank you," she said, and burst out laughing. Gam3r tried to stifle his laughter, but failed, and for a few seconds they giggled uncontrollably.

Gam3r plugged the ID into his handheld control pad, and typed away for a few minutes. "How about, 'Pernikus'? That sounds Kadrafian, right?"

"I like it. Very fitting. And clever. And now I have to turn around and drop you off. You can't come to Kadrafia."

"Oh, I'm going with you. I'm not finalizing this ID until we get there. It's password protected. Look, I've been to Kadrafia before. I just keep my helmet on."

The nagging voice in Freeda's head was telling her to take Gam3r back down, so she decided to take him with her. Just then the radio came on. Laneeko was asking if Gam3r was with her. Freeda shut the radio off and powered up the hyperdrive.

At the security checkpoint, Freeda and Gam3r climbed out of their ship and approached the desk. Gam3r would only need his space suit for being outside in Kadrafia's atmosphere, so they removed their helmets and handed their ID cards to the agent. The agent balked. "Nice ship, but you're going to have to fly it right back out of here. You know you can't bring a human child here."

Gam3r's tone was indignant. "I'm not a child. I'm a Zee."

The agent kept his eyes on Freeda, not looking at Gam3r. "You can't bring a Zee here, either."

"He has a security clearance. He's consulting the KCF on some tech issues," Freeda said, feigning confidence.

The agent was holding both ID cards, but hadn't looked down at them. He finally read over the cards, and sure enough, the Zee's had the hologram denoting a top security clearance. He grunted. "Tech, eh? Yeah, go ahead."

As Freeda and Gam3r got in their ship to pass through to

the planet below, Freeda whispered to Gam3r, "I seriously cannot believe that worked."

"Sometimes stereotypes come in handy. But also, if a Gam3rDud3 ID can't get you there, it's nowhere you want to go anyway."

"Huh?"

"That was my slogan back in the day. I told you my ID's are good. I got into ID making so I could join the Navy, but that was the only thing they couldn't get me into. Because of course if my ID convinced them that I wasn't a Zee, that just meant I was a child. I had plenty of recruiters promising to enlist me the day I came of age, but I'd show up on that day with my ID and they'd be like, how come you still look like you're 13? And I'd be like, good genes, I guess? Late bloomer? I don't know why I ever thought that would work, but I wanted to fly so bad. So where are we going, anyway? A KCF base?"

"Nah. The public library. It's more discreet, and I can log into my old KCF network account from there. You'll have to wait in the ship. Security clearance or not, I can't bring you into the library without causing a stir."

A short while later, Freeda was sitting at a computer booth in the library, off in a corner. For several months she had worn the purple coveralls supplied by the twins, but the Pacifist logo was likely not as popular on Kadrafia as Hedon. She hadn't packed any civilian clothes when she rushed off of New Belgium, but she found a collection of Lumano floral-printed shirts in the storage compartment of the hot rod.

On a whim, she checked the newsfeeds on the computer and discovered that the Pacifists' activity over the last few months had enjoyed a similar reception on Kadrafia as it had everywhere else in the galaxy: mixed reviews, but largely positive.

Smiling to know that her work was appreciated on her

home world, she logged herself into the KCF network, but she was having no luck getting the location of her fleet. She had been at it for a quarter of an hour when she felt a tap on the shoulder. "Need any help, ma'am?" She turned to see Gam3r standing next to her. He had painted his face blue and was grinning from ear to ear. He had also changed into civilian attire.

"Gam3r, that is offensive," she hissed.

"It is not," he whispered. "I told you, I've been to concerts here before. It's easy. I don't have to do tattoos because I look like a youth."

"Yeah, with your light brown, spiky hair?" she whispered.

"Oh, please. Get with the times and look around. The civilians don't keep their hair jet black like you warriors. There's a whole gaggle of emo teenagers over there with bleached white hair. I bet you I could score kadrafalene off them before you're done here."

"Please don't," Freeda muttered, and turned to the console. "Actually, I'm glad you're here. I'm kind of stumped with this."

"Slide over," said Gam3r, pushing himself into the chair with her. It took him a few minutes, but Gam3r was able to unlock Freeda's message inbox, which contained the daily logs from her ship. From there, they'd be able to track the fleet and find Freeda's carrier, which is where General Dalton would be. While Freeda downloaded the coordinates, Gam3r wandered around the library.

There was a Kadrafian girl setting up a history display. Gam3r sidled up to ask her about it. Freeda rolled her eyes at him, but Gam3r's attention was on the Raif'yan. "Cool display," he said. "What's it about?"

The girl smiled at him. "It's a project I've been working on for a while. The main focus is on the revolt that brought the original generation our freedom. It takes you through the group of Kadraf Mining Corporation executives that were subsequently indicted for the crime of enslaving a species. So, these are the four conspirators. You of course know of the three main perpetrators and the just end that they all met–"

"Yeah. Of course. Those three," said Gam3r.

The Kadrafian girl scrunched her eyebrows and studied Gam3r's face more closely for a second before she went on. "But there was a fourth conspirator who was largely left out of the history books, other than perhaps as a footnote. The CFO of the Kadraf Corporation, Joe Dunham, escaped prosecution after the Kadrafian uprising, and was never found by the authorities. My project takes a more comprehensive view of the Joe Dunham mystery."

As she explained it, she continued to hang up pictures of the conspirator in question. He was a middle-aged human with bright white hair and a severe demeanor. "There's something about this guy's face," Gam3r mused, and trailed off. He then turned and walked over to Freeda without saying another word. The Kadrafian girl resumed her history lesson, but when she looked up from hanging her pictures, her audience was no longer present. She looked around embarrassed for a moment before returning to her project.

"How much do you know about Joe Dunham?" Gam3r asked Freeda.

"Not much. Just that they never caught him. Why?"

"Go look at his picture for a second, would you?"

Freeda walked over to the display and smiled politely at Gam3r's latest crush. She stared at the picture of Dunham for a minute and felt her heart sink into her stomach. After lingering on the picture long enough to be sure of what she'd seen, she went to the computer, where Gam3r had already brought up pictures of Joe Dunham and General Dalton side by side.

"But that's not possible," Freeda whispered. "Maybe Dalton shares some lineage with Dunham? We are evolved from humans after all. They couldn't be the same person.

Kadrafians weren't changed over from live humans. We're evolved from humans, but born as Kadrafians. And he'd be over 500 years old. It couldn't be."

Gam3r's whisper got even quieter, and Freeda had to lean in to hear him. "The Conspiracy Theorists of Skepton claim to have evidence that the process that created us Zees was eventually perfected, and it is possible to eliminate the aging process in humans. But of course it would only be available to the super rich, because you can't have the masses living forever. It would be bad for the economy or whatever. If Dalton had access to that kind of genetic lab and could also make himself into a Kadrafian, he would have the best hiding spot ever. That's why he never got busted."

"Gam3r, it can't be. Someone would have noticed this similarity before now."

"Not if they weren't looking for it. Dude has fought pretty hard for the KCF. It wasn't until you knew he was a traitor that you could see it. How much do you know about the general's history, like his early life?"

"I mean, nothing significant. He's got warrior tattoos, but he joined the Combat Force later in life. I think he was like a prize fighter or something before that."

Gam3r turned his focus back to the computer. "Let's see what we can find out, shall we?"

Once he knew what to look for, it took Gam3r less than an hour to confirm that there was very little information about the general's life further back than ten years, and what was there was contradictory. He would have had it faster, but the cute librarian came by more than once to see if he needed any help, and to let him know she had finished the display if he would like to critique the final product. Freeda rolled her eyes again. "I seriously cannot believe she can't see through your offensive makeup job."

"It's just like with the general. It's only obvious once you know what to look for."

Freeda took the information Gam3r had gathered and loaded it onto a data chip, which she hung on a string around her neck before leaving. The library opened into a cavernous indoor town square, and down a corridor from there was the ship hangar where they had parked. Right as they came out the door into the square, Freeda bumped face first into Treshler. "Hello, Freeda," he said quietly.

Freeda gasped, and said in a loud whisper, "What are you doing here?"

Treshler blushed a dark blue and pointed to Gam3r. "This Zee...Kadrafian child messaged me on my fan page. He said that you would be here, and I should come see you now before you go do something really stupid." Freeda looked open-mouthed at Gam3r, but Treshler continued, his voice cracking. "They told me you were dead, Freeda. That was months ago. I–I wrote a song about it and everything. You could have at least told me."

"I'm sorry, Tresh." Freeda made quick eye contact and looked at the ground. "I got shot down over Galeria, and there was a whole thing where I was lost in the jungle with this Lumano who I'm trying to rescue right now and he's got these crazy twin brothers and I helped form the Pacifists and I wish you could have seen it all because you could write the most beautiful songs about it, but General Dalton is a traitor and possibly 500 years old and there's a Purist army and we have to stop them, and by the way this is Gam3r, he's also in the Pacifists..." Freeda trailed off and buried her face into Treshler's chest. He hugged her tightly and didn't say anything.

Gam3r stood to the side awkwardly. After a minute he broke the silence, saying, "I really dig your music."

After a minute, Treshler stepped back and faced Freeda. "Is there anything I can do to get you to stay here and not go do whatever crazy dangerous thing you're about to do?"

"If there was anyone that could, Tresh, it's you. But I have to save my friend, and then the Kadrafian people, and then the galaxy. In that order. Don't worry. By the time I get back, this whole war will be over, and I'll be able to retire and follow you as a tour groupie full time." She kissed him on the cheek. Then she grabbed Gam3r by the ear and dragged him screaming toward their ship. A few passersby stopped to stare and consider whether to intervene. Freeda smiled and gave them a polite nod of the head, but did not let go of Gam3r's ear.

Chapter 36

Brandine was last to climb into the Navy transport. As she pulled the door closed behind her, she said, "Looks like you're finally gonna fly on a Navy carrier, eh Gam3r?" She looked around in a panic, and her heart dropped into her stomach. "Where's Gam3r?"

Everyone piled out of the ship and looked around. "I saw him right before Freeda left," said Laneeko. "He couldn't have gone with her, could he?"

Brandine groaned. "That's exactly the sort of thing he'd do." Laneeko got no response from Freeda on the radio, and after fifteen minutes of looking they agreed he must have gone in the hot rod, so the group loaded into the transport.

The mood was sullen, so Lytess offered, "I know this looks bad, but it's always darkest just before dawn, right?"

"Thanks, Lytess," replied Brandine. "Do you really believe that?"

"I mean, no. On New Belgium, just before dawn is when two of our moons are up. Just after dusk we have one moon in the process of setting. Here it's always darkest about a third of the way between dusk and dawn."

Ashley jumped the Navy transport to the Republic system and headed in to land on the *Centauri*, but her scanners lit up with hostile ships. "They couldn't be here already, could they?" she asked.

She landed in the shuttle hangar, where Admiral Garcia, Commander Greenblatt, and Chief Schultz were waiting for them. As they stepped out of the transport, the launch sirens were already calling pilots to their fighters. The admiral looked grim, and seemed oblivious to the sirens as he addressed the group. "So, you're the ones who have been a thorn in our side for the last couple months, and now you want our help?"

"We're not asking for help, Admiral. We're offering it," answered Lytess. "Our intel clearly checked out if the Purist army is already here."

"Your intel?" the admiral asked. "You hear those launch sirens? I was already getting distress calls from the Republic, son. The Purists beat us here, and it's you renegades that kicked the hornet's nest and brought them out of dormancy."

"Admiral," complained Brandine, "you're not suggesting that we should have let a Purist army go about their merry way of planning a genocide?"

"No, ma'am. I'm not suggesting that. I'm suggesting that you and your friends have been committing war crimes for months, and now you want me to have amnesia about that? After we deal with this Purist threat, you are going to answer for your deeds."

Brandine seethed. "War crimes? We're not the ones who ordered a long-range bombing mission, Admiral."

"But you are the ones being arrested for terrorism," retorted the admiral, as a team of military police marched into the room. "Put these criminals in the brig until further order."

The Lumanos placed their hands on their heads to comply, but Brandine charged forward in a rage. An MP brought his baton into Brandine's stomach, and she buckled to the floor. Bear stepped between the two and pushed the MP hard against the wall. The rest of the MP's raised their rifles, and Bear dropped to his knees with his hands on his head.

"Very well," Admiral Garcia said to Bear. "Apparently you've made your choice. You'll join these derelicts in the brig." The admiral then turned to Chief Schultz and added, "And I don't think for one second, Chief, that Monk couldn't have pulled off his little desertion stunt without some help. I'll deal with you later, but right now get back to work. Lieutenant Sokolov, I suggest you meet up with your squad and get ready to launch."

"Yes, sir."

The launch sirens continued to sing the song of their ancestors as Brandine, Bear, and the twins marched down the hallways toward the brig. Pilots ran past them in the other direction, taking barely a notice of the group of prisoners. Once the cell door slammed shut, Brandine slumped onto one bench, and the twins sat opposite her on the other. Bear stood with folded arms.

Seeing that the cell guard was distracted by the excitement of the imminent action, and having nothing better to do during their incarceration, Brandine slipped the screen showing Copernicus' video feed out of her pocket, and the three other prisoners crowded around her shoulder to watch.

***

Copernicus was sitting up on his bunk when the laser grid locking him in flickered off and a new entourage entered his cell. It was led by a human woman in a dark, pin-striped suit, whose age was impossible to tell other than to say she was likely older than she looked. When she spoke, her voice was stern and commanding.

"So, you're Monk. Do you know who I am?"

Copernicus hesitated. "I believe your name is Willow. Bowing is your husband."

"Very good. You and I need to have a serious conversation, Mr. Monk. I'm sure you understand how many lives are at stake here. I'll give you the opportunity to save a few of them." Copernicus remained silent, so she continued. "I've been giving my husband the chance to prove himself, but he's going about it all wrong. He wants to torture you. He means well, you understand, but he's just a silly boy. I've gotten where I am by understanding what makes people tick, and I know you would gladly be a martyr for your cause. Torture will get us nowhere.

"You should know, Mr. Monk, that my army is going to obliterate the Navy with or without your technology. The battle is beginning now, and there's nothing you can do to stop that. I don't need your shield designs for this battle, but I do want them in the long term. So let's at least frame our negotiations in the context that your martyrdom won't save a single life today, but if you work with me I will allow you to save many, many lives. Can we at least have that as our starting point, Mr. Monk?"

Copernicus finally looked up and met Willow's eyes, but then looked down again. "But why the Republic? There are millions of pure humans there."

"There are, but they are so overwhelmingly blended with all other species, there's no way to filter them out. It's the perfect starting point because it's a mess of every species all jammed together."

Copernicus' gave her an icy stare and said, "It's also the most protected system in the galaxy. Your shiny new carrier is not going to make it through tomorrow, and I don't care if I go down with it."

Willow laughed. "You think you're on a carrier right now, do you? Mr. Monk, this ship we're on is one of a kind. This is the *Purist Organization Ship Citadel*. We've got two carriers parked on our hangar deck. But the *POS Citadel* isn't in the Republic anyway. I was going to threaten to use it to destroy New Belgium, but I've changed my mind. I know you were hanging out with that cute little Kadrafian, so while the Navy is distracted by the attack on the Republic, you're going to watch the destruction of the Kadrafian home world on this ship.

"Oh, don't look so forlorn, Mr. Monk. I'm going to make your choice easy. The GNC and KCF have been weakening each other for decades, and my Purist army is on the verge of conquering them both in one fell swoop. Give me the shield designs, and I'll let you choose a species that I will consider endangered. They'll be confined to one planet and stripped of legal rights, of course, but we won't eliminate them. Lumanos, Kadrafians, Zees, whoever you want. If you don't choose one species and cooperate with us, then we will wipe the galaxy clean of all of them, and you can die with the rest. You can save literally trillions of lives by turning over one small blueprint. If you don't want to save those lives, their deaths are on you."

Copernicus scoffed. "You try to force me into an impossible choice and then hand me some guilt? Loomies don't play that game. No one is forcing you to murder innocent people. Their deaths will be squarely on you. I may be altruistic, but I'm not naive. Even if this is just about money and power, I have no reason to believe you would spare anyone. If you want to murder entire species, you're not going to do it while hiding behind my brothers' shield design."

The crime boss smirked. "Fool. You think you Lumanos are so innocent? Do you really believe Lumanos were the first new species evolved from humans? How do you suppose the original New Belgians were able to come up with a cure to your plague so quickly? You think they were building brand new genetic labs while they were quarantined and dying off whole cities at a time?

"Your little scientific community was able to come up with a cure because they had been engaging in genetic alterations for decades. The New Belgian Genetic Company designed slave species for the Kadraf Mining Corporation for a generation. Planet Kadrafia should really be called Kadrafia VI. No one ever discovered the first five because after they extracted the resources from those planets, the species was eliminated. So spare me your little morality lecture, Loomy. You might as well save yourself, because your people aren't the saints you think they are."

Copernicus wouldn't look up, but he interrupted. "That was thousands of years ago. If that's true, Lumanos won't hide from it. We'll put it in our museums and teach it in our history classes. We learn from our past."

Willow erupted. "*I* funded the original genetic lab on your planet. They were hired to find a way to reverse the human aging process, but they weren't working fast enough. That plague wasn't indigenous to New Belgium, Mr. Monk. It was designed. I had my people release it on the planet as a motivator to speed them up. In retrospect, I'm not sure what I was thinking," she admitted. "Finding a cure to the plague so quickly was impressive, but it wasn't a cure to aging. I motivated them to work on the wrong problem. Obviously they eventually found a way to overcome human aging as well, which is why I'm standing here with perfect skin and talking to you.

"So here is my offer. We're building a new world. I'm not just creating a galaxy of only pure humans; I'm creating a utopia of immortal humans. For 500 years there has been a handful of elites who don't age. Once we seize control of the galaxy and purify it of all abominations, we'll be able to control the population enough that we can offer many more humans an unending lifespan. If you stay on as my science officer, Mr. Monk, I'm offering you the chance to live forever. We can even change your DNA to pure human, so you can enjoy the sexual pleasures. Or refuse, and right now while my fleet attacks the Republic, this ship will travel to Kadrafia and release a new plague upon the entire planet. This one is designed to target that disgusting moss from which they were born. It is deadly to your tattooed friends. You've got less than a half hour to decide, Mr. Monk."

The laser grid flickered on, and Willow and her entourage walked off down the hallway. Monk collapsed onto his bunk facing the wall. *I thought I could stop a war*, he thought to himself, *but instead I brought about a genocide. I'm paying for my hubris. I should have stuck with race cars.* He closed his eyes to hold in the tears, but in the darkness of his eyelids his mind was drawn to the error message icon of his HUD display. He couldn't shake the feeling that he had seen the symbol before, but he just couldn't place it.

***

In the brig of the *Centauri*, the four observers in the room sat with mouths agape at the revelations of the crime boss to Copernicus.

"We need to stop the *Citadel* from releasing that plague," whispered Lytess.

"How are we supposed to do that from inside a cell?" asked Laneeko, looking despondent.

Lytess minimized the video on the screen and brought up his messenger. "I can send a message to the Kadrafian fleet from here," he said. "The tricky part is making it look legit. They'll probably think this is a hoax."

Bear looked over Lytess' shoulder. "Yeah," he said. "It probably doesn't help that your messenger handle is Prankster_420. There's no way they're going to take you seriously."

Chapter 37

Freeda and Gam3r were in the hot rod, approaching the Kadrafian carrier group. "You could have at least told me you were contacting Treshler. That caught me completely off guard."

"Yeah, sorry about that. It was kind of a spur of the moment thing. I was sitting in the ship listening to his songs while you were in the library. By the way, I fixed your Sugar Cane before we left New Belgium." Gam3r brought the staff out from behind the seat.

"Gam3r, you are simultaneously the most infuriating and the most endearing member of our group. You know that, right?"

"Yeah, I get that a lot." Gam3r fidgeted with the console for a moment, accidentally opening a hidden panel. "Hey, check it out," he exclaimed. "They rigged this thing with shields and Inerters! That could come in handy if we fail to talk our way onto your carrier."

"Let's hope it doesn't come to that."

Gam3r paused for a minute, then changed the subject. "You're not going to kill him, are you? Remember, we took an oath."

Freeda gave Gam3r an odd look. "Didn't you spend a good chunk of your life trying to get into the Navy to be a fighter pilot? You've sure had a change of heart."

Gam3r shrugged. "You're all a bad influence on me, I guess."

"I'm not going to kill him. All I care about is finding Copernicus, and I need the general alive if I'm going to get any information."

"Do you love him?"

"Who, the general?" Freeda asked.

"No. Copernicus."

"Yeah, of course I love him. Not romantically, if that's what you mean. I love you too, Gam3r. You're my family now. Copernicus risked his life to save me at the very moment that my own fleet had abandoned me. I will do whatever it takes to not abandon him. You understand?"

"Yeah. Same," said Gam3r. "Whatever it takes."

As they approached the carrier, Freeda asked permission to land, which was instantly denied.

"Look, rich kid," came the reply, "it's a nice ship, but you're in a military zone. Get that thing out of here before a patrol finds and vacuums you. That ship is a piece of art. I'd hate to see it get mangled."

Freeda did not slow down her approach. "I have an appointment with General Dalton."

"I sincerely doubt that. I don't have anything in my book about the general clearing a civilian craft for landing on this carrier. Get lost."

"Tell the general it's about Dunham." Something about the name rang a faint bell in the watchman's mind. It piqued his curiosity enough to run it up his chain of command with a high priority tag. A few minutes later the order authorizing the landing clearance came down, all the way from the top.

Freeda landed the hot rod in an empty bay on the carrier and took off her flight suit. A Pacifist uniform would be even more inappropriate on a KCF carrier than in a civilian library. She grabbed her knife and staff and told Gam3r to wait in the ship, just in case it went sour and they needed to make an escape from the carrier.

"I thought you said you wouldn't fight him alone this time," Gam3r protested.

"I said I may not have to. I don't want to involve the entire KCF until I know where Copernicus is. After that they can do whatever they want with Dunham. I'll just threaten him with revealing his secret."

"But you said yourself you're going to reveal his secret no matter what. Look, you're not going to bluff this guy. Let's take a second to think about this."

"I don't have a second, Gam3r. I'm not a philosopher. I have a situation, and I react to it, simple as that. I let my friend get captured, and now he doesn't have time for me to hesitate."

"Freeda, hold on. Let's get one thing straight. You didn't let your friend get captured. He gave himself up willingly, and we wouldn't know about this Purist threat if he hadn't. These videos aren't just going to be used to warn the Navy. We'll broadcast these to the whole galaxy, send them to the news outlets, blow the whole thing open. It's about to get real. So let's take a moment and think about what we're doing before we go get ourselves sliced open by this general."

"Those are all good points, Gam3r. Thank you. Now wait here."

Freeda stepped out of the cockpit and onto the flight deck. She was greeted by Kamber, her old platoonmate.

"Welcome aboard, ma'am. I'm told you have–Freeda?"

Freeda barely acknowledged him. "Where's the general?"

"He's waiting for you on the observation deck. Ma'am, is that really you? Where did you get that shirt?"

Freeda, still in her Lumano floral print, strode past him toward the observation deck, directly above the bridge.

"Ma'am, wait!" She kept walking, but Kamber caught up and walked beside her. "I knew you were alive. I just knew it. After you were shot down, the general ordered the retreat. Four of us in the platoon asked for a transport to look for you on Galeria, but we were denied clearance. Next day we stole a transport and followed your distress signal. Found your ship but not your body." Freeda kept walking, and Kamber got annoyed. "I'll have you know, ma'am, we did a month in the brig for that stunt. They only let us out to let us fly front lines in the Battle of the Republic. We all know the odds of survival on the front line in a battle that size. Mind you we volunteered, of course, because a noble death is better than sitting in the brig. Anyway, I should be dead right now if the Pacifists hadn't mucked up that whole battle."

Freeda stopped and turned toward him. "Kamber, that was me. I'm a Pacifist." Kamber's eyes widened. Freeda turned and continued walking toward the bridge. She added, "Thank you for looking for me. I'm sorry you paid for it dearly. We have a lot to talk about, but I have something I need to do first." Kamber slowed to a stop and watched her walk away.

***

Gam3r sat on the ship for a few minutes, but had no intention on staying put. He had overheard Freeda and Kamber's conversation and knew that his destination was the observation deck. After washing off his makeup, he felt Freeda had enough of a head start that he could go unnoticed, so he hopped out of the cockpit and looked around. The only person in the hangar was a mechanic working on a fighter five stalls away. Gam3r approached him and asked which way to the observation deck.

The mechanic looked over at Gam3r, started to answer, then noticed his appearance. "A human child? How did you in get here?"

Gam3r flashed his ID. "I'm not a child. I'm a Zee. I got called in to do some tech consulting for your general."

The mechanic didn't even look at the ID. "Tech, eh? Yeah, so take a left out this door, and take the corridor to the end. The observation deck is two decks up from there."

"Thanks."

When Freeda entered the observation deck, the general was standing at the window, looking out. His left arm was outstretched, holding on to a fighting staff that stood propped on the floor next to him. He turned around when she entered, and studied her face. "Freeda?" he said. "You were shot down over Galeria."

She walked toward him. "I was rescued by the Monk, who you recently kidnapped. I need to know where he is, General."

"You must be the Pacifist pilot we encountered before we landed on your base, eh? You always were a loose cannon, kid, but that's what I liked about you. I don't know where your Monk is, and of course I wouldn't tell you if I did."

"I know who you are, General. I can expose you. I have proof."

Dalton smirked. "You're about five centuries too late to expose me. Come tomorrow I'll be done with this identity. If you know who I am, then you know that I'm over 500 years old. What makes you think you're the chosen one who can come in here and intimidate me?"

"I don't know," Freeda mumbled. "I mean, at 500, you're probably not as fast as you used to be?"

The general laughed out loud. "I don't age, kid. If anything, I get faster every year."

Freeda lowered her staff toward Dalton. "I just want to know where the Monk is, Dunham. That's all I care about. Just tell me where he is, or you'll be spending your 600th birthday in the med bay."

"Ha. I was right to promote you. You got a true warrior's spirit, but my memory of the last time we faced each other, it didn't end well for you."

"Last time we faced each other? You mean when I was fighting six commandos at once and you swept me from my blindside? That time?"

The general raised his staff and pointed it at Freeda in a manner that triggered her instincts. She jumped just in time, while from the end of Dalton's staff came a hair-thin beam of glowing orange plasma. The beam missed Freeda, and the plasma burned a perfectly round hole through the floor. "You like that?" asked the general. "After I saw yours in action on that asteroid, I had my science officers build this for me. It links to the center of a small yellow star. It's a little more effective than the dirty water fountain that dribbles out of yours."

He shot another beam of plasma. She rolled under and let out a burst of water as she came up. The Sugar Cane missed to the side of Dalton, and the two warriors came together, locking staffs. Dalton was stronger than Freeda, but she was faster.

Freeda fought valiantly, holding the traitorous Dalton off for a time, but the general was wearing her down. He swung his staff from the side. Freeda blocked with hers. The general pulled away, letting out a burst of plasma as he did so. The beam missed wide of Freeda's shoulder, but close enough that the heat of it burned through her sleeve, searing her skin. She faltered, and Dalton spun and kicked the Sugar Cane from her hands. The staff flew into the back corner of the room.

The next thing Freeda knew she was on her back with Dalton on top of her, preparing to deliver his final blow. Before he brought down his staff, Dalton noticed the data chip hanging around Freeda's neck, and he was overcome with arrogant laughter.

He yanked the chip off her neck and remarked, "Please tell me this isn't where you're keeping your proof of who I am?" Freeda winced, but didn't answer. "You warriors never think ahead, do you?" The general tossed the data chip into the air and disintegrated it with a beam of plasma. The noise that followed was a groan, then a thud. Freeda looked backwards from her position on the floor just in time to see Gam3r collapse. He had walked into the room just as Dalton threw the data chip, and the beam of plasma cut a pinpoint hole straight through Gam3r's chest and into the wall at the far end of the room.

Seeing a human child caused Dalton to look up in confusion long enough for Freeda to scream with rage and plunge her knife into the back of his hand. He grunted, and his staff popped out of his grip, bounced twice, and rolled toward the back of the room, resting against Freeda's Sugar Cane. While Dalton pulled the knife out of his hand, Freeda took the opportunity to spring to her feet and regroup.

She allowed herself one more moment's glance toward her friend's body, then bared her teeth at Dalton and went at him with the fury of a thousand warriors. Her first kick knocked the knife out of the general's hand. He blocked the second. Dalton continued to block blow after blow, but Freeda kept coming at him. Finally he parried, caught her off balance, and struck a fist to her head so hard that she flew backwards and skidded to a landing on her side. Dalton pulled out his own knife and charged her before she could get her wits, but he was stopped in his tracks as a beam of yellow plasma cut in a sweeping motion across his torso, waist to shoulder. The general didn't have time to form a surprised look on his face before his body crumpled to the floor, short yellow flames flickering out of its bifurcation.

Gam3r was sitting propped up against the back wall, holding the general's staff in his lap. Freeda screamed his name and ran toward him. His breath was shallow, and as she leaned in close, he whispered, "Shit, wrong one," and closed his eyes.

Freeda picked up Gam3r's body and carried him down to the bridge, causing quite the scene. The carrier's executive officer, Colonel Torgue, rushed over to her. "What's going on here? Freeda? Is that you? What are you doing here? Who is this child?"

"He's not a child. He's a Zee," Freeda said. "His name is XxXGam3rDud3-69, and he died a hero in battle. I want him to be given a warrior's funeral."

Unsurprisingly, such an answer didn't satisfy the colonel. "Where is the general?" he asked.

"The general is dead. He was a traitor."

"A traitor? Can you prove that?"

Freeda shook her head. "No, Colonel. But you can, if you order an autopsy of his body."

Torgue and Freeda looked at each other, neither flinching. Soldiers accumulated behind Freeda. They drew their rifles and looked to the colonel, awaiting orders. One of them blurted out, "She's the traitor, Colonel. We should kill her on the spot."

The colonel held up his hand to silence the soldier. "Take her to the brig. Keep her isolated." The colonel paused and gritted his teeth for a moment. "No one talks to her until I give the order. And get the ship's surgeon up here. I want a full autopsy performed."

"And my friend?" asked Freeda.

Colonel Torgue hesitated, then reached out his arms and took the Zee. "I'll take him to the med bay for now. If you somehow turn out to be right, he'll get his warrior's funeral."

The colonel turned to leave, and the soldiers bound Freeda's arms behind her back and marched her toward the brig.

Chapter 38

Copernicus stared at the floor of his cell. He'd gotten used to the crack in his vision, but the icon of the guy with big ears nagged him. He glanced around his cell in case there might be the user manual for a CGV480 cyborg eye lying around, but no dice. Perhaps the young guard sitting outside the cell playing video games would let him borrow her radio so he could call customer service. Looking for a distraction to his despair, Copernicus walked to the front of the cell and watched over the guard's shoulder as she played "Orbit Kart," a cartoonish orbit racing simulator designed and programmed by none other than XxxGam3rDud3-69.

Watching the game, Copernicus couldn't help himself but to be a kibitzer. "You need to take those turns lower if you don't want to lose speed. No, don't use your goo launcher power-up in turn three. You'll only get one or two other racers with it. Drop it in pit row, and you'll get everyone."

The guard pretended to ignore him, but she did lower her line on the turns. She turned to say something over her shoulder, but Copernicus didn't hear it, because his eyes were fixed on the upper right corner of her HUD on the screen, where a familiar symbol was blinking green. "Hey, what is that icon?" Copernicus asked. "The little guy with the big ears."

The guard paused the game and turned around. "Wow, old timer," she said. "It's not a guy with big ears. It's a radio tower. That's telling me I'm connected to another user. I'm racing against my girlfriend back home."

Another user. Copernicus let the thought sink into his brain. Someone was connected to his eye? And then it hit him. His prankster brothers. Memories came flooding into his head. He had seen the same icon shortly after first getting his eye, when he had been having horrible hallucinations.

Those weren't hallucinations at all, but his brothers' pranks. They must be connected right now.

His head sprung up straight, and he broadened his shoulders. His brothers were alive. If they were connected to his feed, they knew about the pending attack. Copernicus' battered mind raced as it pulled itself from the oblivion of hopelessness. The next step would be to get a message to them. He looked over at the guard outside his cell. She was looking at her game, but well within earshot. He didn't want to risk communicating audibly, so he looked around the cell, hoping for a brainstorm. The bunk didn't have sheets or a pillow, so instead he approached the laser grid and attempted to reach through it to tap the guard on the shoulder. The outside of his hand made contact with a beam, which let out a loud burst of sparks. He pulled back his hand with a pained grunt, and the girl turned from her game to bark at him to get back from the grid. Copernicus obeyed, but he had what he wanted.

He went and sat on the floor next to his bed with his back to the guard, and used his opposite finger to smear the char from the burn on his hand. With the ash from his damaged skin, he drew two symbols on the floor. Three concentric circles was the accepted symbol for a wormhole in space, and Copernicus drew two of them right next to each other. Finally, he drew an arrow from the first symbol to the second, then sat in a meditation pose in front of the symbols, keeping his back to the cell door to obscure the writing. He stared at the symbols for a full five minutes, then wiped the char from the floor and got into bed.

***

The twins were at the cell door, trying to eavesdrop on the guards and learn the status of the pending battle. Brandine and Bear sat on the bench together, when in her peripheral

The Pacifists

vision Brandine caught sight of Copernicus drawing on the screen. She could tell he was trying to tell them something, but she didn't know what. She took a snapshot of the symbols, then showed it to the twins. Laneeko whispered something in Lytess's ear.

"Tell me," demanded Brandine.

In a low voice, Lytess answered, "A long time ago, when we were working on our scrubbers, we worked out a way to open two stable wormholes right next to each other. We only did it a couple times, because it does serious damage to space-time. You have to use more than two extra dimensions to do it, and it has an exponential effect on the fabric of the universe. Theoretically, we figured out a way to open a wormhole within another wormhole, but we didn't dare experiment with it. A wormhole traveling through another wormhole would get space and time so twisted up around themselves that you'd be left with some permanent kinks and tears, catch yourself in a time loop, have to go back in time and prevent your parents from ever meeting to avoid a paradox, all that. There'd be no amount of inter-dimensional ironing and starching you could do to ever make our three dimensions wearable again after that. Problem is, the applications were virtually endless. If the corporate world knew about it, they'd destroy the galaxy in a matter of months, so we kept it secret."

Laneeko explained further, "Our brother is reminding us of some of those applications, and it reminded me of something else I saw recently. A double wormhole could come in handy right about now, but we have to get out of this cell, and we don't have much time. Have we gotten a response from the Kadrafian fleet?"

"Negative," answered Bear.

"It's going to be up to us," said Lytess.

"I don't know if you've noticed," said Laneeko, "but we're kind of incarcerated at the moment."

"Come on, brother," Lytess pleaded. "You're the one who

251

wouldn't give up when we were stranded on an asteroid. This is a simple jail cell. We've been locked in any number of cells in our LARP games. How do we always get out of them?"

Laneeko perked up. "We prank our way out," he said. "You got one in mind?"

"I've been thinking about it, but it'll take all of us. Bear, how are your acting skills? Think you can play the role of a Prince from the Nigerian IX star system?"

The three other prisoners huddled around Lytess, and he whispered his plan. When they had it down, Bear leaned against the cell door and called out to the guard. The jailkeeper approached, and Bear punched him through the cell door, knocking him out cold.

Lytess leaped from the bench and practically shouted, "What did you do that for?"

Bear shrugged. "I forgot my lines, so I pulled my own prank. Pretty funny, right?"

Lytess slapped his hand onto his forehead, exasperated. "That's not a prank."

"Sure it is. It's hilarious. Help me grab the keycard from him." Together they pulled the guard's body up to the cell door and went through his pockets, but there was no keycard. "Oh, right," said Bear. "The button to open the door is on his desk. I suppose your prank might have worked better."

"We'll never know now," said Brandine. "But I got his radio." She clicked on the radio to broadcast all frequencies and in the sweetest voice she could muster announced into it, "Bing bong bing, Chief Schultz to the brig. Chief Schultz to the brig, over."

Schultz walked into the brig area and looked at the guard on the floor. He sighed and hit the button to open the cell door. "Now what?" he asked.

"The situation has gotten worse, Chief," said Bear. "The Purists are using this battle as a distraction to launch a plague on Kadrafia. It'll be a complete genocide if we don't stop it."

"You got a plan?" asked Schultz.

Laneeko answered, "Can we borrow a transport ship and one of those long-range bombers?"

"I can make that happen," answered the chief.

Lytess turned to Brandine. "You and Bear will be flying the bomber."

Bear frowned. "Hate to be a pedant about military strategy or anything, but if that *Citadel* is as big as they said, one bomber won't scratch the paint."

"That's where we come in," said Laneeko. "Get your bomber to the Kadrafian system, get up to whatever speed you can in the time you have, and launch all ordnance at its bridge. We'll meet you there in the transport. Chief, we also need this list of parts, and we need an hour to get rigged up. We've got one stop to make before Kadrafia."

"I don't know if you have an hour, but where are you going?" asked Brandine.

The twins answered in unison, "The abandoned WID-2 station."

"To do what?"

Laneeko's eyes got misty as he responded. "To play the most important prank of our lives on these Purist Luddites."

"A prank for the history books," whispered Lytess, staring off into space.

Chapter 39

Freeda sprang to attention when her cell door slid open and Colonel Torgue walked in with a confused look on his face. "The ship's surgeon is beside herself," he said. "She says General Dalton couldn't have been born a Kadrafian, but she doesn't know how that's possible. Now she doesn't trust you either. She wants to examine you."

"That's fine," said Freeda. "I have a favor to ask her anyway."

"This whole thing has left me with a lot more questions than answers. Who or what is General Dalton?"

Freeda shrugged. "Long story. For now just call him a Purist spy, I guess, who transformed himself into a Raif'yan. All I know is he was selling us out to a Purist army that is about to attack the Republic in–what time is it?"

"Early morning. A Purist army?"

"They've probably begun their attack already. They've been playing us against the Navy for generations, weakening us both. We should take our fleet to the Republic and give the Navy support."

The colonel scoffed. "Support the Navy? Look, Freeda, I don't know where you've been or how you know any of this, but you've clearly lost your mind. So the general was a traitor. That's good enough to get you out of this cell, but I'm not mobilizing this fleet without some hard intel. So far, the only thing you've proven is that Dalton wasn't who he claimed to be."

"May I have permission to go myself? I'll take the ship I came in."

"Fine, granted, but not until the surgeon confirms who you are. I'll be calling an emergency muster on the flight deck in one hour to explain that the general is dead, and how and why. Word about that is already spreading like moss, so I'll need to set the record straight. After that it's probably better for both of us if you go. For now, I'm having you escorted to the medical bay for examination."

The ship's surgeon had been with the carrier a long time, and Freeda remembered her from being patched up after previous scuffles. They always had a good rapport, but the doctor looked grim when Freeda entered the room. There were two examination tables in the med bay. On one lay General Dalton, and on the other was Gam3r.

Dr. Wentree didn't say much to Freeda until she finished her exam. It didn't take long. She explained that because of the major differences in human and Kadrafian puberties, the distinction of a true Raif'yan compared with a Yoomy modified to Kadrafian in adulthood were easy to spot once you knew what you were looking for. General Dalton got away with his ruse for so long because no one ever looked for it. And the whole not aging thing also helped keep him out of doctors' offices when he wasn't getting himself purposely slashed in battle.

The doctor dismissed the guards and Colonel Torgue with a wave. Torgue nodded and said, "Very well. I'll see you at muster."

Once they were alone, Dr. Wentree relaxed her shoulders. "I am happy you're back from the dead, Freeda. There's all sorts of rumors circulating upstairs. Is it true you're with the Pacifists?"

"It's true," admitted Freeda.

"That's so exciting. I want to hear about it."

"I'll tell you, Doc, but I have a favor to ask first. Are you stocked to treat battle scars?"

"Of course."

"I could use your help with something before muster, right after I stop at my ship." Freeda got up, kissed Gam3r on the forehead, and ran to the hot rod.

Freeda got to her ship and tried to raise the twins on the radio, but got no response. She dialed in Brandine's code next. "Brandine, come in. Have you found Copernicus? Brandine?" No response. *Dammit*, she thought to herself. *I've come on a fool's errand, and I have lost Copernicus. If he's alive, I'll find him at the Republic if I have to tear through every single Purist ship with only my knife to do it.*

An hour later, the crew of the carrier was crammed together on the flight deck, squished in wherever they could find room. Some sat on the floor underneath fighters and bombers, while others had climbed up and sat on top of the ships parked on the deck. Colonel Torgue, soon to be General Torgue, stood at the podium. The news had already spread that General Dalton was dead, that he was a traitor, and several other mostly correct details of the previous few hours. When Freeda arrived, the flight deck was in commotion as these topics were discussed and speculated about by the gathered crew.

Freeda wore her purple flight suit with the Pacifist logo on the chest, but she had cut off the sleeves at the shoulders. When she stepped through the hatch to the hangar, a wave of silence swept across the deck. A few oblivious pilots failed to notice the sudden drop in volume of the room and kept chattering until their friends swatted them on the arms and pointed in the direction of Freeda. She walked toward the podium with her head held high. All eyes were on the Raif'yan Pacifist, and most mouths hung open.

Freeda no longer wore the solid orange lines of a warrior, but had turned her tattoo lines into an explosion of color. Her two most prominent scars met at a point at the center of her forehead, then split to drop down her face across her eyes and cheeks. These two scars she had made into a thick dotted line of alternating purple and white dashes. The rest of the scars on her face and arms she had tattooed with all of the colors of

the rainbow, each fading gradually into the next[12]. Her face
and body were a whirlwind of hues that would eventually
become a trend among a younger generation of Raif'yans.

Colonel Torgue stared at her all the way to the podium.
She came up beside him, and the two of them whispered for a
minute before Torgue returned to the lectern. "By now you all
know that General Dalton is dead," began the soon-to-be
general. "You've probably also heard the rumor that he was a
traitor. It has been confirmed by the ship's surgeon that
General Dalton was not born a Kadrafian. He was a spy
working for a secret Purist army, which is currently
mobilizing." At this, a fresh commotion broke out across the
hangar. Colonel Torgue put his hands up to silence the
crowd, but it was pandemonium, so Freeda stepped up to the
microphone.

"RAIF'YANS," she shouted. The volume in the room
dropped–not to silence, but enough for Freeda to shout over
top of the chatter. "For those of you who don't know me, I
am Freeda. I was a pilot on this ship until I crashed on
Galeria. I was rescued by the Navy pilot known as the Monk,
and since then I have flown with the Pacifists." At this point
she had gained the attention of the entire room. "I'm sure I've
encountered some of you in that role. Some of you I have
probably humiliated, and for that I'm sorry. Others I may
have prevented your deaths."

There were a few grunts and a few responses of "hear,
hear."

"A Purist army has formed in the shadows," Freeda
continued. "The Monk has chased them out into the light, but
he's been captured in the process. As we stand here, the
Purists are beginning an attack on the Navy fleet at the
Republic. If they defeat the Navy, they will surely face us

---

[12]   And presumably the rest of her body, though that's really nobody's
business but hers.

next." The word "Purists" was met with gasps.

"Raif'yans," Freeda continued, "I know we've had mixed feelings for a long time about the Monk. He spares us our lives, but also turns the tides of battles against us. I assure you that in drawing these Purist bastards out from their holes, he's done us a service we'll likely never repay.

"All my life I've been proud of being a warrior, proud of my tattoos, but with what I've learned over the last few months, the orange of my tattoos has begun to disgust me. We get locked into a life path and leave ourselves no room for change and growth. We give ourselves no class mobility, no chance to learn new outlooks. How is that freedom? I may be a warrior, but I am a free Kadrafian first.

"I am going to find the Pacifists and fly with them against the Purists. I believe it's in our best interest to support the GNC in their fight at the Republic, and stop the Purists before they–" Here Freeda lost control of her audience, and the deck burst into an angry chaos. Some were shouting that they would never help the Navy, while others responded that killing Purists sounded like a pleasant way to spend the day.

After a moment, the shouting tapering off, Kamber pushed his way toward the front. "Freeda," he shouted, making sure he could be heard throughout the whole hangar, "If not for you and the Pacifists, I would probably be dead. Of course we want to stop a Purist army, but doesn't it make more sense to let the Navy fight them first? Whoever wins, they'll be weakened far too much to take us on. We should go finish them off after they're done killing each other!" This was met with huge cheers from the crew.

Freeda raised her arms, and the volume lowered enough to give her another chance. "Don't you see? That's what the Purists have been doing to us for decades, pitting us against the Navy. They've been behind the whole war, profiteering off of it. They own the weapon manufacturers that sell to both sides. They run the propaganda campaigns. The war has been orchestrated by them to thin us out for this very moment, and we've been playing into their bigoted hands!"

This last part quieted the crowd. The chatter continued, but with a more somber tone than before. Freeda concluded, "My shipmates, you can do what you please, but I am going to take down some Purist scum once and for all."

Colonel Torgue returned to the microphone to issue his orders. "I'm sorry, Freeda," he said, more to the crew than to her, "but I can't put Kadrafian lives in the line of fire to save the GNC's ass. I have a sworn duty to our species."

"General Torgue, it's our governments that are at war, not our species. I know that's easy to forget sometimes."

"All the same, we're not prepared to rush into a new battlefront with a brand new enemy. We need more intel on this situation. It could be a trap." This brought more murmurs from the crowd. Torgue raised his volume and finished, "But mark my words, if there is a real Purist threat, we'll be sending them into the vacuum before the week is out!" This final statement drew huge cheers, over top of which General Torgue shouted, "Dismissed."

The crowd continued cheering. Freeda turned to head for her ship. Kamber tried to flag her down, but she didn't see him. Minutes later she was suited up and heading for the Republic.

Chapter 40

In all the excitement, no one looked twice at Chief Schultz leading a group of civilians to the long-range bomber bay. Brandine and Bear climbed into their G suits while the chief loaded torpedoes.

"Thank you for this, sir," Brandine said to Schultz.

"Don't call me 'sir.' I work for a living," said the chief, rushing around the ship. "The problem here is you don't have a hyperdrive. You'll have to figure out your own way to jump to the Kadrafian system."

"How are we supposed to do that?" asked Brandine.

"You'll have to sweet talk your way through the mass transit station," said Laneeko, who was sitting on the floor with Lytess assembling devices out of spare parts. "We'll be in the transport. Do not fire on the *Citadel* until we give you the go ahead. When you get to the Kadrafian system, get up as much speed as you can and stay near the planet. If you go in a straight line you'll be out of range, and probably blow through a minefield."

"Wait," said Brandine. "You want me to orbit race around a planet? That's too tight. It can't be done."

"Not with that attitude," chimed in Lytess. "If anyone can do it, it's you, champ. Laneeko and I have an impossible task of our own to pull off, if that's any consolation."

Lytess stood up and slapped a small device on both Brandine's and Bear's G-suits. "Holopaint generators," he said. "We're making a bunch anyway, had a couple leftover parts. They're too small to be useful on anything big, otherwise I'd put them on your bomber." He activated the devices, and both Navy-issued G-suits changed to purple with the Pacifist logo.

Bear stayed quiet as he climbed into the ship. He took the bombardier seat next to Brandine and closed the canopy. The launch tube opened, and Brandine punched the accelerator.

Once they were clear of the carrier, Bear said, "I wouldn't normally fly second seat in a bomber with a civilian pilot, but I know you from the races."

"You a racing fan?"

"Not really. My brother-in-law is into it. I used to watch with him. Your flying is something else. When I flew with Monk, I knew he'd crewed for you, but he wouldn't talk about racing. But anyway, if the crew and pilot that won that insane championship in '72 say this can be done and it will prevent a genocide, then I'm in."

Brandine tried to look casually down at the controls. "Your brother-in-law?"

"My sister's husband," replied Bear, equally as casually.

Brandine and Bear beelined for the mass transit station. Small ships without hyperspace drives could land on the station, input their desired coordinates, pay the requisite fees, and the station would open a wormhole that the pilot could drift through after powering down their WID drives. The Navy bomber, with its crimson red and loaded weapons racks, stuck out among the civilian ships waiting in line.

When they got to the front of the line, Brandine landed the bomber on the station, where the station agent came running out, waving her arms and shouting. "You can't land that here. No military craft!"

Brandine and Bear stepped out of the cockpit in unison in their purple G-suits, and the agent stopped in her tracks.

"The Pacifists? What are you doing in a Navy ship? What is going on here?"

Brandine started to speak, then caught herself. The station agent was a Sheeple with dark skin. Her fleece, naturally pitch black, was shaved into a mohawk and dyed glow-in-the-dark purple. Brandine knew many a dirty barroom limerick about Black Sheeples and their rebellious ways, but she'd never met one in person. She thanked her lucky stars at this turn of good fortune, as no one would be more likely to bend the rules to stop a Purist threat than this natural-born rebel with her purple hair and spiky wristbands.

"Yes, ma'am. We are the Pacifists," Brandine answered.

"That's so awesome," gushed the station agent. "I love you guys! I went to Nightmare Fest dressed as a Pacifist just last week!" She put up her hand for a high five, and Brandine returned it.

"So, listen, Miss...?"

"Harriet."

"Miss Harriet, we're kind of on our way to save the entire galaxy at the moment, and we could really use a hand."

"You want me to break the rules and send a fully armed warship through my station? That'll come with a price, you know."

"Name it."

"I want honorary Pacifist status. You folks recruiting?"

"Done."

Harriet blurted out, "Squee!" and punched Brandine lightly on the arm. "So, what are we saving the galaxy from today, fellow Pacifist?"

"A Purist army is about to attack civilian targets. Here's the coordinates we need."

Harriet's eyes went wide. "Purists? You're serious?" She looked at the coordinates, and then furrowed her brow. "These coordinates are in the Kadrafian system."

"You knew that just from the numbers?"

"I'm a mass transit station agent. Knowing coordinates is my thang. That's just one of many awesome skills I bring to the table as a member of this team," she said with rising excitement. Then more soberly she said, "Seriously, though, I can't send a Navy warship to the Kadrafian system through my station. That's taking a pretty hard-core risk. How do I know you two are the real Pacifists?"

Brandine slapped Bear on the shoulder and said, "Technically, he just joined this morning." Then she thought for a second, leaned in close, and spoke quietly, even though Bear was the only other person present. "After this is over, this video is going to hit the news cycles. We recovered this yesterday." Brandine pulled out her screen and played a short clip of the video from Copernicus' eye of Willow threatening the attack on Kadrafia.

Saying nothing, Harriet punched the coordinates into her console. Then she whistled low and said, "You're going to save the Kadrafian home world in a Navy bomber. It's so poetic. I mean, they're going to blast you out of the ether the second you show up in their star system in that thing, but it's so punk rawk." She looked off into the distance for a second and then said, "You two better suit up and get moving. You've got some Purist balls to cut off!"

Brandine started to put on her helmet, but stopped before bringing it down over her head. "Actually, Harriet, we don't kill people as Pacifists. Not really our thang."

Harriet punched a few more keys on her console. "Who said anything about killing? Just cut off their balls. Let's go, Pacifists! Make Love, Not War!"

Brandine held her helmet over her head, still hesitating. "Wait. What?"

"That's my slogan I came up with for us, like just now. You are not going to be sorry that you let me join. I've got dozens of those. You want me to follow you to these coordinates as soon as my shift is over?"

"That won't be necessary, but thank you. Tell you what, when this is over, if you ever need some ship repairs, head to Brothers Repair Shop on New Belgium and tell them Brandine sent you. They'll hook you up with the Pacifist discount." She winked, and finally pulled her helmet down over her head.

Brandine brought the bomber into position and prepared for hyperspace. The ship's electronics whirred themselves down to a silence, and the bomber drifted forward. Through the stillness, Hassan asked, "How do we know she's going to send us to our coordinates? She could be dropping us into a GNC prison."

Brandine chuckled. "That sweetheart? No way. She's as real as they get. Relax, Bear. You make it sound like this is your first time committing treason against the Navy."

"It's not treason. I'm just taking an unsanctioned side mission and going AWOL to save the home planet of our sworn enemies while my shipmates are busy fighting a very important battle. There's a difference."

The bomber dropped out of the wormhole, and the blue planet loomed in front of them. Brandine and Bear worked in unison flipping switches to power on all systems, while every warning light in the cabin lit up to let them know surface-to-space missiles were being launched by the planet's defenses, and fighter patrols were scrambling to their location.

Brandine set her throttle all the way forward and banked hard to the left. They scanned the system for the *Citadel*, but it was nowhere to be seen. "This is my first time in combat without a shield," she confessed to Bear.

"Try to stay alive. This is my first time orbit racing," he offered.

"Try to stay conscious."

The fighters closed in, and the bomber pulled away with its acceleration dampers off. Brandine leaned hard to the left to hold her ship in orbit. With the increasing speed of her bomber, her orbit got looser and looser. All they could do was await the arrival of the *Citadel* and focus on staying awake under the forces.

Four minutes into their orbit, Bear focused on his bombardier's scope, panting and sweating. "I have something to confess," he gasped.

"What's that?"

"I never considered the races to be a real sport before, but I've changed my mind. You are a true athlete if you do this every day."

Brandine smiled. If only she could convince all the haters of that same thing, she thought to herself. "We could be doing this for a while," she said. "We haven't talked about our exit strategy. If we leave this orbit, we hit a minefield. If we slow down, they shoot us down. We can't go around in circles forever."

Bear frowned. "We might have to surrender," he said. "But if we're successful against the *Citadel*, maybe the Raif'yans will be forgiving about us being in their system."

***

The bridge of the *Citadel* was massive–as large as the hangar bays, but without the ship stalls and launch tubes. The ceiling was three stories high and made entirely of windows, giving a feeling not just of cavernousness, but of being right out in the vacuum. The view was as fantastic as it was unsettling.

As the *Citadel* dropped out of hyperspace, the unmistakable form of Planet Kadrafia came into view, overcast as usual. Between the clouds here and there could be seen the main continents covered in the famed purplish-blue moss.

Willow stood alone on a raised platform in the center of the giant room. Her stage overlooked the hundreds of technicians working away frantically at their stations, preparing for the assault. The technicians wore solid white uniforms, a stark contrast to Willow's dark suit. The bridge was large enough that between the lines of technician workstations were rows of potted plants. It was brightly lit, giving the impression that this was a place of commerce, rather than a terrorist warship preparing to bring death to countless civilians.

Some technicians chatted on headsets, while others in the adjacent cubicles tried to concentrate on their work, furious that the manager had forbidden the use of headphones to drown out the din of the shared office space. The business-like work environment with the upbeat atmosphere and the adult contemporary music playing over the PA system was not just a matter of décor, but strategy. It helped the technicians forget that they were each a cog in the machinery of death, and helped them believe they were simply working a job, supporting their families, and being good patriots.

After all, in their minds, aligning with the Purists was the moral thing to do. Humanity had made a mistake by messing around with genomes and creating species never intended by nature, and that needed to be rectified. Civilian deaths were never a pleasant thing to think about, but it wasn't like these technicians were the ones pulling the trigger; they were just building the circuitry or writing the code or designing the websites. And the jobs they were doing were good for the economy, of course. After all, at the end of the day, a strong economy was all that really mattered.

A technician climbed the stairs onto Willow's platform and whispered something in her ear. She frowned, but dismissed him without comment. Apparently, the Navy had gotten some intel on their presence. An annoying revelation, but it wouldn't much matter. The Purist forces would overrun the GNC at the Republic, and General Dalton would keep the KCF out of the way.

Willow's threat to Copernicus had been genuine, but of course she was planning on wiping out the Kadrafians no matter what. He wasn't stupid enough to fall for her lie, but it was worth a shot. They would eventually get the shield designs out of him, she was confident.

The *Citadel* was capable of launching two carriers and a

fleet of ships, but their pilots were engaging the Navy at the Republic. Instead, the *Citadel* would launch a barrage of missiles at the planet below. Large "citybuster" ballistics were aimed at the dense population centers of the planet, but to ensure total annihilation they would also launch a flock of biological warheads equipped with a plague specifically designed to target the Kadrafian moss and all its progeny, i.e. the Kadrafian species. There would be no chance for escape.

Willow leaned against the rail and watched as the *Citadel* was brought into position to launch its attack, when the same technician returned and whispered a new message into her ear.

"No, the KCF won't be able to scramble in time to reach us. We've gone through every scenario," she said. The technician whispered something else, and Willow's face dropped. "What?" she exclaimed. "The Navy? Why would they send ships here? Speak up, man. I can't hear you."

The technician stopped whispering and spoke out loud. "It's just one ship, ma'am. A long-range bomber. We clocked it at 30% of lightspeed. It's a Navy bomber, but it's alone. It could be doing recon..."

Willow grimaced. "Very strange. A lone bomber. Is it flying with the KCF ships?"

"No, ma'am. The KCF is chasing it. If anything, the Navy bomber is drawing them off of us."

"Very strange, indeed," she trailed off. "None of those ships can scratch the paint on us, but keep me updated. I want this taken seriously. They must be up to something."

"They're coming around the planet. They'll be in range in six minutes of our time."

"Which direction did they come from?"

"Orbit, ma'am. They were already here. We looked, but there's no carriers. We're checking into it as fast as we can."

***

Brandine switched on her radio. "Laneeko, come in," she said. "The *Citadel* is here. We need you here now. I don't know how long after hyperspace they'll be ready to drop their payload, but we can't take our chances."

"You made it?" came the response. "You made it to the system? We didn't think you could pull it off."

"Where are you?" asked Brandine.

"Be there in a minute."

Bear looked into his scope again and took the radio. "We don't have a minute," he said. "The *Citadel*'s torpedo tubes are opening. We have to take it down before it can launch, or an entire planet is going to perish. Get here now."

The *Citadel* adjusted its position to face the planet. Warning strobes flashed around its torpedo tubes. Just then, Laneeko and Lytess dropped out of hyperspace in their transport, a microscopic speck next to the giant Purist ship. "Fire, now," Laneeko said over the radio. "Aim for the bridge."

Bear made one minor adjustment to their course, then pulled the trigger. "Fish are in the water," he called out over the radio, releasing the payload. "Let's get out of here. This whole situation gives me the creeps."

With their faith entirely in the twins and the fate of the galaxy in the balance, Brandine and Bear watched the torpedoes close in on the *Citadel*. A target that size is hard to damage, but it's also difficult to miss. In the final seconds before the torpedoes hit, Bear and Brandine held their breath. When the two projectiles plunged into the side and bridge of the *Citadel*, they caused a brief explosion that looked like nothing more than a few sparks of static electricity compared to the size of the target, and then the *Citadel*, as Laneeko and Lytess had promised it would, blinked out of existence and left an eerie void of empty space in its place.

Chapter 41

Ashley sprinted to the fighter bay, where the rest of her squad was suited up and ready to launch.

"Where's Lieutenant Amador?" asked Flips.

"No time to explain, Flips," barked Ashley. "Our fighters launched ten minutes ago. I hate being late to the party. Let's go."

Flips was so used to being called by her real name by her squad leader that she froze. Flare nudged her in the elbow, and she turned and climbed into her ship.

Once they were spaceborne, Ashley got on the radio. "You all know I'm not much for speeches," she began, "but this is a big moment. Flips became an ace last week with her fifteenth kill. Flare, how many are you at?"

"Fourteen, ma'am."

"One more and you're an ace. All right, diamond formation, India Squad. We haven't run this one before. I'm up front, high altitude. Flips and Flare, you're on the sides. Wild Bill, you're the tail with your bomber, and fly it low on the vertical axis. That gives everyone a clear shot to the front and we don't get in each other's way. Questions?"

"No, ma'am," they said in unison.

A dozen Purist ships were already in the system, including three carriers, and more were arriving every few seconds. The Navy was badly outnumbered. Ashley cued up Delta Squad on the radio. "Riff, are you seeing this?"

"Sure am. That's a lot of ships. Good thing you got Delta with you, eh? We gonna puree these puries."

"Well, I wasn't planning on leaving you any kills today, but there seems to be enough to go around. I suppose I can let you have a couple."

"Funny you should mention that," said Riff. "Did you hear about Lima Squad? They're gone. AWOL. Deserted."

"Wow," said Ashley. "I mean, Porter is a lot of things, but I didn't think he was a coward.""Don't you get it, Sokolov?" asked Riff. "Porter's fighting in this battle, just not on our side. That's why I've been looking for you, to call dibs. You find him out here, let me know his location, but leave him for Delta squad."

"There's no such thing as dibs. But man, Porter is a purie? I mean, he's an awful person, but a purie?"

"My squad has known all along," Riff said. "Didn't know he was going to go join a secret Purist army, but he's obviously a specist. But you're a human. He was only kind of awful to you, and even then only because of your Lumano squadmate. He was ten times worse to us. He tortured our squad, especially me. Purists hate Mesozoids most of all because we're not evolved directly from humans. We're a double abomination in their eyes."

Ashley thought about it for a minute. Her initial instinct was to be defensive, until Riff's speech stirred memories in her mind–things Porter had said and done that seemed like standard ribbing. In light of him having deserted to join a Purist army, they no longer seemed like standard ribbing.

"Gosh, Riff," she said. "I'm sorry. If I'd known that, I would have stuck up for you more. I know we've had our disagreements, but we both thrive on a little rivalry. If I find Porter, you'll be the first to know." To her squad she said, "That goes for all of India Squad. That's an order."

"Thank you, Lieutenant."

"Hey, Riff," continued Ashley, needing the last word.

"Yeah?"

"You should know...I'll save Porter for you, but that's probably the only kill you're getting today. The rest of the leaderboard is going to be India Squad."

"Careful, Lieutenant. I know you're one of the good ones, but as a Yoomy I'm not sure you get the fury that I have for these specist bastards. I'll talk it over with my squad and see if I can talk them into leaving you any."

Purist capital ships continued arriving in the system, and Ashley turned her radio to her squad. "Looks like we might be outnumbered, but these puries are not combat hardened. Almost everyone coming at us today is flying in their first real battle. Sure, they've got a few Navy veterans and deserters in some leadership roles, but no matter how much training this army has been doing wherever they came from, none of them have any notches on the side of their fighters. Be patient, take your evasive moves first, and we'll take these shiny new ships down by the dozens." She was met with huzzahs and ooh-rahs from the radio, and her squad pushed forward to the front lines.

The battle spanned the entire thirteen-planet system, with the Navy positioned between the Purist army and each planet. Both fleets spread out through the system like a tangled fight between two Galeradecapuses. Even at a glance from afar it was clear the Purist army had the advantage in numbers, spreading around and completely surrounding the Republic star system. But just as Ashley had suggested, the Navy had the advantage in the skill and experience of its pilots.

India Squad waded into the fray behind Delta, holding their fire and assessing the enemy fleet on approach. Purie capital ships advanced toward the *Centauri* carrier group, so the Navy pilots' first priority was protecting their carrier. As expected, one nervous, green-behind-the-ears Purist pilot laid into his guns well before they were in range of each other, giving himself away as a rookie and catching the attention of every veteran Navy pilot hoping to pad their stats with that first easy kill.

"Leave him for the vultures," Ashley said to her squad. "There's plenty of fish in this barrel. Follow me in. We'll run a McTwist." Ashley broke from behind Delta, and her squad followed in formation. She inputted a pattern route into her ship's computer, and it came up as a twisting line on their HUD displays, allowing her wingmates to keep their place in formation without constantly watching the squad leader.

Flare was on the starboard side of the diamond. As they cut into the battle Ashley pulled her formation behind a wing of puries and marked them on her HUD. Just as a shiny silver ship spun around to fire, Flare was flipping above the fighter and shooting down into its roof. The Purist fighter broke apart in a burst of yellow, and Flare resumed formation. "Fifteen, ma'am," he announced.

"Roger that. India Squad, weapons free. Let's make sure Delta gets that coveted second row on the leaderboard today. And Flare, congratulations, ace."

Receiving the go-ahead from the *Centauri* that the carrier was defended, Ashley went on the offensive and weaved her way through the chaos, picking lines and calling routes to her wingmates. Little by little they worked their way in to give Wild Bill clean shots on the Purist capital ships with his bomber. Along the way the three fighters scored points for the leaderboard, punishing any purie within range of their now ace squadron. Wild Bill dealt out damage where he could, but the single laser equipped on his bomber only caused an annoying distraction while his squadmates swooped in for the kill.

Nearing range of the first Purist cruiser, they loosened their formation to be harder targets for the turrets. They also attracted the attention of the cruiser's fighter escort. "Twenty," Flips called out as she took down a fighter. "How's that one go again, ma'am? The poor bastards have us surrounded again?"

Ashley smiled and narrowed her eyes. Flips was catching up to her kill count for the day. As squad leader she had to pay attention to navigating through the battle, while the rest of them got to follow her lines and fire relentlessly at the swarm of fighters around them. Monk had always made doing both look so easy.

"Firing," Wild Bill announced as he let his first two plasma torpedoes go. Ashley called a new route to take them out of the turret range. As they banked their fighter trajectories around, they all spun to face the cruiser and watch it break apart.

Over the radio, Ashley heard someone providing the sound effects for the exploding cruiser. "Shhhhhhhh-blam. Kerplowzer. Kaaaaa-bloomp."

"Watson," she said, "is that you?"

There was a pause, and then Wild Bill's voice again. "Ummm, yes, ma'am. Didn't realize my radio was on. The silence in space freaks me out, so I, um, add my own sounds. Sorry."

"Don't be sorry, son. From now on keep your microphone on. That's an order."

All around the star system, Navy bombers wore down the Purist fleet little by little, creating quite the spectacle for the civilians looking up at the night skies of the planets of the Republic.

Commander Greenblatt radioed Ashley from the carrier and asked her for a status. "We're outfighting them at every turn, Commander, but the sheer numbers we're up against are becoming an issue."

"I know," said the commander. "And I've got some bad news. There's another wave of Purists entering the system." There was a pause as Greenblatt surveyed the holomap. "Statement be damned," he said, "this will turn the tide against us. I don't know how much more the *Centauri* can take, but we need to do everything we can to protect the civilians in this system before we're overrun."

"That's about to get more difficult, sir," said Ashley,

scanning the battle. "There's a Purist battleship breaking away from the fleet. It's targeting the planet."

"That's a purposeful distraction to spread out our defenses."

"Yes, sir. It is."

"But it's a distraction that can't be ignored. Get that battleship now. You may not have a carrier to return to, but my fleet does not allow a vessel of war to drop its payload on civilians unchecked."

"Aye, sir."

India and Delta turned toward the battleship, joining their squads together to pursue the threat.

"How many fish you got left, WB?" asked Ashley.

"Two, ma'am."

Ashley cursed under breath, then realized how silly that was, and cursed out loud. "That's a big ship, but if you hit them just right, two will be enough. Let's see how close we can get."

Pursuing the battleship meant following it away from the rest of the fleet, out into the open, and oddly enough, out of the safety and security of the chaotic battle. Even before being assigned with Monk, Ashley had survived a long time by knowing how to tumble and dance through a battle without telegraphing her intentions. A little misdirection combined with a healthy dose of bobbing and weaving usually brought her through the chaos unscathed. Pursuing a battleship out in the open meant its fighter escort knew exactly what her squad's target was, and they immediately swarmed toward the approaching Delta and India squads.

The two Navy squadrons were several hundred kilometers from the capital ship when they were surrounded by its escort fighters. Delta Squad was flying above India Squad, and the pilots kept their backs toward the center, rotating the entire diamond clockwise and inching their way toward the battleship. Flare had taken out six purie fighters before a laser finally ripped through his cockpit. At the same time, Steve of Delta Squad pulled his eject lever milliseconds too late as his ship broke apart. Down two fighters, Ashley assumed command and ordered the two squads to join into one five-ship formation with Wild Bill in the center.

Ashley shouted orders into the radio, simultaneously picking purie fighters apart and lining up new routes toward the battleship depending on where the holes opened up in the purie defenses. "All right, listen up," she said. "Even if we do cut through these fighters, we'll be up against the massive line of defensive turrets on this battleship. These jagoffs are firing on civilians, so we have no choice but to press forward." The calmness in her voice didn't reflect the whiteness of her knuckles as she squeezed her trigger as hard as she could, carving enemy pilots out of their cockpits and into the vacuum. "We're running out of time here, and I don't know how to get my 'it's been an honor serving with you' speech down to fewer words than that, but I'm proud of you rook–"

As she spoke, Ashley caught several shots to her upper port side engine. Her controls went jerky, and white smoke billowed from the engine. Ashley fought with the controls as her ship lurched around. She was trying to relearn her controls, shoot down fighters, and navigate for the entire squad.

The Purist pilots turned and concentrated their fire on the damaged GNC ship. The second hit connected with Ashley's lower starboard engine, and her controls deteriorated. Ashley looked up from her dashboard to see a solid wall of laser fire raining down on her in slow motion, so she keyed up her radio to instruct Riff that he was the new squad leader.

Before she could speak, a blinding flash of pink absorbed the laser fire intended for her cockpit. The twins' purple hot rod slid sideways through the fray, catching laser fire, and laid into the Purist fighters with the Purple Inerter. The Navy ships then finished off the disabled purie fighters with their lethal Gatling lasers.

The radio squelched. "This statement isn't false just yet, ma'am."

"Freeda? Is that you?"

"Present and accounted for, Ms. Ashley."

"I don't suppose you brought any backup with you?"

"No, ma'am. I tried. Have you found Copernicus?"

"No. I've been a little busy."

"I must find him," said Freeda.

"Please, Freeda," said Ashley, "we need to take down this battleship that's firing on civilians, but we have to get through its turret defenses."

"The engines are too big to neutralize," Freeda said, "but if you can hang on for a couple minutes, I can take out the turrets. Those are WID-powered and vulnerable to my beam."

"No time like the present," Ashley responded, as she and her squad regrouped and prepared for the next wave of Purist fighters.

Freeda pulled ahead of the formation and got into range of the battleship's defenses. The anti-spacecraft laser turrets pummeled into her flashy sportship, and her shield lit up bright pink with the thudding of laser rounds. "Ms. Ashley," she called out over the radio, "keep your distance, but I'm going to need a spotter. I can't hardly see through the laser fire."

"I'm a little busy here," Ashley responded, while trying to catch a glance of Freeda's position. "Looks like you need to rotate 30 degrees to port, and five meters upwards. Good. Now lay on the trigger and rotate to starboard. You'll take down a whole line."

Freeda squeezed her trigger and turned gradually to the right.

After a minute, Ashley called out again, "You've got the whole row. Now drop 15 meters straight down and turn to port. That should clear out the entire starboard side of the battleship."

After dropping the 15 meters, the laser fire on her shields let up a bit, as the top row of turrets could fire but not aim, and were now firing over her head. Freeda squeezed the trigger again, this time rotating to her left. After strafing the whole row, she slid to the side and was clear of turret fire. "Send your bomber in now, over the top, Ms. Ashley."

The battleship continued firing on the planet. Wild Bill didn't wait for the order to be repeated. He slammed on the throttle and climbed his bomber over top of the battleship's defensive turrets. The fighters fell in behind him to give cover. When Wild Bill was within range, he launched his torpedoes at the joint just below the bridge of the battleship. Before turning back, he waited to make sure they reached their target.

The bridge of the battleship went up in an orange fireball that took most of the aft section with it, breaking into pieces and leaving the forward section of the ship to drift dead and lifeless away. Over top of the cheers that erupted over the radio, Wild Bill added, "Shablamaphone. Kerplobberbloooooooosh." While they all laughed merrily at Wild Bill's antics, on the bridge of the battleship the flesh of Bowing and his men burned from their bodies as they were sucked into the vacuum.

"I'm out of fish, ma'am," Wild Bill added. "Not much more I can do now."

Ashley was adapting to her limping controls. With a shielded ship taking point, she might just hang on a bit longer. "Roger that. Let's fall back and support the carriers for as long as we can."

Chapter 42

Willow stood on her platform and listened to the updates from the floor. "Torpedoes inbound. Sixty seconds to impact–no, time dilation is–twenty seconds to impact. Brace for impact." Willow grabbed the rail of her platform, though she knew there was little need for it.

She looked up at the windows just in time to watch the orange burst of a torpedo exploding against the glass, followed by a cloud of dark black smoke, but not the slightest tremor was felt below her feet. A slight rumbling sounded like thunder in a distant mountain range. Then, almost a full two-Mississippi count later, the *Citadel* jerked to port, throwing Willow completely off her platform. She careened to the floor below, bounced, then hovered in the air with her skirt riding up around her hips. The gravity and the lights had gone out. Being in a similar predicament, the crew was spared the awkwardness of seeing their boss's exposed underpants.

For a few long seconds, everyone waved their arms to steady themselves and float down to their workstations. They could do little when they got there, however, as all sensors turned off with the gravity and lights. After what felt like an eternity, but was less than four seconds, the power whirred on, and everyone crashed to the deck with a chorus of painful grunts. Willow picked herself up off a pile of groaning technicians, straightened her suit jacket out as she climbed up to her platform, and yelled for a situation report. The thick black smoke over the windows dissipated out into the ether, again revealing the sight of the overcast Kadrafian home world below.

The sitreps came in rapid-fire. All systems were functional. The blow from the Navy bomber was impressive for only two torpedoes, but they left no discernible damage in their wake.

Within a minute, Willow had the situation under control, and the technicians, nursing their bumps and bruises, got busy with their tasks.

***

Copernicus was reclined on his bunk when he heard the impact alarms blaring. He sat up, rubbed his eyes, and was about to plop back down when the ship jerked sideways, flinging him off his bunk and toward the laser grid at the front of his cell. As he hurtled through the air, he closed his eyes and waited to be cut into ribbons by the lasers. Instead, he slammed into the far wall outside of his cell. When he opened his eyes, the room was dim, and he was floating a few feet above the floor.

The guard was nowhere to be seen, so Copernicus began pulling himself along the corridor. When the gravity and lights flickered on, he collapsed to the floor face first. Getting up and brushing himself off, he looked around, then followed the hallway.

Copernicus began by looking for a shuttle bay and a means of escape. He passed by a corridor that obviously led up to the bridge. Tempted to investigate further, he snuck toward the entrance to watch. The hallways were eerily empty, as the *Citadel* was left with a skeleton crew to accomplish their side mission to Kadrafia. Copernicus was peeking his head through an entrance to the bridge, still in his slightly torn purple Pacifist uniform, when a technician in white came up behind him and passed right by without looking up from her handheld screen. Copernicus stepped out of cover and marched into the massive room. Technicians hurried by him in all directions without notice.

The first thing Copernicus was struck by was the sheer size of the bridge. Willow stood on a raised platform that brought her feet to everyone else's shoulders, and she was going rapidly back and forth between yelling orders across the room and whispering orders in the ear of a technician who stood on the platform with her.

The windows that made up the ceiling of the bridge displayed the planet Kadrafia as the lone object in the sky. None of the technicians running back and forth noticed that there was no longer a response of KCF ships racing toward this oversized warship to demonstrate how unwelcome the *Citadel* was in this sector. Copernicus did notice, however, and smiled to himself.

Willow looked over at the Lumano approaching the platform, and waved at him. "Mr. Monk, so glad you could join us. I must apologize, I meant to have you brought up here to watch the show, but in all the excitement I completely forgot. Guards," she called out, and Copernicus was surrounded by four commandos with rifles.

"Just hold him right there for now," Willow instructed the guards. Then to Copernicus, "I'll be with you in a second, Mr. Monk. I have a few matters to attend to."

Copernicus crossed his arms and waited while Willow murmured orders to the technician on the platform. Turning to her captive, she said, "What you're about to witness could have been avoided. Contrary to what you may think, I don't believe that genocide is the final solution to fix the galaxy. We just need better control over some of these more problematic species. If I could equip this *Citadel* with an energy shield, I would have a much easier time exerting that control without resorting to these more extreme measures." Here she waved her arm broadly toward the windows. "Give me the designs to the shield, and I won't need to expunge any more whole planets. Refuse, and I'll build you a cell right in this room and make you watch as we cleanse the entire galaxy."

A technician interrupted and whispered something in Willow's ear. She turned to Copernicus and smiled. "I'm informed that your precious Navy is currently being overrun,

Mr. Monk. My husband is commanding a battleship in the assault." As an aside she added, "I made sure I gave him a task he can't possibly screw up."

She looked up at the windows, then back. "Now, as for this miserable planet before us, the cities are being targeted with explosive ordnance. They're the lucky ones. The rest of the planet will fall to the plague. Bombs away, Mr. Monk."

On the surface of the planet below, explosions large enough to be seen from orbit lit up in a brilliant orange. Copernicus had been holding a grim face, but now he allowed a smirk to creep through. "This was never about shields, was it, Willow? You're retaliating because we messed up your plans. You want me to know you have power over me, is that it?"

"Perhaps, Mr. Monk. Do you find that humorous?"

"Not really. But you should take another look out the window."

Down on the planet, the explosions continued on the surface, but the clouds flickered. After a few seconds they went blank, as did the blue surfaces of the continents. What was left was a dull gray orb.

Willow's jaw dropped. "What is that?"

"I've never seen it in person," Copernicus answered, "but from pictures that looks to me like the old WID-2 station."

Willow didn't try to hide her panic. "But how?"

"Those torpedoes were a smoke screen. They didn't knock out your gravity; the fail-safes did. My brothers opened two adjacent wormholes, one large enough to bring this ship to an orbit around the abandoned WID-2 station, the other supplying the gravity to pull it through. They holopainted WID-2 to look like Kadrafia. You were too busy to notice that all three Kadrafian moons disappeared, or that their planetary defense systems were not responding to you, or that we're in deep space and there's no local star anywhere to be seen.

"The result is that you Luddites just hit an unstable ancient WID device the size of a planet with enough explosives to render this whole entire statement false. The station has already shrunk to half its original size. I don't think your plague will do much good inside of the black hole that WID-2 is currently imploding into, unless there's some moss on this ship you want to kill. This *Citadel* is about to get sucked in like a megalomaniac Yoomie with some purie propaganda."

Out the windows, the WID-2 station was visibly crumpling in on itself. Streams of lightning arced into it from every direction. Willow gasped. "But, your brothers...they killed you?"

"If they sent us to an unoccupied planet, they would have saved Kadrafia, but they'd still have to deal with your *Citadel*. They know stopping a Purist genocide is a cause I'm willing to die for. They're not killing me; they're saving everyone."

Willow stared mesmerized at Copernicus for a moment, finally snapping out of it and turning to the technicians around her. "Get us out of here, now!" she yelled.

"Already trying, ma'am," came the reply. "We're spinning up the hyperdrive, but we're caught in an immense gravitational field. Our size is working against us. We have enough power to open a wormhole, but not one big enough for the whole ship."

Across the bridge, technicians flew into a panic. Most sprinted from the bridge–some for the shuttle bay, some to contact their families, others to the Tautologist chapel to make their peace with the Statement. As the remaining techs continued in their attempts to engage the hyperdrive, the gravity and lights went off in preparation for a jump, and the running Purists launched comically into the air.

The *Citadel* was a magnificent feat of engineering, and would have been a formidable force in any battle, but no ship has ever been victorious in a military conflict against the laws of physics. The technicians who remained at their posts tried everything they could to draw power to their hyperspace drive. Under the drastic conditions of a nearby black hole formation, their drive core sputtered and coughed while the imploding WID-2 station reached out and swallowed the *Citadel* whole.

Chapter 43

India and Delta Squads raced toward their carrier group, Freeda leading the charge with her shielded pleasure cruiser. On the way, Ashley surveyed the scene and remarked, "How could the Navy have gotten caught so off guard by a Purist army?"

Flips had been mostly quiet, but she finally broke in with, "I'm not surprised at all. If you really think specism is dead, come to Thanksgiving with my family."

Riff's wingman, Adam, spoke up for the first time. "You got puries in your family?"

"Not card-carrying Purists, but I've got an uncle who's an ice cream social away from membership. He's subtle about it, of course, but all the classic prejudices are there, the us-against-them attitude. I don't think my cousins would go join a purie army, but you know what I mean. The Raif'yans have been demonized our entire lives, and one just saved us. Speaking of which, I haven't thanked you."

"Nothing of it," responded Freeda. "Your Monk has this theory that–" Before Freeda could finish the thought her shield lit up pink, and a split second later a purie sloop came barreling into her from underneath, knocking her out of formation, and coming face-to-face with Ashley's limping ship.

"Riff," called out Ashley, "it's Porter."

Porter grinned toward Ashley's fighter, and the two turret gunners on his sloop opened fire. Ashley dodged her ship upwards in a backflip, and as she came around, she took the extra millisecond to aim at the sloop's port engine, shooting it clean off. Meanwhile, Freeda righted herself and showered the sloop with Inerter fire. The starboard turret kept a bead on Ashley. She dodged again and let loose with her Gatling laser into the turret, spilling the gunner out into the vacuum.

Ashley leaned forward and squinted into the dark, swearing she could make out the lifeless form of an athletic male body in salmon-colored shorts with a knee brace and expensive sunglasses floating away from the sloop.

"Huh. Small world," Freeda mused over the radio.

"I'm sorry. What?" asked Ashley.

"Oh, nothing."

"All right, Riff," said Ashley. "I said I'd leave him for you. He's all yours."

Riff and Adam butted their ships against the disabled sloop, and in unison pushed Porter and his remaining turret gunner in a trajectory toward the central star of the Republic system. Porter tried hailing Riff over the radio, but the Mesozoid only switched the radio on long enough to say, "Sorry, Porter, but we better go radio silent," and flicked it off. When Delta Squad had accelerated the sloop sufficiently toward the white dwarf, they let the doomed vessel coast, and returned to formation.

***

In the fleet, standing on the bridge of the GNS Mars was Vice Admiral Keiko Akiyama, a woman of mixed descent, with a Caveman father and human mother. Through narrowed eyes she watched as the Navy continued to lose control of the battle. Her ship's executive officer, a Mesozoid named Commander Steggs, stood next to her.

"Admiral Garcia has ordered the abandon ship of the Centauri, ma'am," said Steggs. "You are now in control of the fleet. Orders?"

"Press forward." Akiyama watched as the Centauri launched its troop transports. Moments later, the purie artillery tore through the Centauri's bridge. "Report," ordered Admiral Akiyama.

"Admiral Garcia was on the bridge, ma'am, but most of the

crew made it off. They'll head for the planets below and set up defensive positions."

As the *Centauri* fell, the *Mars* pulled forward into the lead position, and began to take its own beating from the Purist artillery fire.

"It's not looking good, ma'am," said Steggs. "If we pull the fleet back, we could regroup and plan a proper attack."

Admiral Akiyama paused. "Commander," she finally said, "did I ever tell you the human side of my family is a bunch of low-class puries? Since I look straight human, they don't acknowledge that I'm mixed. Growing up they were never shy about their leanings."

"That must have been confusing, ma'am."

Admiral Akiyama turned and announced to the rest of the officers on the bridge, "Press forward. We're not going to just roll over and let them have the Republic. Whatever else they say about us, they'll know we fought the good fight."

The *Mars* was taking heavy damage, and the bridge was a chorus of situations being reported and orders being shouted, but one voice rose above the rest enough to momentarily quiet the room. "Admiral, a Kadrafian carrier just jumped into the system."

"What?"

Before Keiko Akiyama could speculate as to what it meant, the same voice rang out again. "Admiral, two more Kadrafian carriers just arrived. Check that. Three Raif'yan capital ships arriving, cruiser class. They're still coming, Admiral. It looks like a whole fleet."

"Well, shit."

Chapter 44

Seven and a Half Minutes Earlier:

After Freeda's speech and departure, Kamber and his squad lingered on the flight deck in a whispered huddle. A slew of other pilots also loitered about, unsure what to make of the new developments. As General Torgue was turning to exit, Kamber called out, "General! Banshee Squad requests permission to go to the Republic system on a volunteer basis and engage the Purist threat."

Torgue scoffed. "And how are you going to get there in your fighters, pilot?"

Before Kamber could answer, another voice called out, "If Banshee Squad gets to go, Grim Reaper Squad is also requesting permission. We want to kill some puries, General!"

"Don't think for a second you're leaving Angel of Death Squad behind," called out another voice. "We're not losing our spot on the leaderboard because they get to go kill puries without us."

"No fair," shouted another. "Soul Collector Squad is coming too."

"Now hang on a minute," cried the general. "I didn't say anyone was going anywhere."

"Count in Boatman of the River Styx Squad," yelled a voice from the far corner of the room.

"And Ladle of the Flying Spaghetti Monster Squad," yelled another.

"Well, you're definitely not going without Harvester of the Statement Squad."

"Silence," shouted the general from the podium. "Why are you all so hellbent on killing puries anyway? If anything, they're less awful to us than every other group. They hate everyone. Everyone else only hates us."

"Hey Doc," yelled a voice hiding in the densest part of the crowd, "You got your tattoo gun? I think the general needs some white tattoos. He wants to be a philosophizer."

The laughter that followed the insubordination should have enraged the new general, but instead Torgue answered with, "All right, you pathetic wastes of moss DNA, you have 360 seconds to get suited up and ready to scramble your fighters before we jump to the Republic to wipe out some purie scum. You just wasted seven of those seconds. Move!"

The pilots let out elated whoops and hollers as they all raced to their fighters.

Five and a half minutes later Kamber was strapped in and ready to launch. His fighter sat at the base of his open launch tube. At the end of the tube he could see the black circle of the vacuum, dotted with stars. Before the carrier could hyperjump to the Republic system, the fighter pilots had to check in and power down their WID drives.

"Azrael Squad, checking in and powering down."

"Davy Jones Squad, checking in and powering down."

Kamber's turn. "Banshee Squad, checking in and powering down."

He turned off the radio and powered down his lights. The temperature dropped, and a single shiver passed through Kamber's shoulders. From within the carrier, three thundering foghorn blasts announced the imminent jump to hyperspace. At the end of the launch tube, three flashes of yellow warning lights reflected off the hull of the carrier, followed by a single flash of red, and then the stars beyond shifted to a new pattern.

A green warning light flashed once, signaling the all clear, and Kamber switched on his power and wedged forward on his accelerator. First out of the tubes, he glanced over his shoulder to see the rest of the squads racing to keep up.

The Kadrafian fleet jumped into the system behind the Purist capital ships, pinning them between the GNC and the newly arrived KCF. Kamber and Banshee Squad cruised by the purie fleet to target their fighters, who were engaged on the opposite front with the Navy.

Kamber's head start was enough to earn him first blood for the day. He came up behind a squad of silver fighters entering the battle, and spun up his guns. The puries having tunnel vision toward the Navy, Kamber got in close, and took all four ships out from point-blank before they could turn to face him. Only then did he turn to look for his squad and give them the chance to form up on his wing.

"All right, Banshee Squad," he said. "Let's herald some death."

***

A silent tension fell over the bridge of the *Mars*. To Admiral Keiko Akiyama's ears, even the artillery pounding on her carrier's hull felt muffled. Her first officer gave updates as the KCF carrier groups moved into range and added their heavy artillery fire to the sterns of the Purist fleet, but the updates weren't necessary. Everyone on the bridge looked up from their assigned tasks, watching the events unfold. The scales of the battle tipped so quickly that a faction of the shiny silver ships retreated from the system before they were hit with a single shell. Following that, several purie carriers jumped out of the system with their fighters still deployed, stranding their own pilots.

With the Purist fleet partially destroyed and the remainder in retreat, the KCF ships were left face-to-face with what was left of the limping GNC. The two forces hung there, facing each other in the most uncomfortable of tableaus. On board the motionless carriers, the crews stood quiet and still, waiting. A lieutenant standing next to Commander Steggs blurted out in the silence, "Well, this is awkward."

"Re-call the fighters," Akiyama said, her voice a whisper.

There was a moment of hesitation, and then Steggs shouted, "You heard the admiral. Re-call the fighters." Then quietly he said to the admiral. "We'll never get them back in time to retreat now, and we've lost two carriers. A lot of these pilots don't have a hangar to return to."

"We stopped the Purists," Akiyama said. "Suddenly, surrendering to the KCF doesn't seem as dishonorable as it would have 12 hours ago."

Across the bridge, the communications officer spoke up. "Admiral, we're being hailed by a General Torgue." Everyone looked to the admiral. Silently, she nodded.

"This is General Torgue with the KCF," a clearly Raif'yan voice announced over the bridge loudspeakers of the *Mars*. "To whom am I speaking?"

"This is Admiral Keiko Akiyama. Thank you for the assist, General."

"I'm just here to kill puries, Admiral," responded the general. "Let's not make this any harder than it needs to be. You're in no position to continue fighting, but in light of this Purist threat, I'm sure we can come to a mutual agreement on the terms of your surrender."

Keiko Akiyama swallowed hard. "General," she began, but Torgue cut her off.

"Beg your pardon, Admiral," he said. "Give me a moment." The sound of his voice in the speaker continued, but muffled as though he had turned away from the microphone. "A Navy bomber?" he asked. "Are you sure? Our home world?" Admiral Akiyama remained silent, but exchanged a glance with Commander Steggs.

After a beat, the Kadrafian general's voice continued. "Why would they–what do you mean, the mic is hot?" There was the "pock, pock" sound of a hand slapping the microphone. Torgue's voice remarked, "It feels fine to me."

After a few seconds of silence, General Torgue's voice returned. "Admiral," he said, "it seems an apology is in order. I just found out now about your bomber mission that protected our home world from a Purist threat. I've received a cease-fire order. Apparently, our governments have entered negotiations."

On the bridge of the *Mars*, Commander Steggs held his hand over the mute button. "What in the Statement is he talking about, ma'am? Navy bomber that protected their planet?"

Akiyama shrugged. "I haven't the foggiest idea."

Steggs pulled his hand off the mute button, and the admiral leaned forward into the microphone and forced her voice to sound confident. "Apology accepted, General," she said. "I'm re-calling my fighters now."

The KCF, as directed by their headquarters, held position and monitored while the Navy ordered any surrendering Purists down to the planets of the Republic to formally surrender. After that, the KCF fleet returned to their home system to wait while the diplomats got down to the difficult task of negotiating the formation of a new entity incorporating the KCF and the GNC into a joint defense force that would cooperate to seek out and expose the remaining Purist combatants and ships, wherever they fled. Tensions don't disappear overnight after decades of conflict, but cooperation would be helped along by a shared goal to work toward. Without a common enemy, the terms of peace would be almost impossible to achieve, but a common enemy is still an enemy, and enemies mean conflict, and on and on it goes.

***

As the Purist forces retreated, India Squad whooped and

hollered, and pulled ahead of Freeda to hunt down the remaining fighters, but Freeda urged them to hold back. "Don't kill them, Ms. Ashley," she pleaded. "Let them surrender."

Ashley scoffed. "Sorry, Freeda, but this is not the time for holding back. We need to cleanse the ether of these bastards."

"Cleanse, Ms. Ashley?"

The radio was silent for a couple beats. "Poor choice of words. But you know what I mean. These puries are evil. We can't show them mercy. I would think a Raif'yan of all people would agree with that."

"Oh, believe me, Ms. Ashley, I want blood from the leaders of this movement, but the pilots in those ships, the boots on the ground, they've been manipulated and exploited, same as you and me. They've been taught their entire lives that we're evil, and vice versa, while the powerful elite sit back and manipulate us."

Ashley started to squeeze the trigger, then slumped her shoulders and relaxed her finger. "India Squad, hold fire," she said. "Let them surrender." Then she added, "Dammit, Freeda. You really have been drinking from Ace's flask."

"Bullshit," barked Riff. "Delta Squad, break and open fire." Riff lurched his ship forward and laid on his trigger, but nothing happened. Freeda had put a burst of her Purple Inerter into his ship, and he floated peacefully forward.

Riff unloaded a long line of expletives into his radio, swearing he would have Freeda executed for war crimes. "Relax, Navy," she said. "I'll give you a tow myself."

Just then the Purist ship Riff was targeting lit up and broke apart in a spectacular ball of fire. A KCF fighter coasted through the wreckage toward the purple ship. "Nice ship, Freeda," it announced.

"Kamber, is that you? I didn't think you were coming to this party. What happened?"

"Right after you left, everyone started getting nervous that the Navy was going to win this battle, especially if they had the Pacifists on their side."

"Yeah, so?"

"The idea of letting the Navy have all the fun was a hard pill to swallow. I'm not sure what happens now, though."

"We're being recalled to our carriers," Ashley informed them, "but we don't have a carrier to return to. We'll have to set down on one of the planets."

"I know of a beach on Planet 5," chimed in Flips. "Went there as a kid. We should relax while we regroup and await further orders. What do you say, ma'am?"

Chapter 45

On a secluded beach on a tropical island just south of the equator of Planet 5 in the Republic System, a miniature fleet of ships is parked on the sand. There's a lifeboat bearing the chief mechanic's insignia under the name *Centauri*, a flashy purple hot rod, and a dozen KCF and GNC fighters facing every which way, as if the valet had gotten drunk and quit halfway through the shift.

The footprints in the sand next to the ships circle each other in a pattern that to the trained eye would suggest the initial meeting of several attendees of this soiree shared hostile introductions. There's no animosity now, though, as a few meters away a fire is lit on the beach, and a gathering of humanoids from various species sit in a circle around it passing a bottle and singing drunken space shanties. Blinking lights appear in the sky above and turn gradually into the shape of a touring vessel painted with brightly colored letters spelling out "Tresh and the Free Miners World Tour" along the sides. It lands on the sand among the chaos of other parked ships, and from the doors emerge a skinny Kadrafian and two ample humans.

A Kadrafian woman rushes at the skinny figure and throws her arms around him. "They made me a temporary diplomat," he can be heard to explain, "and allowed me to transport these two POW's to their own territory and release them."

The four figures make their way to the fire, where a guitar is thrust into the skinny Raif'yan's hands. He gestures ineffectively that he simply couldn't, then takes the instrument and leads the group in song.

After a few melodies, someone stands up to say a few words of lament about a fallen comrade, and the mood turns somber until one more ship, this one a Navy transport, appears in the sky above, and sets down on the far side of the fire. Three figures emerge from the ship, and the group erupts into raucous and emotional cheers. The Raif'yan with the guitar shouts that he has the perfect song for the occasion, and by the time he gets to the second verse, the rest of the humanoids have learned the chorus and are singing along.

Chapter 46 – Epilogue

After the space dust settled on the Purist attack, some of the more salient revelations from the video taken by Copernicus' cyborg eye were released to the press, which effectively turned galactic politics on its head. It also had annoying side effects in the form of the Conspiracy Theorists briefly being taken seriously by the rest of the galaxy.

It's undisputed that the *Citadel* was pulled into the imploding WID-2 station, and nothing could have survived. Now, when a black hole is forming, the laws of physics aren't exactly their normal, organized selves. The laws of physics around the formation of a black hole tend to wake up with a bit of a hangover, and though they do their best to drag themselves out of bed and into their normal routine, they generally show up to work an hour late, and they don't put in their best effort. It's better for everyone if you leave the laws of physics alone in their cubicle and try not to bother them too much if they've been up late forming black holes the night before. Things like time and gravity tend to get forgotten at home next to their half-finished coffee, and if you have something you absolutely need them to do that day, you can expect a whole lot of electromagnetic interference to come with it.

For this reason, the very end of the broadcast from Copernicus' eye recording was not the best quality video, and was the subject of countless debate over the centuries. Billions of unqualified laypeople discussed millions of ridiculous theories about what exactly could be seen in the final moments of the pixelated and staticky video.

Admittedly, what could be seen was difficult to explain. There is no sound, but as the WID-2 station implodes in the background, through the static on the video could be seen what the Conspiracy Theorists of Skepton unanimously agreed was a Navy transport vessel hyperjumping into the vast bridge of the *Citadel* (and what every sane citizen of the galaxy agreed was not a Navy ship at all, but simple electromagnetic distortion). After that, the more moderate Conspiracy Theorists would admit that it was impossible to make anything else out, but the more zealous Theorists swore you could then see the bay door of the transport open, and a figure wearing a purple jumpsuit standing at a mounted machine gun, laughing maniacally and raining a storm of gray foam at whatever Purists on the bridge were still standing.

At that point, almost all of the Conspiracy Theorists would begrudgingly admit that nothing more could be divined, but there is one final static-filled single frame that most experts would tell you is a hoax, that only the absolute most delusional wishful thinkers believed to be a first-person view of Copernicus diving into the bay door of the transport. And after that, no matter how hard anyone tries to recover more, it's nothing but cosmic fuzz.

Two months after the fall of the *Citadel*, Harriet the mass transit station agent traveled to New Belgium to visit the Brothers Repair Shop. She arrived to find several Lumanos and a pair of Kadrafians working on ships of various classes and sizes, all of which were painted a bright purple. She looked up to see Brandine and Hassan on the roof, leaning against the railing together. Brandine spotted Harriet and hurried down the ladder to greet her. The racing pilot brought the newcomer into the garage, where the group of Loomies and Raif'yans stood in a circle, debating something about locations within the galaxy. Brandine interrupted them with a boisterous greeting.

After introductions, Harriet asked if they'd been discussing where to find the fleeing Purist army. The group hesitated, but Brandine answered, "Nah, the GNC and KCF joint forces are working together on that. They've got it covered. We could use your help with some coordinates, though." One of the Lumanos started to stop Brandine, but she cut him off. "Don't worry. She's cool. She got us through to Kadrafia to stop the *Citadel*. She basically saved the whole galaxy."

Brandine turned to Harriet. "We need to find a secret lab that the Purists had control of. Everyone we know of who would know where it is died in the Battle of the Republic, so we're back to square one."

"Coordinates, you say? Well, you've come to the right Sheeple. Running the transit station gets a little boring, so I notice anomalies in coordinates–people going to places they don't seem to belong, like rich people going to very impoverished regions and vice versa, or even just coordinates that I don't immediately recognize will often catch my attention.

"It's rare that the exceedingly wealthy fly ships that don't have their own hyperdrives, but there's the occasional collector that will come through my station with some ancient ship that they paid way too much for. I think I have some places you could start looking. What kind of lab is it?"

"Harriet, do you want to live forever?" one of the Lumanos asked seriously.

Unsure if it was a trick question, Harriet thought about it before giving the honest answer. "No, not really. I think I'd lose my mind."

"Good," replied the Lumano. "In that case, it's a lab that has the kind of power in it that the galaxy isn't ready for. We need to destroy it before it falls into the wrong hands."

"And whose hands are those? Purists'?"

"Anyone's. Are you with us?"

"All the way."

###

About the Author

Kevin Carlin is the host of the Denver Moth StorySLAMs. He has been featured on as well as guest hosted the Moth Podcast. *The Pacifists* is his first book, but he hopes to finish his next work soon!

Thank you so much for reading The Pacifists. If you enjoyed it, won't you please take a moment to leave me a review at your favorite retailer?

Thanks!

Kevin Carlin

Made in the USA
Columbia, SC
15 July 2023

20510514R00167